Odriel's Heirs

HAYLEY REESE CHOW

ISBN: 9781652953302

Editing by Mica Scotti Kole
Cover Design by Dominique Wesson
Map Design by William G. Reese

DEDICATION

For my dad, who read it first...
And then a hundred more times until I finally got it right.

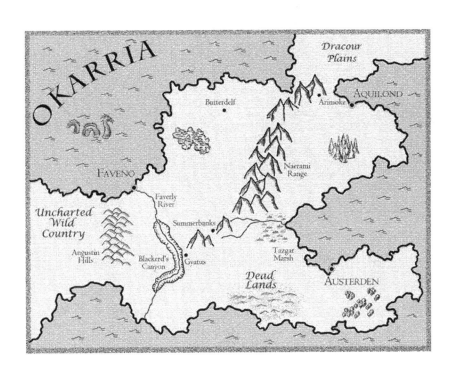

The brave, burning with fire,

Harnessed the dragon's rage.

The cunning, veiled from the world,

Stole the shadow's step.

The gentle, blessed with life,

Healed like time itself.

- The Heirs' Way, Chapter 2, Passage 36

PART ONE

BURNING WITH FIRE

CHAPTER 1
DRAGON HEIR

Kaia Dashul wove a ball of fire between her fingertips, feeling the rage simmering beneath a tangle of excited nerves as she watched the festival from the shadowed wood. Bright, fluttery decorations tied to tents of every color greeted the mountain folk coming from miles around to shop among the wares of silks, candles, fireworks, and other goods. The competitions of strength, speed, and skill were held on the other side of the clearing, but the laughter and applause carried over the crowd like a ray of sunlight.

An acting troupe readied a traveling stage closer by, joking and smiling in their outrageous costumes as they hung the backdrop and arranged their props. The smell of caramelized sugar, baking bread, and roasting meat swirled through the crisp mountain breeze. Kaia inhaled the sweet air. Her fingers tingled with exhilaration, but still, beneath it, she was acutely aware of the Dragon's Rage smoldering within her.

Her ragehound's wet nose snuffled up into her side, his big eyes questioning. All ok?

Kaia let the fire in her hand dissolve into the air before reaching out to pat the shaggy red fur of her enormous dog.

"It's fine, Gus." She stroked one of his bat-like ears. "I'm just nervous is all."

She pulled at the sleeve of her borrowed dress, a lovely remnant of her mother's past as a noblewoman in the old monarchy, before her father and the other Heirs brought it crashing down. The deep blue of the hooded dress suited her tanned complexion, but it was still tight around the shoulders and about a hand too short, revealing her craggy leather boots. She hadn't been able to find any matching shoes in her mother's closet.

1

She took a deep breath and fingered the side braid pulled back above her ear, a rope of copper-red nestled in her brown locks. "I'm just going to walk out there like a normal villager."

"This isn't a good idea." Her 12-year-old brother, Layf stumbled through the brush behind her, panting slightly after chasing her down the slope on his short legs.

Kaia rolled her eyes. "Then stop following me and go home." She pulled the hood up over her coiled chestnut hair before stepping out into the field towards the tents.

Layf wiped his forehead with a sleeve as he trailed behind her, Gus close on his heels. "C'mon, Kaia, you know Papa said you're not allowed to go into town."

"But Papa's not here." She took in the bright blue tent on the edge of the field filled with ceramic pottery of strange shapes and designs. A slim young man gestured wildly with his hands as he engaged a customer. Gus' nose twitched eagerly towards another tent selling sizzling skewers of hedge hens further down the row.

"He'll find out when he gets back."

If he gets back. Kaia opened her mouth but then closed it, her agitation seeping out in a sigh instead. They hadn't gotten a letter from Papa in months. She pushed the dark thought away. Not today. Today, she was going to enjoy the festival.

She paused in the back of a crowd gathered to watch a juggler toss gold rings into the air, not quite daring to enter the throng yet. Her heart hammered at their closeness. What if the locals recognized her?

Layf caught her hesitation. "You don't think something's happened to Papa, do you?"

"No." Kaia glanced at her brother's face, creased with worry as he eyed the mass of mountain folk swirling in front of them. She sighed again, her shoulders falling. "But something big must be happening to keep the other Heirs away." The juggler performed a backflip before catching his rings once more, and Kaia clapped along with everyone else. "No one's missed a Triennial before."

The Triennial, after all, was the only opportunity for all the Heirs to meet and practice tactics, skills, and swordplay. Fourteen at the last Triennial, she had been the weakest fighter by far, but she had trained fiercely for the last three years and had been sorely disappointed that she hadn't gotten the chance to redeem herself.

"But if it were something big, he would've taken you," Layf said, eyeing his sister carefully.

Kaia winced as the sting of her father's abandonment slapped her once more.

Oh, how she had begged and bargained to accompany her father on his journey. After all, she would take his place as Dragon Heir one day. She had a duty to check in on Klaus and Jago, her Shadow and Time Heir counterparts. Her father claimed she was too young still, but Klaus had been patrolling the land since he was fourteen! Her row with Papa over it had shaken the house before he left.

Gus whined and gave her palm a lick. Let it go.

Kaia scratched his ears and cast about for another distraction. Her eyes landed on a small puppet booth, and she moved towards it.

"Kaia!" her brother hissed as she walked into the crowd. He shadowed her so closely she almost tripped on him. "Remember what happened last time?"

Her fists clenched. It had been five years since she had last tried to sneak into the village, but she could still hear their voices spitting hate—*devil's spit, witch wart, demon bastard*. Full grown men had reached for rocks to keep her at bay, but their hands had been trembling too badly to hit their mark. Kaia's palms itched, but she suppressed the urge to allow them to flame.

"Of course, I remember, Layf," she snapped. Exiled by the people she was sworn to protect—the unfairness of it rubbed her raw. "But it's my turn to dance in the Eventide this year, and I'm not going to miss it." It was a tradition in Arimoke for the new adults of the town to kick off the Eventide dance at dusk. Kaia had often daydreamed of the town cheering her name as she stepped onstage and a handsome suitor stepped forward to lead her into the dance.

"You honestly think they're going to let you dance?" a deeper voice said from her other side.

Kaia jumped at the sound of her twin brother's sudden closeness. "How'd you find us?"

Bram ruffled Gus' fur roughly. "It's hard to miss a ragehound." Gus' tongue lolled out in pleasure.

She sniffed. "No one else seems to mind."

Bram crossed his arms, annoyance and amusement mixing on his face. "Yet."

Kaia's lips twitched. "I can at least watch the dance." Her voice sounded weak even to her own ears.

Layf pulled on her arm. "It's not worth it, Kaia. It's just a boring old dance anyway."

She looked down at her little brother. With freckled cheeks and almond-shaped eyes, Layf looked just like her, but he was a world apart. Of course, the dance bored Layf. He went to the spring festival every year. He went to school in town and had more friends than she could count. But all of those things were foreign to her. The Dragon's fire only fell to the eldest child. An honor she had stolen from Bram by six minutes.

A booming voice drew her eyes to the puppet show once more. She smiled humorlessly at the familiar tale. The legend of how three ordinary men had stepped forward to confront Nifras, the demon necromancer, and his army of the Lost.

The puppeteer lowered a wooden hawk into his small set. "And then the high spirit, Odriel, blessed them with great gifts to pass down to their Heirs. To the bravest, he gave the power of the Dragon—of *fire*."

Kaia could feel the embers churn within her at the very mention of it.

"He cloaked the cunning in shadow—to walk unseen. And to the kind, he gave his healing touch."

A little girl in front of Kaia leaned towards the stooped old woman next to her. "Where are the Heirs now, Gama?"

"They were banished after they turned on the royal family, my love." The woman's voice creaked with age. "Who knows where they ended up."

On distant mountainsides, along the southern border, and remote buffalen farms, Kaia thought. Keeping watch on the legendary magi's yanai barrier that protected the world from Nifras' return. Bringing down the lawless gangs that roamed between the three State-cities. Secretly. Thanklessly.

"But won't Nifras come back?" The little girl edged closer to her grandmother.

The old woman chuckled. "Of course not, my dearie. He hasn't been seen or heard in thousands of years."

Kaia grimaced. That didn't stop the Lost from squeezing through the yanai barrier in the south every now and then. Nothing Guardian Brigg and Jago, the Time Heirs, couldn't handle, but the Lost weren't creatures to be taken lightly.

A strong hand clamped down on Kaia's shoulder, snapping her out of her thoughts. "What in Odriel's name are you doing here, Kaia?"

Kaia groaned as she turned to face her mother, her accusing glare practically burning a hole into her head.

"And is that my dress?"

She winced. This day wasn't going at all like she'd planned.

Her nine-year-old sister, Eleni, shrugged apologetically from behind her mother's muddied pants. "Sorry, Kaia, it slipped out." Her blusheep lamb bleated by her knee, a shiny first-place medallion tied around its cerulean neck.

"Well, I...." Kaia started, grappling for some pardonable excuse. She looked at her brothers for inspiration. Bram looked at Kaia with a poorly veiled smile on his lips, and Layf carefully averted his eyes.

Gus looked up his long nose at her. You knew this would be a short visit.

Kaia threw up her hands. "I just wanted to look around for once, Mama. I'm not causing any trouble."

"Kaia!" Her mother seized her elbow, guiding her back towards the edge of the festival. "You know you're not supposed to be here. And today especially, I don't have a good feel—"

An inhuman screech pierced through the air, followed by another, and another. As one, the family pivoted toward the cries. The sound froze Kaia's already scattered thoughts and a spike of panicked adrenaline shot through her limbs. For a brief, tense moment, the clamor of the festival fell quiet.

"It can't be," Kaia's mother whispered. "Not this far north already."

And in that moment, Kaia knew the Lost had arrived in Arimoke.

CHAPTER 2
THE LOST

A blood-curdling human shriek sliced through the silence, and the crowd erupted. Screams of panic and terror shredded what was left of the festive air, and in a wave of shouts and cries, the crowd turned to flee. Kaia stood, frozen in shock with Layf clinging to her arm, as the crowd buffeted them about in their eagerness to escape the unknown terror.

Her mother shook her by the elbow, "Kaia, snap out it!" she yelled, still clutching a frightened Eleni. Her mother's eyes locked on her daughter's. Two identical sets of russet eyes boring into one another. "This is what you've been trained for." She gave Kaia's elbow another squeeze before reaching out to pull Layf away from her. "Now go!"

A jolt of adrenaline shot through Kaia, breaking through the ice of fear, and she picked up her leaden feet. Gus barked excitedly and ran in front of her toward the screams, encouraging her to move faster. The crowd avoided the ragehound as he tore through the throng with Kaia following close behind, grateful now to be in her boots. When they finally broke free from the mob, Kaia skidded to a halt, taking in the nightmarish scene before her.

A swarm of animated corpses had infested the festival. The creatures wore damaged armor and carried rusted swords. Dead, gray skin dangled from their bodies and faces like a half-peeled, rotted fruit. Where their eyes should've been, black holes stared out from long stringy hair that hung limply from their scalps. A green aura of *yanaa* curled around the white sheen of bone that glimmered through patchy, decaying flesh. Blood already smeared their jagged teeth from the victims they had caught unawares, and the nauseating stench of graveyard rot was almost unbearable.

These could only be Nifras' corpse soldiers—the Lost.

The creature's movements were jerky as if they were not of their own volition, but they lurched quickly in a shambling run after the living.

Kaia pitched forward as something ran into her from behind. She leapt to her feet, her dress ripping along the shoulder seams and fire springing to her hands, only to see Bram brandishing a tent pole. "What are you doing? Use your fire!" he yelled, before charging to the defense of a bleeding woman trying to fend off one of the creatures with a butcher's knife.

Kaia nodded and focused on the yanaa within her, nestled in the ball of rage she nursed in the core of her being. Her heart careened around her ribcage as she remembered her training. She glanced at Gus standing next to her, and the dog seemed to nod at her. Control it.

As the fire grew in her hands, the dead turned towards her, drawn to her yanaa. Their red-stained limbs, orchestrated by a vicious, unseen puppeteer, jolted into motion as they whipped towards her. Suddenly, they seemed all too close, and Kaia released her blaze in a rush. An uncanny, high-pitched keen rang across the field as the dead burned. Still, they came. A second volley of fire launched through the first while still burning corpses stalked towards her. One of the creatures collapsed into a nearby tent, setting the canvas alight.

Kaia spooled more fire into her palms faster than she thought was possible, her hands shaking with adrenaline, and unleashed the blaze again. Her vision narrowed as she focused. Another volley. And then another, until the whole field seemed to be on fire, and the smell of burning flesh and hair stung her nose.

She scanned the ground for more, but a strange gurgle from behind her caught her off guard. She turned to find a corpse tilting towards her at full speed—its leering eye sockets and unnaturally grinning smile only a few paces away. Suddenly, from beside her, Bram heaved his makeshift spear, impaling the creature through the neck and knocking it to the ground.

Kaia shook herself from her surprise and dispatched the creature with a quick burst of flame. She clamped her hands to her ears as its death screech rent the air.

Her eyes swiveled once more around the field, hunting for stragglers. The festival tents were still alight, but the Lost had already burned down to a fine ash, scattering in the mountain breeze. Sweating and out of breath, Kaia turned to her brother with a broad smile, her eyes gleaming with triumph.

But his face darkened as his gray eyes studied her, looking like the spit image of their father—the spit image of the Dragon Heir. "Six minutes," he whispered. "And it would have been me." With that, he turned and strode away.

Kaia's face fell, and she looked to where a crowd had gathered a safe distance away. Still, she could hear them.

"That witch led those demons right to us."

"She set the festival on fire."

"Don't get any closer, we don't know if she can control herself."

The ecstasy of her first victory drained away, and once again Kaia could feel the Dragon Rage bubbling within. Gus yipped beside her, lifted up his front paws to rest on her shoulders, and licked her cheek with his big sloppy tongue.

"Gus," Kaia protested.

He snuffled her neck affectionately. Don't let it get to you.

Kaia smiled ruefully and shoved the big brute away. "Thanks, bud."

But as she walked back up the mountain slope in her ripped dress, the festival still smoldering behind her, Kaia couldn't help but notice the townsfolk shrinking away from her.

"*Hellspawn*," someone hissed as she passed.

Six minutes, she thought. If only I could have waited six minutes.

***

Kaia's mother whirled around the house, shoving supplies into canvas bags and trying to goad her children into action. "Eleni, go help Bram get the blusheep in. Layf, take this bag for your things."

Still in her ripped dress with her hair falling down on her shoulder, Kaia sat at their crimson oak dinner table, chin on fist, trying to collect her thoughts. She rubbed her stocking feet over Gus' belly where he lay spread out on the floor. Her mind spun in a loop—the crowds, the screams, the Lost. Even with her mother running about, their modest farmhouse seemed strangely peaceful after the grim festival. Still, something kept sticking in her mind.

"Mama—"

"We're going to cross the mountain and stay with Cressida's tribe until your father returns." Her mother opened the door to the pantry and shoved food into a bag.

Kaia nodded. With the sinuous four-legged body of a dragon, the scaly torso of a man, and a set of murderous horns, the Dracour were the fiercest warriors in the land, bar none. They were a proud and vicious people but considered her father one of their own. Her family had spent many summers honing their combat skills with the Dracour while her father was patrolling. "Yes, but—"

"The Rogerson boys will watch the flock, they're always grateful for the work."

"Ye—" Kaia tried, but her mother cut her off.

"And I'll—"

"Mama!" Kaia stood and snagged her mother's wrist, forcing her to meet her eyes. In the moment of stillness, she could hear the mellow song of the ridge robins outside the farmhouse window. "You weren't surprised to see the Lost."

Her mother looked away. "Of course, I was."

"But you said, 'Not this far north *already*.'" Kaia's brow furrowed. "You got a letter from Papa."

The flint eased from her mother's eyes, and she sagged into the chair next to Kaia. "Yes."

Relief and anger swirled through Kaia. "Why didn't you tell us?"

Her mother slapped the table. "Because he asked me not to!" She rubbed her temples, her voice thick with emotion. "And there's nothing you'd want to hear."

"I'm not a child. Of course, I want to hear it!" Kaia nearly shouted.

"Do you?" Her mother bit back, her voice rising. "You want to hear that the Lost are running rampant on the southern border? That someone else is raising a dead army to try to defeat them? Do you want to hear that Pryor Brigg is dead and Jago is missing? Do you!" Her mother turned away and hid her face in her hands, choking on a suppressed sob.

Kaia sat down heavily in her chair. Shock wiped her mind blank. The Time Heir dead and his son missing? How was that possible? When she spoke, her voice was soft. "When did you get the letter?"

Her mother took in a shaky breath. "Only a few days ago." She wiped at her dry eyes and folded her hands in her lap. "Your father and Klaus are looking for the mortal necromancer, he calls himself Ariston, while the magus, Everard, searches the south for Jago." She rolled her neck in a slow circle, her voice once again steady, but now coated with acid. "I'd imagine those dead we saw today were the work of Ariston. He doesn't understand what he's unleashed. All dark yanaa stems from Nifras. Fighting fire with fire will only build the blaze."

Kaia's heart pounded in her ears. "Does this mean Nifras has returned?"

Her mother turned to her. "If he had, we'd know it." She reached out to take her daughter's hand. "But it seems now like it's only a matter of time."

Kaia squeezed her mother's calloused palm. "Then I must go to them."

Her mother drew her hand away. "This is why your father didn't want me to tell you."

"They need me." Kaia pounded the table, her fist smoking.

Her mother stood up. "Absolutely not."

Kaia followed her, knocking the chair over in her haste while Gus scrambled to get out of the way. "But I'm the Dragon Heir."

Her mother whirled to face her. "Not yet!" her mother thundered, her nose only inches from Kaia's face. "You're not ready."

Kaia took a step back, struck speechless. Her mother's red face creased— worry, anger, and sadness, all mixed into an iron will. There would be no changing her mind.

Her mother took a deep breath and lowered her voice. "You're going to pack your bag and ready to leave tomorrow for the Dracour camp." Her mother thrust the bag into her hands. "Do you understand?"

Kaia nodded with gritted teeth. "Yes, Mama."

With that, she turned on her heel and stormed up the stairs to her room, Gus trailing behind her. She opened the door for the ragehound before closing it behind him and leaning against it. Slowly, haltingly, she let herself slide to the floor.

Gus' wet nose snuffled against her cheek and she scratched his neck numbly, trying to absorb her mother's news. A Time Heir dead, another missing, Lost roaming the land, and Nifras' return imminent—the ancient legends had broken open like old wounds.

With a wringing twinge of the heart, she thought of the Time Heirs. During the Triennial, she had often sat on Pryor Brigg's knee as he filled her with stories of the Heirs' youth on the run from the murderous King Candon. Guardian Brigg had been her father's best friend, and she had adored his son, Jago. Jago had such a kind face, with beautiful cocoa skin and a deep, resonating voice that always made her blush. He couldn't be dead. He had to be out there somewhere. With her father. And Klaus. And the Lost.

She looked out the window at dusk falling over the verdant mountain fields. Not seeing any answers, she drew a small candle-sized flame to her palm, watching it flicker as grief, confusion, and anger swirled and eddied within her. Just the thought of running north burned her with shame. But then again, she had never been south of Arimoke. Could she find her way alone?

Gus placed a huge paw on her knee with a huff. He sat on his haunches, tall and proud, beside her. Not alone.

Resolve hardened her heart and steadied her hand. She had to go.

She rose from the floor and packed her bag, just like her mother had instructed. She cast off the torn dress, giving it one last wistful glance before replacing it with her usual shirt and breeches, buckled her father's hand-me-down sword to her waist, and drew her bag closed.

The soft knock on the door almost made her jump out of her skin. The hinges creaked as Layf slipped in the room. Her little brother took in the sword strapped to her waist and her bulging pack. His doubtful eyes met Kaia's, and she could see the indecision weighing on him. "You're going south, aren't you?"

"You heard the fight?"

He nodded soberly. "I brought you something." He stepped forward, holding out a folded square of paper.

The thick parchment crackled when she opened it. "A map of Okarria." She spread it out on the bed and brought a small flame to her fist. Light danced across the weathered page as she bent over it. She tapped a small dot circled in the north midlands, squinting at the scrawl next to it. "What's this?"

Layf leaned over beside her. "Butterdelf—it's where Papa's letter came from."

Kaia straightened in surprise. "But how did you—"

"I was in town with Mama when the harehawks flew in." Layf chewed his lip. "When I saw how close it was on the map, I thought Papa was going to come home and surprise us."

Kaia tapped her chin; that's why he had brought it up at the festival. A knot of anxiety loosened itself in her chest. They were closer than she thought. At least now she had a direction, a trail to follow.

Layf ran a finger from Arimoke southwest across the mountains. "If you take the Glim Pass, you can make it in five days."

Kaia drew in a deep breath. "I'll push hard. Papa will probably already have moved on by the time I get there." She let the flame fade from her fingers and folded the map. "I don't want to fall too far behind." She turned to her brother; his face full of shadows in the darkening room.

"I already saddled Thornbite for you." His voice wobbled.

Kaia's heart squeezed in her chest, and she reached out to wrap him in a hug. "Thank you, Layf," She rested a cheek on his soft hair—her little brother, her best friend. "Tell Mama and the others I'll miss them."

Layf, nodded, pulling away. He smiled through moist eyes. "But you have to bring me back something good for my birthday."

Kaia laughed. "Deal." She hefted her bag on her shoulder and clicked her tongue for Gus to follow. Turning away, she offered the old Dracour parting. "Till our horns lock again, brother."

"Odriel protect you," he whispered.

With that, Kaia slipped down the stairs and out the back door, where she found their gray mule, Thornbite, waiting for her in the gathering dusk. "Thank Odriel for Layf," she said under her breath as she tied her bag to the saddle.

"So, you are going."

Kaia turned to find Bram leaning against the corner of the house, his face unreadable. Her stomach flopped as guilty butterflies scrabbled within. She looked back to the worn saddle. "To keep the dead from our doorstep, I must ride out to meet them." Kaia winced at the tremor in her voice.

She swung into the saddle, not meeting her brother's stony stare. "You could come, too," she offered, trying to appease him. Then, considering it, she warmed to the idea. "We could fight together, like we did today." It'd be nice to have someone watch her back, even if he was moody.

Bram looked out to the darkening forest stretching below their home. "There could be more on the mountain." He turned back to her; his face shadowed. "Someone will have to protect the family."

Kaia shifted. She hadn't thought of that. Her family would be safe with the Dracour tribe, but anything could happen on the day's journey over the ridge. The thought of the Lost slinking after Layf and Eleni in the darkness sent a chill through her. Then again, staying would put her another two days behind her father and Klaus.

A soul-releasing sigh eased out of her brother as he let his forehead fall onto Thornbite's neck. "I have to stay. You have to go." He straightened, and his hands moved to tighten the straps on her saddlebags. "I've always known this is how it would be." A humorless laugh escaped him. "But I still hate it." He stilled, his eyes staring into nothing. "Don't do anything stupid. Mother would fry me for letting you go."

Kaia smiled, feeling a surge of affection for her twin. "Thank you, Bram."

He turned and dismissed her with a wave. "Get out of here, ugly. And give my best to the old man when you find him."

She nodded. "Stay safe, Brother." With that, she dug her heels and spurred Thornbite into the growing night, Gus racing ahead, his tail wagging with excitement. They dashed away from the cozy town that had spat on her face and the cheerfully lit home that had hidden her for the last seventeen years. Finally freed into the vast world, the weight of those unseen fetters lifted from her shoulders, and she did not dare look back.

CHAPTER 3
MEMORIES

The days passed quickly as Kaia pushed Thornbite through the winding Naerami trails. She rode until she threatened to topple out of the saddle, rested on the side of the road, and passed quickly through the foothill villages, pausing only briefly to replenish supplies. Gus' ears remained on a swivel, his nose ever-twitching for any sign of the Lost. Mercifully, they found no trace of the creatures, and Kaia found the monotony of the journey wearing her instead.

The road was little traveled, and the still mountain air only seemed to magnify the crowding thoughts that scrabbled at her mind. Guardian Brigg was dead, Jago was missing, the Lost crawled the land, and still, her father hadn't sent for her. Why? Her father had trained her as a Dragon Heir since before she could remember. He taught her how to draw the flames from within, and read her *The Heirs' Way*, the history of the Heirs, until she could recite it by heart.

Then there were the Triennials. Of course, she was the youngest of the Heirs, but she had always given it her all. Her thoughts turned to Jago and Klaus. What did her father see in them that she lacked? She cocked her head as she considered them. She could barely imagine two people more different than her counterparts.

Jago was the eldest of the three at 28 and the kindest, by far. Kaia had been five when her father allowed her to participate in her first Triennial. After weeks of looking forward to the gathering, it had been a crushing blow to discover the adults were too busy for her, and Klaus' teasing had been merciless.

But Jago had gone out of his way to compliment her on the faint glow she sweated to produce, and he often took her aside to ease the pain of skinned knees, bruised shins, and minor bumps earned in their training exercises.

Kaia had been in awe of his strange and wondrous gift. A touch of his smoky cornflower aura triggered a maddening itch that stole away the pain and then gifted a surge of yanaa instead. How Kaia had wished she could be the Time Heir just like him. Even from the very beginning, his winks and friendly jokes had made her blush.

Klaus, on the other hand, had been a different story. Possessing the power of invisibility, Klaus proved a terror even at the precocious age of eight. He pulled the usual pranks—blowing in her ears, pouring salt in her cocoa, and popping out of thin air to scare her—but he also told Kaia that Bram must have been the real Heir, went on about fireflies that could best her, and teased that no one really liked the Dragon Heir. Of course, that last bit was true, but hearing it stung all the same.

Still, for better or for worse, they were stuck with each other as sparring partners. Their training sessions had been more like games, but they were games that Klaus always won; losses he did not let her forget easily. Luckily, she always had Jago to mend her pride just as well as her scrapes.

During Kaia's second Triennial, Jago arrived with his father as usual, but the blood plague had stolen away Klaus' parents that winter, leaving their son stony with grief as he trailed behind Everard up the mountain. She remembered little of his ascension ceremony, only that the newly christened Guardian Thane did not cry.

A pall fell over that summer as Guardian Brigg and her father quietly mourned. Klaus would disappear for days at a time and spoke to her only when forced while training with unforgiving intensity in their drills. Once again, Kaia was embarrassingly grateful to Jago for curing the bruises and sprains Klaus dealt her.

At eleven, the Dracour clan arrived to teach them weaponry. Some of Klaus' cheek had returned, and he flaunted his prowess with blade, bow, and spear. But Kaia had grown a spirit of her own and worked tirelessly to match him. The compliments from their teachers, Cressida and Lazander, made her swell with pride, even though Klaus' superior strength proved unbeatable.

Jago merely shook his head. "You're both strong, but remember you're on the same side."

At fourteen, it was Kaia who changed. Filled with adolescent rage fueled by the injustice of her exile, Bram's jealous resentment, and her father's secretive sheltering, she faced Klaus's taunts with rage. Fire and shadow skills weren't allowed, so the two Heirs turned to staves or blunted blades wrapped in leather. Their bouts took hours and ranged the cliffs and fields.

Klaus continued to best her, but Kaia could see him sweating. A glimmer of excitement at the challenge replaced the Shadow Heir's usual bored look while Jago continued to heal her increasingly worsening injuries. "Take it easy before you get hurt." His voice rumbled with concern. "You're three years younger. You can't expect so much of yourself."

But she couldn't slow down, and the Triennial came to a fever pitch with only two weeks left in the summer. Kaia and Klaus traded hand-to-hand blows for hours near the mountain peak, but Kaia couldn't seem to gain ground. Close to exhaustion, her control slipped from her fingers. Her body heated, flames flickering through her closed fists. Alarm widened Klaus' eyes, but it only excited her as red filled her vision.

Distantly she could hear the ragehound pup, Gus, begin to bark, and a remote part of her registered she couldn't stop herself. The Dragon's Rage, the bane of the Dragon Heirs, had begun to grab hold. But she could see Klaus, himself exhausted, struggling to beat her back. She was so close.

Then, abruptly, he disappeared. Her rage, which had been simmering just below the surface, erupted. Fire bloomed from her hands and swirled around her. Gus nipped at her legs, oblivious to the danger, but too small to knock her out of her trance.

A blunt object sang through the air and stole the wind from her lungs, quelling her firestorm. With another unseen blow to the jaw, she staggered backward, stunned, but the flurry of invisible blows continued unchecked. One last powerful kick to the chest sent her soaring into the air. Except the ground didn't come when she expected it. The air whistled by her ears as she continued to fall, the sound of barking faded, and she glimpsed a frantic Klaus reaching for her over the cliff edge far too late—a crunch, and then blackness.

That episode ended the Triennial for Kaia and Klaus that year. Kaia awoke three days later to see Jago smiling tiredly at her. "I told you to take it easy." She tried to sit up and realized in a panic that she could not. Her whole body itched furiously. "Hold on there, firecracker," Jago gently pushed her back with a hand on her shoulder. "It's still going to take me another few days to fix you up. Broken bones take a lot out of me, and you broke forty-seven."

The events flooded back to Kaia, and hot tears she thought she'd outgrown leaked from her eyes. "I'm so sorry."

"Hush now," Jago said. "Everyone's all right. That's why the Dragon Heirs have the ragehounds—to snap you out of your fits." He glanced at the red ball of fur at the foot of her bed. "Gus just isn't quite big enough yet to do his job right."

"Klaus must be furious..." Kaia whispered. "And Papa...." Her face fell.

"Don't worry. Everyone's just glad that you're all right." Jago squeezed her shoulder. "It gave us all a fright to hear Klaus barreling down the mountain, screaming like a harehawk." He chuckled. "And you certainly tested my skills." Jago pulled the copper side-braid hanging along her cheek, and she couldn't help but return his grin.

All in all, Kaia needed ten days to fully recover, and she only saw Klaus once more before he departed. While shame filled her, she couldn't seem to find the words to apologize. Meanwhile, Klaus had donned his unreadable mask once again. Kaia bristled under his gaze.

"Next time," Kaia burst out, "I'll be strong enough."

His mouth had quirked up into an almost smile. "Me too, Firefly."

A sharp wind kicked dust in her eyes, dragging Kaia back from the past. She took in the long-necked *llamow* grazing on the grassy hills fields and the harmonized chorus of a flock of red and indigo *childae* cutting through the sky on their long, prickly wings. The gusting spring breeze rippled the green hills all around her, and she pulled her cloak tighter around her shoulders.

The Dragon Rage… was that why Papa left her behind? She sighed and shook her head, trying to dislodge the bitter thoughts that poked at her like sharp burrs.

Sensing her mood, Gus yipped beside her, his tongue lolling out happily. The sun is shining, and we are free! He yipped again. We should be happy.

Kaia offered her canine friend a weak smile. "I know, Gus." She sighed again. "This just isn't how I thought it would be."

She had always dreamed of the day she would leave Arimoke, but she had pictured friendly Jago and the difficult Klaus beside her. In her father's stories, the Dragon, the Shadow and the Time were always together—closer than brothers.

But Jago was missing, and she had left her real brothers behind.

Kaia clenched her fists and rode on, spinning her memories about her like a cocoon to keep the loneliness at bay, but still longing for her father's steady strength, Jago's deep laugh, or even Klaus' taunts to fill the maddening silence. She blew out another long breath. Soon, they would be reunited, Kaia told herself as she chewed on her chapped lips. Klaus would say something insulting, and her father might be cross at first, but she would tell him about the Lost in Arimoke, and then he would be proud. She would tell him how far she had traveled, and he would realize she was ready to fight alongside him as the Dragon Heir he had trained her to be. Then together, there wasn't an evil known to man that couldn't be overcome by three Heirs.

Or so she hoped.

CHAPTER 4
BUTTERDELF

On the fifth day, Kaia left the towering Naerami peaks behind and approached the neat little hamlet of Butterdelf on a warm and overcast evening. The sinking sun painted the low clouds deep shades of persimmon and rose. Looking down upon the cozy, stone cottages from a nearby hill, Kaia brought Thornbite to a sudden halt. Her stomach flipped at the town's resemblance to Arimoke. She could almost feel the rough hands of the schoolboys grinding her face into the dirt. She shifted in the saddle, her sore backside twinging in protest.

She leaned her head back towards the sky and groaned. "I hate these little towns."

Gus bark-howled softly in agreement. We can do this.

Kaia rolled her neck from side to side. "It's been almost a week since we got the letter, so they probably won't even be here."

The ragehound snorted and shook his head. You're stalling.

"Ok, ok." She edged Thornbite forward. "We'll start at the inn. Someone must have seen them."

Less than an hour later, Kaia had almost reached the first houses when a diminutive black cat dashed out of the grass and alighted nimbly on Thornbite's haunches. Gus' head swiveled sharply, and Kaia pulled the mule to a stop, turning in the saddle. "What—"

"Not exactly who I was hoping for, but I'll take it," the cat said in a cool, velvety voice. His eyes glowed sapphire in his jet-black face.

Recognition flickered in Kaia's wide eyes. You never forgot a talking cat, but it had been nearly a decade since she'd last seen him. "You're Everard's cat."

Eighty years ago, Shad had been a young man, until he tried to steal precious relics from the ill-tempered magus. As punishment, Everard had sentenced him to 100 years as a pet cat, spy, and servant.

"Shadmundar, right?"

"Yes, yes." The cat's ears twitched impatiently. "If we could skip the niceties, I'm in a bit of a rush."

Gus put his front paws up on Thornbite's flank to get a better look at the creature.

Shadmundar's black nose wrinkled. "That flame resist charm smells like singed fur." He lifted his chin. "Not Everard's best work."

The ragehound sat back on his haunches with a low whine.

Kaia looked back up the road towards the town and nudged Thornbite forward. "Is Everard here then? Or my father and Klaus?"

"No, they are not." The cat's tail flicked back and forth. "And I would not go into this town if I were you."

Kaia twisted back to him.

"As far as I know, Everard is still in the south, looking for Jago." He turned his face, not meeting her gaze. "But I was serving as a guide for your father and Klaus when they were captured here four days ago."

"C...captured?" Nausea bubbled in Kaia's stomach. "But that's impossible!"

The cat's ears flattened. "There's no need to shout, I'm right here."

Kaia resisted the urge to swat the cat from the back of the mule. Her heart thumped in her chest as she barked out panicked questions. "How? By who? Where are they now? Are they ok?"

"They were poisoned at the inn. Ariston is holding them in the dungeons of Butterdelf Castle, ten miles north of here." Shad examined his claws. "To what end, I don't know, but last I heard, they were alive." His eyes flicked to her, solemn and steady. "I've tried to get a message to Everard, but most of the people here are loyal to Ariston." He paused. "So it seems Odriel has sent me the Dragon hatchling in his stead."

Kaia's chest heaved as if she had run a mile. Her hands felt frozen on the reins and her legs stiff. The fireflies blinking lazily in the long grass stood in stark contrast to the panicked buzzing filling her ears. "Ariston is the one that can raise the dead, right?"

Shadmundar nodded. "They say he has already raised his corpse army." His whiskers twitched. "But he is a poor shepherd, and his flock terrorizes the countryside. Though he blames it on Nifras, of course, and then, in turn, the Heirs for not protecting the people." The cat was so matter-of-fact, he could have been discussing the weather.

Kaia rubbed her forehead. "They attacked Arimoke."

The cat's eyes narrowed. "That doesn't sound like a coincidence." He cocked his head. "But you handled it, I hope?"

She nodded. "There were only a dozen or so."

He sighed. "Well, I suppose that's better than no experience at all." Shadmundar looked towards the west, where the sunset was already fading to shadow. "But we must hurry. If we move quickly, we can reach the castle while the moon is high."

Kaia fumbled with Thornbite's reins, her heart jumping nervously. "And once we get there? What then?"

"Then, little dragon," Shadmundar purred, "we'll see just how well your father taught you."

CHAPTER 5
RESCUE

They reached the old castle just as the crescent moon peeked through the spindly fingers of the tree branches. Kaia dismounted as she studied the structure. The castle stood as a simple, tall rectangle of stone with two short chimneys poking out of the crown like ears. A crumbling stone wall, perhaps thrice Kaia's height, surrounded the building. Kaia breathed a silent sigh of relief—much too small to contain an army. Even so, it was a castle, and she was just one girl. Not even Bram was here to watch her back this time. Her stomach twisted in a painful knot.

"So, what's the plan?" she whispered, consciously trying to keep her voice steady.

Shadmundar looked at her from his perch in Thornbite's saddle bag. "Find Tam and Klaus and free them."

She snorted. "You say that like it's child's play."

He rolled his eyes. "Well, considering you are a child, we best hope so."

She stuck her tongue out at him.

Shad considered the castle. "Most of Ariston's followers are deluded simpletons, so try not to kill the idiots, but don't underestimate the Lost." His ears flicked. "When a body is raised, the darkest part of that person's soul is also raised to inhabit it." Every hair on Kaia's body rose to attention. "And keep the dog close. Klaus and Tam will be too weak to protect themselves if the Dragon's Rage seizes you."

If possible, Kaia tensed even more. The last time the rage took her had been only months before, when Bram had accidentally slammed Layf in the neck during a sparring match. For a moment, Kaia had thought Layf's neck was broken, and she had snapped. Luckily, Gus had been there.

Shad cut into her thoughts. "Well, what are you waiting for?"

Kaia shook her head in annoyance. "Thanks for the encouragement, Shad."

She gripped the hilt of her sword and took a step forward. Everything depended on her. She took a deep breath. *Courage*, she thought to herself, remembering her father's words. *The first battle is in your head.*

She jerked her head at the cat. "See you soon." She clicked her tongue softly. "Come on, Gus."

Girl and hound crept through the trees to the west wall. Staying low to the ground, she silently crossed from the cover of the wood to the shadow of the wall. The aged, crumbling stone was easy to scale compared to some of the rock faces on her mountain at home. Gus sat patiently by the wall as Kaia scrambled up and over the top. She edged a short way down the other side before impatiently jumping to the ground, only to find herself crouched at the feet of two guards.

The first guard's eyes widened just before Kaia slammed her elbow into his jaw. While the first guard collapsed, the second swung his oversized broad sword at her head, but the swipe looked almost sluggish to Kaia as she ducked beneath it and countered with a low kick. Already off balance from his clumsy attack, the guard fell heavily onto his back. Her boot to his temple left him unconscious on the castle stones.

Kaia straightened in time to hear the gatehouse guard cry for help. Cursing her lack of stealth, she ran to the gate, drawing her sword as she crossed the courtyard. Instead of holding his post, the gate guard fled to the stables, and Kaia felt a pang of pity. Layf could put up more of a fight than this.

Lights flickered through the castle as she cut through the gate's iron lock with an intense blue flame. Flinging it open, she let out a low whistle, and Gus bounded through the gap to meet her as if it were a game. Giving him a pat, she turned to the castle; a dozen men streamed out with lanterns and candles. A handful darted toward the stables while the remaining rushed her with swords held high.

Now, she thought, *it's time to flash.* She widened her stance and let flames engulf her blade. Bram had once said that she reminded him of a demon when her sword blazed, and the very sight of the flames filled her with a glow of pride. As the flickering light illuminated the fearful faces of her attackers, she returned a smug smile. The spectacle was more ostentatious than dangerous, but only Kaia and her father knew that.

With a yell, the first man charged her straight on. Kaia knocked his blade to the side and smashed her hilt into the side of his head. Just as the first fell, the next man ran at her. Kaia parried his thrust, and the blade flew into the darkness. With a slash to his strong arm, Kaia ensured he couldn't pick it up again. The third tried to chop at her as if he were splitting a log. Kaia sidestepped him, and the oaf managed to bury the blade in the soft earth beside him. Her jump-kick connected with his jaw, snapping his face up and knocking him on his back. Whining like a beaten dog, he scrambled towards the stables without even trying to recover his weapon.

The last three rushed her simultaneously from all sides. As they drew close, she extinguished the bright flame of her sword. Engulfed in blackness, the men stumbled about, bleating and flailing like lost sheep.

Although her own night vision was spotty, Kaia was ready. She shoved one of the brutes into his comrade. Thinking they had found their prey, the pair attacked each other, and one cried out in pain.

"Odriel's Teeth! Out of the way!" the other cursed.

The last guard managed to trip over poor Gus, his weapon landing on the grass with a soft thud. Kaia used the pommel of her blade to quietly dispatch the inept trio before they could injure themselves any further.

A shout and an indignant bray sounded from the stables, but drumming hoofbeats drew her eyes turned towards the open gate, announcing the hasty departure of the remaining guards. Before she could catch her breath, the shuffle of many uneven footsteps approached through the darkness from the rear of the castle. Gus whined and pawed at her leg, but the smell of rotting humanity had already reached her—the nauseating stench of an open grave.

In a desperate last effort to stop her, they had released the Lost.

Adrenaline sung through her limbs as she allowed her sword to flame again and illuminate the yard. Not thirty yards distant, a score of corpses stumbled towards her with jerky, involuntary movements. They looked almost identical to the dead she had dispatched in the Arimoke: ashen skin, frayed flesh, dirty rags, and empty black eye sockets.

She released a breath she hadn't realized she was holding. Not so many— she could handle this. The flame encircling her blade grew until it resembled a small tornado, its crackling drowning out the low keening of the Lost. Shad had said the things were evil, but they showed no sign of intelligence. As the hot vortex of flame before her grew to the size of a small house, it still gave them no pause. She let the shambling horde of Lost come within twenty paces before she swung the sword, whipping the cyclone blaze into their midst. A high-pitched wail rang through the air as the hungry flames consumed their flesh faster than dry tinder, the scorching fangs snapping zealously.

Kaia took it in with short breaths and a thumping heart. *Odriel has indeed blessed the Dragon Heir,* she thought.

Within seconds, the bodies of the Lost crumbled to dust, and the fire receded. For the first time in her young life, Kaia felt a grave kinship with her ancestor.

Gus nipped at her shirt, breaking her trance. The others must be inside. Move!

Glancing up at the looming tower, Kaia broke into a sprint, bursting through the open castle door with Gus close at her heels. The flame from her sword cast a flickering shadow against the mossy stone walls.

She passed through a low entryway into what she supposed was the great hall. Perhaps, in its time, it had been grand, but now it held only a few scattered chairs and a small table. The light danced along on the walls, illuminating two staircases in the corners of the room leading higher into the castle. She dismissed these. In the stories, the prisoners were held in the dungeons, and the dungeons were below the castle. Weren't they?

She contemplated calling out to her father and Klaus, but the thought of attracting further trouble kept her silent. Meanwhile, Gus bustled around the room, his nose snuffling along the floor. He came to a stop in front of a tapestry that seemed out of place in the barren hall.

He looked at Kaia and whined. Here.

The tapestry depicted the original confrontation of the three Heirs and Nifras—three beacons of light facing a monstrous demon. Although frayed, the moss and age that plagued the rest of the wall had spared it. Moving the cloth aside with a finger, Kaia discovered a hidden staircase plunging down into the dark. A miasma of decay emanated from the chilled air below.

"Stay behind me, Gussy," she whispered, her voice wavering. She wiped her brow and inhaled again. This smell of rot was different from her Lost encounter—lighter, more natural. She blew out the stink and bent her head to venture down the cramped passage. Her left hand trailed along the inner wall to balance her on the uneven steps while she held her glowing sword before her. When she came to the last step, she found a chubby guard in front of a tiny gated cell.

He nervously wiped sweat from his eyes, brandishing his shaking sword in front of him. "D-don't come any c-closer."

"Skies above," Kaia swore in exasperation. She had faced more ferocious barn cats. With two steps, she knocked his weapon aside and delivered an uppercut to his jaw with the pommel of her blade. He collapsed with a thump.

"It's… about… time," the cell's prisoner wheezed.

Kaia didn't need to see him to recognize his voice. She stepped over the incapacitated guard and approached the cell—little more than a hole in the wall.

"I can't believe you let these fools kidnap you," Kaia taunted, grinning as she melted the lock and opened the door. "The cunning Shadow Heir was tricked." She lifted her light and immediately regretted her words.

They had shaved Klaus' head to the scalp and chained him to ceiling, arms stretched up so high that he could only stand on his toes. Each foot was chained to a heavy ball, and the manacle had rubbed his skin raw at the ankle. Blood stained his tattered clothes, a swollen purple bruise dominated the whole left side of his face, and a deep slash cut across his right eyebrow.

Gus whined beside her. Oh no.

Outrage choked Kaia's chest. "Who did this to you?" *Surely not that harmless halfwit outside the cell.* She sheathed her sword and knelt. Extending an index finger, she produced a fine blue stream of fire to delicately cut through the manacles without burning his raw flesh.

"Mogens," he rasped, lifting his head with a weak grimace. "You'd know if you saw him." He erupted in a spasm of coughing, and his hazel eyes glazed with fatigue. The top of Kaia's head only reached his jaw, so she had to step on one of the balls to reach his wrists. She could hear him wheeze with every breath.

Gus nuzzled his leg. Hold on.

"It's okay, Gus," Kaia reassured him breathlessly. Klaus' left hand fell to his side like a broken wing. She switched to work on his right. "Do you know where my father is?" She tried to keep her voice steady, but it shook in spite of her.

"West Wing," he murmured. As the final manacle broke, Klaus collapsed against her shoulder, and she staggered under his weight. Heirs were nearly twice as strong as the average man, so she could carry him if she had to, but it would leave them vulnerable to attack. After seeing the work of this Mogens character, she didn't want to take that risk.

"Can you walk?"

He raised his battered head and managed a few steps before stumbling and catching himself on the wall. Kaia blanched at the sight of the ugly gashes that crisscrossed his back, crimson lines across his bronze skin.

Klaus winced. "A little help here, Firefly."

She rolled her eyes and hoisted one of his arms over her shoulders before unceremoniously dragging him out of the cell and up the stairs.

"Hey, come on, easy!" he protested.

Kaia pushed the tapestry to the side as she half-carried him into the great hall. "You know I hate that nickn—"

A sneering rasp echoed in the dank chamber. "I was *so* hoping it would be you."

CHAPTER 6
MOGENS

Klaus swore darkly, and Gus barked with a wild fury she had never heard from the gentle dog before. Kaia looked up, and a part of her died.

Her father struggled to lift his head, peering at her through the slit of his left eye. The right was missing. Kaia's stomach churned, and bile rose in her throat. Blood gushed from countless, oddly patterned gashes. With a start, Kaia realized words had been etched into his flesh with a knife. Where his fingers and toes should have been, only nubs remaining, and his right knee was bending the wrong way. His left ear was missing while the other hung by a strand and his face was so swollen it looked disfigured. In all respects, he was unrecognizable... to anyone, that is, but his child.

Tearing her gaze away, she looked to the man who had spoken. His appearance was nearly as disturbing as her father's. He had no lips, no nose, no eyebrows or ears, and he bared his teeth and gums in a grotesque smile. His wide eyes bulged unnaturally out of his bald head, and wrinkled, pink scar tissue covered every inch of him. He propped her father up as if they were close friends. *So, this* thing *was Mogens.*

"Ariston said we were supposed to keep them pretty until he got here, but I just couldn't help myself," he rasped cheerily. "Besides, wouldn't Guardian Dashul want me to return the favor after all these years? Justice is beautiful, after all,".

Her father tried to speak, but his words were unintelligible through his enflamed lips, and he let his head drop in exhaustion. The pool of blood burgeoning beneath him shined black in the shadows of Kaia's fire

"Put him down," she growled, letting the flames engulf her free hand. "Or I'll finish the job my father started."

Mogens produced a bloody, serrated dagger from his grimy vest and held the blade to her father's throat. "Now, now, let's not be hasty. I have a deal I think you might find interesting." Kaia let the fire in her palm grow, but Mogens seemed unperturbed. "It's simple, really. If you serve Ariston, I will let your father and your friend go free."

"And if I don't?" Kaia snarled.

"Then I torture your dear father until he dies, and we use his body as part of our Lost army," Mogens returned. "I'd prefer that really." His eyes bulged even further, and his unnatural grin widened.

Kaia hesitated, her fire receding. Her father was a protector of the land, a good man. He didn't deserve this. She couldn't let this happen to him. This was her father—her teacher, her partner, her friend. He had taught her everything—dried her every tear, bandaged her scrapes, calmed her fears. It wasn't a choice. She would pay any price for his life. *Any price.*

"Kaia, he's lying to you," Klaus croaked as loudly as his raw voice would allow. "He'll kill us all." At the sound of Klaus' voice, Kaia's father yanked his head up to gaze at them with his good eye. The sight of his mutilated face was too much for Kaia to bear.

"*Papa...*" she sobbed, and let the flame die.

At that, a strangled cry erupted from her father, and with one final burst of strength, Tam clamped onto Mogens' arm with his bloody palms and dragged the wicked knife across his own throat.

Both Kaia and Klaus cried out as Mogens let Tam slide to the floor with a look of disgust. The young Heirs stood frozen, transfixed by the sight of the Dragon Heir's broken and ruined body lying motionless on the blood-slicked stone.

Then, inexplicably, Mogens began to laugh—a bloodcurdling, ugly sound. The cackles rebounded on the stone walls and echoed endlessly in Kaia's ears.

Kaia cracked. Her muscles bunched, and a boiling cauldron of white-hot rage roared to life from her toes to her fingertips as a nimbus of blue flame encased her body. Agonizing pressure built within her until it felt as if her skin would split. In her last willful act before giving herself over to the fury, she shoved Klaus against the wall. An invisible giant hand forced open her gritted teeth, and she unleashed an earsplitting scream of anguished rage as the flames flared higher around her.

Still smiling, Mogens fled the room on quick feet.

Klaus threw up his arms to shield himself from the flames. "He's gone, Kaia! Stop! YOU'LL BRING THE CASTLE DOWN AROUND US!"

Vision red and ears filled with her own screams, Kaia heard none of it. Its walls buckling, the castle rocked on its foundations, and Klaus flinched away from the searing flames and falling rocks. With a panicked yelp, Gus leapt against Kaia, using his ten-stone weight to knock her to the ground. Kaia's head whipped against the flagstone floor with a *crack*, and the flames extinguished instantly with Gus licking her face in quick, rough strokes. As the red haze filling her vision receded, Kaia hugged the singed Gus around his neck and broke into painful, uncontrollable sobs.

Gus whined, his enchanted fur smoking ever so slightly. I'm sorry, my girl. Sorry, sorry, sorry.

Klaus collapsed to the floor in relief. A bead of sweat dripped from his chin onto the cold stone. "Earth below," he whispered. "Thank Odriel for you, Gus."

***

Kaia extended her hands and attacked the funeral pyre with vigor. The fire burned bright and hot in the chill of the pre-dawn air.

Kaia's eyes were sore and puffy, but her face was expressionless. "Would anyone care to say anything?"

Her heart had been torn apart and trampled until she had become an emotionless husk. Her grief—and anger—were spent. She felt nothing.

Gus leaned against her, sharing her grief. I am with you.

Kaia wiped at her face with a sleeve and tangled her fingers in his singed fur.

Shadmundar flicked his tail silently as he sat beside her feet, his cat eyes unreadable. Thornbite had fled in the midst of the battle when the soldiers had tried to mount him. Kaia distantly hoped the poor mule found his way to safety.

Klaus looked at Kaia with glistening eyes. Grief thickened his voice. "I wish I knew what to say."

"Nothing?" Kaia's unfocused eyes stared into the fire. "Let us be on our way then."

She turned her back on the pyre, but Shad's voice, ringing through the misty air, halted her. Kaia recognized the somber words, slow and measured, from *The Heirs' Way*:

> *This man journeys far to the great unknown,*
> *Where, bitterly, we will one day follow,*
> *But until then, we are left here alone,*
> *Our only companion is dark sorrow.*

> *The Dragon Heir has passed and been reborn,*
> *Here, his courageous heart continues on,*
> *But his noble sacrifice is now mourned,*
> *Odriel's guidance we must call upon.*

The echo of the cat's requiem lingered in the stillness. Klaus bowed his head, and Kaia trembled with the emotion she had thought spent. How many times had she been lulled to sleep by her father's smooth voice recounting the tales of the Heirs from that very book?

Shadmundar padded over to stand in front of Kaia. He dropped his head until the tips of his ears brushed the earth.

Guardian Dashul, Dragon Heir, we humbly ask for your protection."

Kaia choked back a sob, and hot tears once again streamed from her eyes. "I grant it freely," she whispered.

The cat raised his eyes and fixed his cobalt eyes on her. "Now, we may go."

Kaia stared vacantly at the ground under her feet, wishing she could become an ant and hide beneath a blade of grass. She felt a childish desire for her mother's embrace, but as soon as she thought this, a hot stab of agony seared her belly. She'd be the one to give her mother the news. *Papa will never come home.*

She felt a hand on the small of her back.

"Come on, Firefly," Klaus urged gently as he guided her out of the courtyard. "I want to show you something."

Outside of the gates, two stag-like steeds stood waiting patiently for them. The powerful beasts stood tall with broad racks of velvet antlers, lionlike manes, and bobbed tails. The palomino shone gold with a milky cream mane, while the roan gleamed a blue-silver. Gus leaned in for a cautious sniff as the creatures considered them with large, intelligent eyes.

The roan trotted up to Klaus on dainty hooves and whickered with a sonorous voice deeper than any horse.

Kaia sighed. "What—"

Klaus patted the roan on its shaggy neck. "They're Naerami Dalteek. Lucky for us, they're quite particular about their riders." He glanced at Kaia. "Your father brought them with him when he came west to find me. They're sure-footed and can run for miles without rest." The roan lipped his cheek. "This is Moonstreak." He nodded at the palomino. "And the doe is called Sunflash, your father's mount."

Kaia eyed the handsome creature's dancing legs and lean body, too burdened with grief to register its beauty. She held a hand out, palm up. The Dalteek edged towards her, it inhaled and then snuffed at her hand before reaching forward to nuzzle her cheek with its velvet nose. Kaia cupped its long jaw in her arms and leaned forward until their foreheads touched. Girl and beast breathed each other in. Sunflash smelled of pine, smoke, and sweat—she smelled like her father.

With another deep breath, she pulled away from the great creature. "Ok." Taking the reins in one hand, Kaia mounted the Dalteek.

Klaus followed suit and Shad leapt onto the roan's flanks behind him before securing himself once again into one of the roan's saddlebags.

"Where to?" Klaus' voice was still hoarse, but already growing stronger.

"We ride south," the cat declared.

And with that, the trio trotted down the dusty path and away from the crumbling castle gate. The pyre smoked at their backs, and before them, a rising sun cast a bloody smear across the horizon.

PART TWO

THE EVIL OF MAN

CHAPTER 7
DESPAIR

Days passed as they rode south, the Dalteek sauntering effortlessly along the dirt road as the aftershock of the Dragon Heir's death washed over their passengers. The landscape rose and fell along gentle green hills dotted with tangles of coral blossoms, but Kaia noticed none of it. Her body stiffened and ached from the agonizing toll of the Dragon Rage, but she savored each jolt and stab of pain. She deserved far worse. Despite the trilling birds and the clear blue sky, Kaia's world was dark.

Her face remained a stoic mask, her eyes staring at Sunflash's shaggy mane, unblinking and vacant. Inwardly, she combed over her father's death obsessively. She scrutinized every choice and action. Where had she gone wrong? If she had gone up the stairs instead of down into the basement, she could have found him sooner. Perhaps, if she hadn't hesitated... if she had just attacked right away, she could have saved him. That's what Bram would have done. Bram would have charged as soon as he laid eyes on Mogens. Kaia stiffened at even the thought of his malformed face—a sickening mixture of fear and rage squeezed her heart.

On the third night, they settled in a small thicket to the side of the road. After their campfire had reduced to embers and Klaus snored softly with his head on his pack, Shad padded over to where Kaia sat awake.

"It's not your fault, you know," he murmured.

Kaia shook her head. "You didn't see it. You don't know."

"This is not my first encounter with Mogens, or his handiwork." Shad's tail swished through the grass. "As you probably gathered, your father and he had quite a history, in the worst way."

Kaia looked sharply at the cat silhouetted by the glowing coals. "What do you mean?"

Shadmundar sighed. "King Candon hired Mogens to hunt down your father and the rightful Prince Beirtolo when they fled the Austerden court all those years ago." His sapphire eyes shined in the dark. "But while the younger Heirs went into exile, the elder generation stayed at the court, still believing Candon's lies."

"You mean my grandfather?" Kaia's brow wrinkled. "My father always turned away when I asked about him."

Shad nodded. "After chasing after the Heirs for months, Mogens realized he had the perfect bait lying right under his nose." He closed his eyes. "Your father and the others raced back, but by the time they got back to court, their loved ones hung from the palace gates."

Kaia covered a gasp with her hand.

Klaus sat up on the other side of the fire, his face hard. "After my parents died, I always wondered what happened to the last generation." His eyes shifted to the fire. "That explains it."

Kaia looked across to the Shadow Heir then back to Shad. "Then my father burned Mogens with dragon fire."

Shad turned his gaze back to Kaia. "These events were set into motion long before you were born." He put a paw on her leg, every word weighted with gravity. "It's. Not. Your. Fault."

Klaus nodded at her from across the cinders. "You did your best, Firefly."

Kaia pressed her lips together and stared into the dying fire. She *had* tried her best. But what did you do when your best wasn't good enough?

***

As they continued their journey in near silence, Kaia could feel the eyes of her companions, watching her as she descended further into herself. Her appetite deserted her and nightmares plagued her in the darkness, but still, her mind spiraled ever deeper. Where was Mogens now? Why was he working for Ariston? What were they planning next? Her eyes glazed as she listed dangerously in her high saddle.

Gus let out two sharp barks. Wake up!

A rough hand seized her wrist, pulling her upright. "Whoah there, Firefly."

She yanked her arm from his grasp. "Stop calling me that. I'm fine." Her voice sounded scratchy from disuse. How many days had they been on the road already—eight? Nine?

"No, you're not." The Shadow Heir pulled his stag in front of Sunflash, bringing them to a halt. "You don't sleep, you barely eat." He looked her up and down. "You probably couldn't light a candle in your condition."

Gus shifted from paw to paw, and Shad peered at them from his saddlebag, but they remained silent.

Kaia set her jaw and dismounted. She turned on her heel and walked back down the path. She didn't need this.

"Hey!" Klaus dismounted, hurling words at her back as he stalked after her. "Pryor is dead, Tam is dead, Jago is probably dead or worse, but we're still alive. Our duties as Heirs have to come before our grief."

Kaia spun around, her face suddenly inches from Klaus. "My father *died*, Klaus."

"And more will die before the end, but that doesn't mean you can just quit." He jabbed a finger into her forehead, and Kaia's rage surged.

"I'm not quitting," she roared, smacking his hand away with one hand, and then throwing a punch with the other.

He dodged easily, a mocking smile dancing across his features. "Still too slow, Firefly."

Kaia howled with anger as she attacked with a flurry of punches, elbows, knees, and kicks. Klaus stepped back, ducking and dodging. Kaia leapt forward with a flying kick, only to skid to the ground when the Shadow Heir vanished.

With a shout of frustration, she let the furious fire within her explode out of her clenched fists

"Welcome back, Guardian Dashul." Klaus reappeared five paces in front of her. "I'd prefer the Dragon any day over a sulking little girl." His smug smile flashed again. "But I thought you were supposed to be training these last few years, you're still as slow as a wartslug."

Kaia's flames surged again. "Just you wait till I get my strength back. Then we'll see who's slow." She let her hands cool before stalking back to her mount. "Let's get going, you're wasting time."

***

As if waking suddenly from a nightmare, Kaia began to live again. She spitefully shoveled food into her mouth like a beast starved. In every spare moment, she cycled through her combat exercises and conjured complex flame patterns until her hands cramped from the strain. She trained to exhaustion and at the end of the day, fell into a sleep too deep for horrors. The silence, too, disappeared as bickering filled the peaceful mountain air.

Klaus' success in saving her from a slow self-imposed death, as he put it, made him insufferable. He harassed her endlessly with childish pranks—bugs in her hair, burrs on her saddle, toads in her bag—until she was forced to flick tiny fireballs at him to keep his distance.

But it was not the same as it had been years before. A newfound emptiness swallowed all the joy she might have taken in tormenting him. Kaia found it difficult to even smile, but Klaus' pranks were quietly reassuring all the same. They allowed Kaia to pretend, if only for a second, that she wasn't the Heir that had witnessed her father's violent death. For just a moment, they could both be the quarreling youths they always had been. Though she'd never admit it, secretly, she was thankful to Klaus for banishing her dangerous melancholy. While thoughts of Mogens and Nifras still loomed large, they did not consume her, and her world became manageable once again.

***

"It's been two weeks since we left the castle." Klaus glanced at Kaia across the fire as they slurped sleek trout stew in the gathering dusk. The Dalteek grazed as the tall grass waved in the whispering wind, but slate grey clouds obscured the stars. His eyes moved where Shad lay curled by the fire, eyes half closed. "It's time we discussed the plan."

Kaia blew on her soup-laden spoon. "What plan?"

Klaus opened his mouth to reply, but Shad spoke first. "The plan is to send word to Everard to meet us on the southern border. The yanai barrier is weakest in the Deadlands, and Nifras will almost surely strike there first."

Kaia sipped the herb-infused broth. "What about Ariston?"

Shad's tail tapped back and forth on the flattened grass. "He's the lesser of the two evils."

Kaia ran her fingers absently through Gus' fur as he stretched out beside her. "How do we know Ariston isn't actually just a pawn of the necromancer?" With a stab of pain, Kaia thought of her last conversation with her mother. "All dark magic stems from Nifras."

Klaus rubbed a scabbed gash on his arm. "Regardless, I think it's safe to say, Ariston is not on our side." He took a deep breath and let it hiss out his even front teeth. "Ariston's army is moving south as well. If we're not careful, we could find ourselves sandwiched between two armies."

For the first time, the gravity of their situation hit Kaia like a brick to the face. "And there's only two of us left." She winced.

Klaus rubbed the scar in his brow where the hair hadn't grown back—a lasting reminder of their vulnerability. He threw another stick into the fire. "We need help."

Kaia stuffed her empty bowl into her pack beside her. "But who?"

Silence stretched between the trio as the fire burned low between them. In the vast open lea, beneath the endless sky, their pitiful fire seemed like a single spar in an ocean of darkness. Gus puffed out his lips in a long sigh that Kaia felt down to her bones.

Shad sat up, ears twitching. "You must ask the Maldibor Tribe to call the warriors of Okarria." His pink tongue flicked out over his black nose. "Only they keep the jackhawks fast enough to carry your message."

Klaus raised his eyebrows. "Where can we find them?"

Shad blinked slowly as he looked out to the Dalteek bending their antlered heads low in the grass. "Their village lies in the shadow of the Naerami, not two days journey from here," he turned to meet Klaus' gaze. "In Carceroc forest."

Now it was Kaia's turn to look up. "Where the magi imprisoned the ancient mankillers?" In the world's youth, bloodthirsty beasts had roamed the land, killing for pleasure and squashing creation in all its forms, until the magi emerged from hiding to imprison them in a spelled wood in the heart of Okarria. The story had been one of Kaia's favorites as a child.

Klaus snorted. "That's suicide."

Shad shrugged his small shoulders. "Maybe you're right, oh wise Shadow Heir." He sank back to the ground. "What do I know? I'm just an 80-year-old cat."

Their words washed over Kaia as she tried to focus her scattered thoughts. With her father gone, only she and Klaus stood between Okarria and two dead armies. She glanced at Klaus. His shirt and vest were ragged, and his breeches were full of holes, but the bruise on his face had disappeared, and the stripes on his back had closed. Short dark hair now covered his head, and his jaw sported a layer of scruff.

Confidence marked his every gesture and movement, but the lines of experience had yet to etch his features. And they would need more than confidence. Kaia fixed her stare on Klaus. "We have to try."

Klaus shook his head. "There's got to be another way. This is a stupid idea."

She shrugged. "If you think of a better way by morning, feel free to share." She lay back on her saddle, but she could still feel Klaus's eyes on her.

His voice was soft in the night. "You don't have to prove anything you know."

Kaia let the breeze take the words over and past her into the field beyond. Three weeks ago, she had daydreamed of going to the Spring Festival while tending her blusheep. Now, fate had tossed her into a maelstrom of danger and evil, and she was drowning. Klaus couldn't understand—he'd assisted her father with missions for years. Of course she had something to prove. She had been born the Dragon Heir, but she had yet to earn it.

Gus reached over and licked her arm. No worry. Rest now.

Kaia wrapped her arms around the dog in a tight hug. Inhaling his scent of earth and smoke, she felt the knot of anxiety loosen in her stomach. Tomorrow, they would go for help. Until then, she could sleep.

As her eyelids drooped, she felt small paws alight on her side and turned to see glowing sapphires staring at her through the darkness.

"Have you courage, girl?" the cat asked.

Kaia swallowed. "I am the Dragon Heir. Of course I have courage," she whispered.

Shad's eyes narrowed into slits. "You will need it."

CHAPTER 8
CARCEROC

Kaia remembered these words vividly when two days later, she stood before the verdant tangle of branch and fern they called Carceroc Forest. Butterflies fluttered cautiously in her ribcage as she recalled her father's stories of the creatures of Carceroc—cyclogres that could hypnotize you with a glance, shadow beasts that could silence your inner thoughts, and strigans that could mimic a child's desperate cries to lure you to your death. As she stared into the dark wood, Kaia became uncomfortably aware of the odd silence, devoid of bird song or insect chatter.

Her eyes shifted to Klaus as he pulled Moonstreak beside her. His full lips pressed together, and tension hardened his hazel eyes. He had voiced his objections again and again over the past two days but had yet to come up with an alternative course. His playful pranks had disappeared as he begrudgingly followed Shad's advisement. Now, sitting atop his majestic stag, with his grave countenance and freshly healed wounds, he looked every bit Odriel's Assassin, the dangerous Shadow Heir of legend.

Kaia tucked her copper braid behind her ear and pushed her mass of tangled hair behind her shoulder. Meanwhile, she still looked like a lost sheep girl.

Gus yipped from her other side, panting exuberantly. Chin up, my girl, chin up.

Klaus' grimace deepened as he regarded the black cat in his saddle bag. "Do you know how to find the Maldibor Tribe once we're inside?"

Shad's tail swung back and forth. "No need. The Maldibor will know as soon as we enter. They will find us."

"As long as something else doesn't find us first," Klaus grumbled. He clicked his tongue to urge Moonstreak forward, with Sunflash following close behind.

The bright afternoon surrendered quickly to dusk as they entered the forest. Color drained from the trees, leaving only silhouettes to line the silent path. Unlike the serenity on her mountain, the silence here felt unsettlingly oppressive. Kaia strained her ears, listening for sounds in the shadows that her eyes could not pierce in the gathering gloom.

Her mind strayed to thoughts of Lost, slinking through the dark with their hellish red eyes following her through the trees. Gus drew close to her, ears pricked, and even the Dalteek seemed nervous as their pace quickened along the ever-narrowing path.

As they rode into the twisting, moss-covered trees, a question prodded Kaia's thoughts. "Shad, why would the Maldibor choose to live in a forest of monsters?"

The cat didn't look back. "Ask one when we get there."

They hadn't gone twenty paces along the narrow trail when Klaus stopped abruptly. "That's odd," he murmured

Kaia leaned in her saddle to peer around him. Not far ahead, the path broke into not two, but five separate paths.

Klaus glanced from one to the other. "Which way?"

The cat considered the paths for a moment. "Isn't this interesting?" he mused to himself as he surveyed the scene. "I have heard of this before, but never experienced it for myself."

The quake of Kaia's heart sent rushes of tingling nerves through her fingers, her fire bubbling just beneath the surface. "What's going on?"

 Shad's whiskers twitched. "This is the work of forest *griegals*."

Kaia cocked her head, not sure if she heard him right. "What's a *griegal*?"

"Take the most irritating parts of an imp, a pixie, and a fairy and mix them together. You get a griegal," said Shad. "They aren't dangerous, mostly, but meeting up with them can make a long day much longer," The cat mewed with impatience. "The pests have altered the appearance of the forest and will play with you until they get bored. I would travel slowly and hope they tire of us sooner rather than later."

A rustle in a bush near the path caught Kaia's attention. Gus bustled noisily through the thin layer of spring shrubs and scared a small midnight squirrel out of its hiding place. They continued on, and a few minutes later, they came to another fork in the path that looked exactly like the one they had just left.

Klaus scanned the paths with knitted brows. "We were just here, but we didn't go far enough to get turned around."

Kaia eyed the darkening canopy. "Leave us alone, griegals,"

The Shadow Heir skewered her with a contemptuous stare. "Right, because I'm sure that'll work."

"You're the one who's leading us in circles," she said. "Let's try this way."

Kaia led Sunflash to the rightmost path. Once again, after an impossibly short time, they arrived back to their starting place.

Klaus rubbed his stubbled chin, then pointed. "Walk down the left path, and I'll wait here for you."

She bristled at his sharp tone. "Hopefully, Gus, he's wrong, and we'll just leave him behind." She turned her back on Klaus, but she didn't have to go far before she saw him and Moonstreak looking towards her expectantly. Kaia dismounted. "What now, oh great Shadow Heir?"

"I don't know. There's probably a reason they're not letting us pass, but what do you think they want?" Klaus massaged his temple with a sigh.

"I have no idea." She shrugged and sat down to ruffle Gus' fur. "You're the crafty one. Aren't you supposed to figure things like this out?"

Klaus rolled his eyes, "I know it's not your strong suit, but you could at least try to help."

"I did, and you snapped at me. So, feel free to struggle all on your—"

"My dear Heirs," Shad cut in, raising his voice. "Let's not air our dirty laundry in front of company." He nodded towards a tree on the edge of the path.

Kaia squinted up at the mossy trunk, trying to make out the eavesdropper. Then, an olive child-sized creature peeked out from behind a lush branch hanging high overhead. The griegal, or so she assumed, resembled a skinny pixie with a stubby, impish tail sticking out of its tunic and vestigial wings far too small for its body. He tilted his head as he edged closer, his black hair sticking out in all directions. He smiled at her innocently with sharp white teeth and chattered something unintelligible. Then he jumped from the branch and, with wings fluttering madly, descended to the forest floor.

Klaus cleared his throat. "Firefly, for your sake, I hope these things are friendly because they've got you surrounded."

She sat back on her heels and saw that Klaus was right. Six or seven of the creatures were cautiously descending from the trees and creeping toward her and Gus, while another dozen pairs of amber eyes glowed in the shadows.

Gus sniffed at one cautiously, then snorted. Interesting smell, but not bad.

"They're only two feet tall, Klaus. I think we could take them." Kaia allowed herself a small smile as the griegals poked at her hair and clothes, tittering to each other in scratchy chirrups.

Klaus tapped a finger on his chin. "Well, you have obviously found your real family."

"You're just jealous that they like me more than you," Kaia said, bending down so the clamoring griegals could hold on to her fingers. They tugged on her with sharp fingers, leading her away from the path. They waved their arms at the Dalteek, and the mounts sauntered after them.

"I'm not sure this is a good idea," Klaus ventured as Moonstreak threaded into the wood after them. "We should stay on the path until the Maldibor find us."

Kaia took in the ever-widening tree-trunks as they passed deeper into the forest. "The Maldibor won't be able to find us if the griegals are casting an illusion."

Shad yawned widely, showing his sharp white teeth. "If griegals are the worst things we find, it'll be a good day."

Kaia's mouth hung ajar as she stared at the branches as thick as Dalteek intertwining into a dense canopy above, while below, ivory flowers dotted the carpet of pine needles and ferns. As the breeze wove through the forest, softly glowing blue butterflies the size of her hand fluttered gaily about them in the honey-scented air.

Still atop Moonstreak, the tension eased from Klaus' features. "Do you hear music?"

The airy low whistle of a flute echoed around them.

"It's beautiful," Kaia whispered.

The griegals brought them to a halt in a small circular grove, where a dozen more appeared to poke and pull at the legs and hands of their visitors. They gibbered and gestured towards one of the enormous trees.

Kaia shrugged. "Seems like as good of a place to wait for the Maldibor as any." She sat down and leaned against an oversized root.

Klaus dismounted and leaned against the smooth trunk, his eyes still scanning the dusky forest. The mounts grazed contentedly on the lush ferns, and Gus stretched out in his usual spot at Kaia's feet.

His tongue lolled out of his mouth as the griegals smothered him with attention. Little people not so bad.

Shad's eyelids drooped as he watched lazily from Moonstreak's back.

The glow of the rising moon lit the grove, and another, lighter melody joined the first. As the sound of the gay flutes drifted through the trees, the green tribesman began to dance in a coordinated and complicated pattern in the silvery clearing. A small crowd pulled on Kaia's fingers to join them.

"Looks like they want you to dance, Firefly," Klaus said.

"I don't think they're going to let you escape either," she called back as a small mob surrounded him. Kaia smiled at their enthusiasm but wasn't quite sure what to do. The creatures wove, spun, and skipped around one another with matchless grace. Kaia watched their steps, and tentatively copied their movements. Klaus raised a mocking eyebrow.

Kaia bowed unsteadily. "Aren't you going to join in?"

The Shadow Heir crossed his scarred arms. "They seem perfectly happy to just dance around me."

"Well, aren't you boring?" Kaia reached her arms above her, spun around, and weaved carefully between the other dancers with slow, dainty steps. "I think I'm getting the hang of it."

The words had barely escaped her lips when the music evaporated, and the griegals froze mid-step. Their large, tapering ears pricked up as they stared furtively into the dark forest with luminescent yellow eyes. Kaia halted along with them, fingers of fear fisting in her belly.

Shad's eyes snapped open, and Klaus sprang to the ready, scanning their surroundings. In the sudden silence, the giant trees towered ominously above them.

Gus whined as he looked from Kaia to Klaus and back. *Something's wrong.*

Kaia glanced around the field of still figures. "Klaus...."

"Shh!" Klaus whipped a hand towards her. "Can you hear that?"

"Hear what?" But then she heard the hissing. The vibrations started low but grew louder with every heartbeat until the sound rattled her very rib cage. She could see nothing through the large trunks, but the noise emanated from all around them.

"What is it?" she whispered.

Then, *it* attacked. An enormous scaly head burst through the ground with gaping jaws lined with rows upon rows of fangs that opened wide as it swallowed a griegal whole. The meadow erupted in panicked flight. Griegals dashed and fluttered, clambering up the thick trees and jabbering in hysterical, high-pitched tones as more wormlike heads broke the ground.

Klaus yanked his sword from its sheath and fire leapt to Kaia's fingertips. She hurled a fireball at a nearby attacker, but its glinting, earth-colored scales deflected her flames. Frustrated, she drew her sword from her waist, but the armored, slimy creatures were too fast, dragging griegals down all around her. Klaus lashed out at one and then another, but even the quick Shadow lagged a beat behind.

With a whinny, Moonstreak reared and brandished his sharp hooves at the nearest worm.

Shad clawed at the saddlebags to stay seated. *"Terraverms!* Run!" he yowled as the mounts bolted for the safety of the forest.

The Dalteek bounded nimbly away from the worms with great leaps, disappearing between the giant trunks.

Gus ran after them, before turning and barking wildly from the tree line. *C'mon, c'mon, c'mon!*

Klaus grabbed her arm. "Run, you fool! Get moving!"

He yanked Kaia away from the slaughter just as a pair of jaws punched through the ground to snap at her heels. Gus ran back and forth from the trees, urging them on, while the terraverms, sensing larger prey eluded them, pursued hotly. The Heirs followed after the ragehound as he ran out in front, weaving through the gargantuan trunks. The fanged predators struck through the earth every few strides, spraying the trio with dirt.

"We have to climb a tree!" Kaia yelled over the rattling.

Klaus weaved to the left, just missing the open jaws of one of the monsters. "We can't climb these trees—we don't have claws!"

"But we can't run forever!" Kaia's flames glanced off the scales of another attacker.

"If you have a better idea, let me know!" he spat. "If you hadn't followed those stupid griegals, we wouldn't be in this mess in the first place."

Kaia opened her mouth to respond when their luck ran out. A worm surged from its hiding place beneath a log and clamped onto Klaus' leg, taking him down. Before Kaia could react, the worm's thorny head retreated into its hole, rattling as it dragged the screaming Klaus with it. Kaia dropped her sword and dove headfirst underneath the log while the Shadow Heir clung to a tree root in a desperate bid to stay above ground. As Kaia slid on her belly over the soft earth, she found herself nose to nose with the nightmarish creature, its jaws tightening around Klaus' oozing calf. Its six yellow, spiderlike eyes met Kaia's, and for a brief, mortifying second, Kaia froze.

Another howl of pain from Klaus snapped Kaia into action. She seized a sharp rock jutting from the tunnel wall and jammed it into the worm's lower right eye. The rattling turned into a squeal as the creature released Klaus' leg and retreated into its burrow. Kaia pushed Klaus out of the way before releasing a stream of flame into the hole. After one last hiss of pain, the sinister rattling finally receded to a whisper. Kaia sprang out from under the log, head whipping from side to side.

The rows of fangs had punctured Klaus' leg in what seemed like a hundred places, but the wounds weren't deep. "Did you kill it?" he asked between gasps of pain.

Kaia's chest heaved as she tried to catch her breath. "No, it's too fast. I think I just scared it." In the light of her glowing fingers, she could make out the black streaks already etching the skin around his wound. Venom. "We need help," she said, wiping sweat from her brow.

Klaus struggled to his feet. "It's fine. I can walk."

Kaia extended a hand to help him up, but he waved her away. "That worm was venomous, Klaus." She shifted her grip on the hilt. "You need an antidote."

Klaus' face remained stony. "Where did Shad and the Dalteek go?"

Gus barked from the darkness. This way! This way! The ragehound turned in tight circles and barked again, urging them on.

Kaia nodded towards him. "Gus smells something."

"Let's hope it's something without teeth." Klaus set off with a limping gait after the ragehound. Following close behind him, Kaia kept her eyes to their rear. Still, her thoughts whirled. Even small cliffsnake bites could cause you to lose a limb if they went untreated. And the terraverms were ten times as big as cliffsnakes. There no longer seemed to be anything beautiful about the Carceroc Forest.

Twenty minutes passed before Klaus lost feeling in the leg and had to lean heavily on her shoulder. Kaia blanched as she thought about the possibility of amputation. She had nothing to sedate Klaus with, and the leg wasn't even broken. Could he survive the shock of sawing through the bone? Even if he did, cauterizing the wound might kill him.

The terraverms' hiss whispered through the trees.

"Oh no," she breathed. She caught a glimpse of Gus' wagging red tail wagging in front of them. Surely, he had to be leading them somewhere. The hissing grew louder.

"You're going to have to leave me," Klaus murmured, his eyelids drooping.

"Don't even think it," Kaia said, stumbling over a root as she searched the nearby trees for a low branch, but the giant trunks offered no such route to safety.

Gus' wild barking ahead of them interrupted her thoughts, and Kaia's head jerked around to find a light flickering between the trees. Her spirits surging, she shuffled as quickly as she could, dragging Klaus behind her. The light bobbed toward them, resolving into a lantern held aloft by a looming cloaked figure, with Gus trotting alongside him.

With the hiss rattling her brain and no other options, Kaia stumbled towards the silhouette. Panting, she nearly fell at the feet of the stranger. "We need help!"

The hood of the figure fell back, revealing oversized teeth, wolf-like ears, and a long snout. Kaia's jaw fell open as she shifted her body, putting her weapon between herself and the beast. His pungent musk burned her nose as he considered her with emerald eyes.

Before she could form another thought, a terraverm struck at her from the dark. Caught off balance, she could only watch in horror as the wide, fanged mouth lunged at her.

But the beast was faster. With one smooth, ringing movement, he drew his cutlass and slashed the creature across its tender eyes. The terraverm's head snapped back, recoiling into the ground with an angry hiss. The hulking beast tipped his muzzle to the sky and unleashed an earsplitting howl. The howl rose and fell like a wave on a shore, flowing and crashing and flowing again, until at it last faded away to nothing. With it, the rattling had silenced as well, leaving the air still and peaceful once more.

Still bristling with suspicion, Kaia regarded the beast. It—or *he*, she supposed—was not a man, nor was he an animal. He wore breeches, and his green eyes sparkled with visible intelligence, but he bore the body of a hulking red-brown bear.

Practically unconscious, Klaus' ragged breathing filled the space between them, while Gus looked from Kaia to the beast, his tail wagging. Good people, this is good people.

Slowly, the beast bowed his head towards the ground. His deep voice vibrated in Kaia's bones. "Greetings, Guardian Dashul." He straightened to his full height, more than two heads taller than Kaia. "I am Tekoa of the Maldibor Clan. Shadmundar and the Dalteek have already made it safely to the village." He nodded his lupine nose towards Klaus. "Come, the sooner we treat Guardian Thane, the better."

Still in shock, Kaia nodded dumbly.

Satisfied, Tekoa turned and led them into the shadowed heart of the wood.

CHAPTER 9
THE MALDIBOR

Kaia sat outside the healer's cabin, her back against the log wall as she tried to shake off the shock of the terraverm attack. It had been her idea to follow the griegals, perhaps if she hadn't, Klaus wouldn't have gotten hurt. Could she do nothing right?

Gus licked her cheek with a slick wet tongue, trying to wash away the shame. You are good. You are right. You are my girl.

She leaned into Gus as she took in the village before her. The animal stench of Tekoa and his kin soaked the air, as they walked along the neat rows of wooden dwellings sprouting up amongst the trees, like a natural part of the forest. The cabins pinned in an open lawn that served as the village square, where human women rotated spits of meat above large fires. Meanwhile, beast and men rolled smoothed tree trunks to form rectangles around the flames, and children lit torches along the pathways. Although the presence of the beast-men was impossible to ignore, they were still far outnumbered by other ordinary folk milling through the square.

Kaia stroked her ragehound's long ears. "What is this place, Gus?"

Gus' wet nose twitched this way and that as he took in their new surroundings. Good place. This is a good place.

Kaia jumped as the cabin door creaked open beside her. Tekoa lumbered out of the tall doorway, Shad padding out close behind.

The beast turned his great wolf-head to Kaia, "Your companion will be fine, but the antidote has given him a much-needed rest. He will not wake until the morning."

He glanced at the black cat. "I understand you wish to speak to Okoni of sending our jackhawks to rally the Okarrian warrior tribes?"

Kaia opened her mouth to speak, but Shad beat her to it. "Tekoa, we really don't want to take you away from a dark moon." His ears twitched. "We know how much this means to your clan."

Kaia's forehead wrinkled. "A dark moon?"

Tekoa's tongue lolled out, revealing his great fangs. "It is a magical night for our people, and there will be much celebration." He looked out at the preparations in the square. "As friends of Everard, you're more than welcome to join us." He held out a thick paw with long claws. "Please, join us for a meal before you turn in for the evening. You're more than welcome at our celebration."

Shad bowed his head. "Thank you, Tekoa, but I'm too old for such revels. I'll stay with the Shadow Heir." He turned to Kaia, yawning widely. "I'll find you in the morning."

Tekoa nodded, opening the cabin door so the cat could slip back inside.

Kaia felt Tekoa's eyes fall to her as she eyed the crowd uncertainly. "If you don't mind, I'd like to check on Sunflash for the night first."

"Of course." The Maldibor bared his teeth once more. "I knew there was a reason Sunflash liked you." He strode off toward the stables, glancing over his shoulder, to meet her curious gaze. "I watched the births of both Sunflash and Moonstreak, you know—both descended from the uncatchable stags of yore."

Kaia nodded, her words lost as the hulking beast led her to the far end of the village. A crowd of children chased after Gus as he weaved happily between their feet, looking for tidbits of food.

She plucked at her sleeve. "There are a lot of children here."

Tekoa dipped his head. "We take in orphans and runaways from miles around. Many come from hard pasts that they wish to escape in the seclusion of the forest. Here, they find acceptance and protection from the reach of their own monsters." Tekoa's laughing bark sounded like rocks grating together.

As Kaia watched a bulky beast embrace a young girl, she could no longer contain her curiosity. "Tekoa, do you mind telling me more about your people? I'm afraid I've never met a Maldibor before."

"Do not fear. Most haven't." Tekoa stepped into the warm, hay-scented stable. Sunflash whickered softly from a doorless stall as Kaia reached out to stroke her soft nose in greeting.

Tekoa rubbed the doe's shaggy mane with a great paw. "All you see here who look like me—my cousins, father, brothers, and uncles—are descendants of my great-grandfather Elika, who foolishly spurned the magus, Ivanora." He reached into a threadbare bag hanging from the wall.

"These are Sunflash's favorites," he said, dropping dried periapple into Kaia's hand. Sunflash's soft lips snapped the fruit from her palm even before Kaia offered.

Tekoa paused, reaching out to scratch the base of Sunflash's branching antlers as the doe loudly smacked the periapple. "As I'm sure you already know, the magi, as a rule, prefer rather…imaginative punishments."

Kaia nodded again, thinking of Shadmundar.

Tekoa called to a nearby beast-child with instructions to stock the saddlebags with food. He returned to Kaia and led her back to the fires. "So, when Ivanora declared her love for Elika, and he told her he loved another, she avowed that she would make certain that no woman would ever love him again. She turned him into a beast like the ones you see before you." He spread his arms wide, gesturing towards his kinsmen. "Luckily, Everard disapproved of her sentence and took pity on Elika and his love. He made a bargain with Ivanora on their behalf."

"Everard was a champion of love?" Kaia's words dripped with disbelief. The cantankerous magus had attended many of their Triennials, but she had never once even seen him smile.

"Indeed." Tekoa let his tongue hang out as he sat down on a log by the fire. A silver-haired woman handed him a plate of food and a cup of wine. He passed it to Kaia before accepting his own dish. He brushed a paw across the old woman's hand. "Thank you, Mother."

She smiled back at him. "You are welcome, Teki," she patted his furry arm before bustling away to serve the others surrounding the fire.

Kaia added her thanks as she sat down next to Tekoa, eating the meat with her fingers and sharing with Gus, whose wet nose had appeared out of nowhere. "What was the bargain?"

"We are allowed one human day every moon cycle, but the curse passes from father to son." Tekoa opened his mouth and dumped the plateful of food straight into his gullet.

Kaia bit into the hunk of meat, succulent juices running down her chin. "That was a good deal?"

Tekoa rumbled with laughter. "Elika thought so, I'm sure. He got to be with his love. And look around you now–I see nothing but happiness."

Kaia sat back and drank in the atmosphere. The air was filled with shrieks of laughter. Smiling faces and people of all ages and shapes sat close and shared tales in the glow of a cozy fire.

She turned back to the grinning Tekoa. "You're right," she murmured. "I'm sorry to have suggested otherwise."

He lolled his tongue out in what Kaia was beginning to recognize as a smile. "We must accept who we are, the good *and* the bad."

Kaia sipped her wine thoughtfully, just as the crowd erupted in shouts of excitement.

"Midnight nears." Tekoa's green eyes glinted in the flickering firelight. "Now that you've seen the bad, you're about to witness the miraculous."

Kaia glanced at the sky peeking through the forest canopy. The clouds had cleared, but the moon wasn't nestled in the heavens tonight. In its place,

Odriel's guiding star winked back at them from a blanket of black. Just as the shouts reached a climax, the beasts transformed. Their great hulking bodies shrank, their thick fur coats and tails disappeared, and the claws, fangs, and ears all receded. In the space of a few seconds, she was looking at a shirtless, broad-shouldered young man, perhaps ten years older than her—Jago's age.

He had shaggy black hair and golden skin taut with muscle, but his emerald eyes still twinkled with joy. The crowd cheered as couples and families embraced. Tekoa picked her up and whirled her around before going to embrace his mother and father on the other side of the fire.

Kaia's face burned to match the flames in front of her. Just seconds ago, she had been surrounded by reeking wolfish beasts, and now a slew of half-naked, green-eyed men circled the fire. Even the smell had vanished.

After embracing everyone in reach—Tekoa sat down beside her once more. "And?" he asked, his words smoother than honey—bearing no resemblance to his previous rumble.

Kaia stared, trying to order her thoughts. Finally, she shook her head. "I just...I mean...this is *incredible*."

Tekoa grinned. "Now you know why Everard and his friends will always have a place at our feast." He paused to drain his mug of wine, and then sighed, his smile lingering. "It's like your flame, Kaia. At once destructive and life-giving."

Kaia's stomach flipped. "You know I'm the Dragon Heir?"

Tekoa laughed, a whole, rich sound like the tolling of a bell. "I can smell the embers in you as easily as you can smell the beast in me."

"Ah," she said, her eyes falling to study the dark loam of the earth around the fire.

"My dear Kaia." Tekoa took her hand. "I see the sorrow that weighs on you, the responsibilities you bear, and I fear you face a difficult future. But enjoy this time while it is ours. Tonight is a happy one. A miraculous night." He squeezed her hand. "Listen, I can hear the fiddle. Let us dance!"

Tekoa yanked her to her feet, and they joined the other villagers in a wild, jubilant jig that had no steps. Kaia whirled from stranger to stranger, from man to woman to child. The world spun, and the wine flowed freely, lightening her heavy load, and for the night, the Dragon Heir and the grandsons of Elika danced until they left their troubles behind.

***

Kaia did not remember falling asleep. But when Tekoa shook her awake, she blinked with heavy eyelids and found herself next to the fire with a thick quilt thrown over her. Gus snored beside her, his wet nose tickling her cheek. She smiled up at Tekoa's kind face, but his eyes were hard.

"Come, Kaia, there is something you must see."

Kaia rubbed her eyes, and Gus rose with a yawn. It was still dark, but a few families still clustered around the glowing fires. Their eyes lingered on Kaia as they murmured to one another.

"What is it?" Kaia asked.

Tekoa grabbed her hands and pulled her up. "This way." Gus shook himself before trailing after them.

The murmurs quieted, and the eyes followed Kaia around the square as they took the main road into the darkness of the wood. Kaia tucked her copper braid behind her ear, her stomach sinking. *They know.* Memories rose like bile in the back of her throat. She remembered the first time her mother had taken her into Arimoke with Pellie, her first ragehound, at her side. The villagers crossed the road to avoid them and ushered their children inside.

One brave woman had approached her mother and seized her elbow. "You can't bring that curse here," she hissed. "A child who summons fire could burn this whole town down in a fit." Kaia could still remember the woman's cringe as they locked eyes. "It's *unnatural.*"

Lost in thought, Kaia almost ran into Tekoa's broad back as he stopped in the middle of the road. "There." He pointed a finger down the dark lane.

Kaia stepped in front of Tekoa and scanned the road, but her eyes couldn't pierce the moonless wood. She chewed her lip and looked back at the Maldibor, his muscles rippling beneath his open vest. He nodded, his gaze softening ever so slightly.

Kaia returned the nod and faced the road once more. She reached out a palm and let the fire flow from her core to her fingertips, lighting the path. In the shadows ahead, she could just make out the silhouettes of two dozen Lost crawling over a wagon-sized mass in the road like wriggling gray maggots. Kaia squinted and craned her head forward, but they had already ravaged the carcass into unrecognizable pieces. The iron stench of blood and rot infected the air.

Gus let out a low whine. Bad, bad smells.

Kaia felt her fire bubble up with shame and rage as the realization dawned on her. "They followed us."

CHAPTER 10
LIGHT THE DARK

Tekoa growled, a low beastly sound that squeezed Kaia's already thrumming heart.

Kaia flinched as Shad padded up behind them to brush against her calf. "They've managed to bring down one of the cyclogres." He turned to Kaia. "Well, go on then."

Kaia shook her head, breaking the strange trance the scene had wrought on her. "Right." She brought her other palm alongside her burning hand as she sized up the gathering. This would be her largest burn yet. She had to be sure to conjure more flames than she needed. After all, the one thing worse than being attacked by a corpse was being attacked by a *flaming* corpse.

She let her rage and guilt at the Lost endangering the Maldibor village flow into her hands. As the flames cut through the darkness, the Lost turned to her, attracted by the yanaa. Their keening call pierced the night air as they shambled towards her at a jerky run.

Kaia released a horse-sized fireball into the advancing creatures, incinerating the fastest chargers. The fire illuminated the gory body in the middle of the road, revealing another two dozen of the dead hiding in the shadows. They rushed her as she spooled another ball of flame before discharging a surging river of fire with a whoosh. They screeched and scurried, only to regroup and come forward once again, scattered on the road and among trees.

Kaia changed tactics, hurling melon-sized balls of flames at the creatures as they closed her in. She threw with her right and then her left, picking them off one by one, until she panted with the effort, sweating in the crisp night. The burning shots knocked them to the ground, screaming as they flailed haplessly. The last corpse edged close enough for Kaia to see the swirling green yanaa in the caverns of his eye sockets before she burned the head from his shoulders.

The Dragon Heir sucked in deep lungfuls of air as she surveyed the scene. Small pockets of flames burned around the bloody mess in the road, devouring the last evidence of the aberrations. But all was quiet, save for the gentle mountain breeze kissing Kaia's damp brow.

"You control the fire well," Tekoa said, breaking the silence.

With another deep breath, Kaia allowed herself a small, victorious grin. She turned to look back at her companions, and her smile faltered.

In the darkness behind Tekoa, the villagers had gathered with lanterns and torches. Kaia choked on her heart as it suddenly leapt into her throat. Families squeezed together in tight bunches, and wide eyes skewered her to the dark. Her fingers searched for Gus at her side, curling into his thick fur.

Gus gruffed softly. It's ok, my girl. The air is good again.

Tekoa's hand on her shoulder brought her focus back to him. "It's not you they fear," he murmured. "It's the dead that walk again before their eyes."

Kaia took a shuddering breath and nodded, but the worry still creased her brow.

Shad's words cut through the shocked silence of the night, from where he sat by her feet. "Tekoa, I think it's time we spoke with Okoni."

Tekoa stroked his chin. "Yes, of course. We'll meet him at the mews."

He gestured toward a small, red-headed girl, and with a nod, she ran back toward the village. With a hand still on Kaia's shoulder, he guided her towards the crowd.

Kaia stiffened as Maldibor and human parted before her, bracing for their hateful whispers. But none came. With a shock she realized they weren't just getting out the way, they were bowing their heads.

"Light the darkness, Dragon," one called out.

"We give thanks," another said.

A blush that was not shame or rage burned from Kaia's toes to her cheeks, filling her with a warm pride she had never felt before. If these people wanted her—she would face Nifras alone for them. She would be the Dragon Heir they needed.

***

The sky grayed with the dawn as they approached the mews, which turned out to be little more than a dozen roosting pillars and a few benches around a table sheltered by a covering pavilion. A jackhawk twice the size of a normal harehawk peered down at Kaia from its roost in the hollowed pillar. Its four taloned legs gripped the rough wooden perch while its tall ears twitched curiously, its long tail swinging below.

The messenger girl sat at the table, quill and parchment at the ready, while

Klaus, freshly clothed and arm bandaged but still looking a bit haggard, sat across from a broad, silver-haired man. Their heads leaned together earnestly, but they looked up when Kaia and the others arrived.

Tekoa gestured to the older Maldibor. "Kaia, may I introduce my uncle, Okoni, chief of our clan."

Okoni rose to his feet, standing even taller than Tekoa. "Guardian Dashul, the news of your father's passing has been on the wind." His face darkened. "Your grief is ours." He bent closer, his words so soft only she could hear. "Your mother wrote, desperate for news of you."

Kaia's eyes swam, letting the words wash over her.

"Would you like us to send her a message for you?"

Kaia tried to swallow the lump in her throat. "Does she already—"

Okoni nodded, his eyes gentle. "She knows of your father."

Kaia breathed deeply. "Could you just tell her that I'm ok? That I love her?"

"That's all?"

Kaia bobbed her head, battling for control of her emotions. The messenger scratched onto a sheet of paper and then handed it to her. Kaia glanced at the elegant looping script before handing it back. "That's perfect, thank you."

Okoni stepped back, raising his voice again. "Now, for other matters." He glanced at the jackhawk's wide eyes peeking from their hollows. "Everard has used the Maldibor jackhawks to rally the warriors to Okarria in times past." He paused. "But there are not many warriors left—the Dracour of the northern plains, the nomads of the southern deserts, the Odriel faithful left in the three State-cities." He looked from Kaia to Shad at her feet. "But will they come?"

Shad scoffed. "The Lost walk the land, Nifras rises, and Odriel's Heirs call upon them." His ears flattened. "I should certainly hope so."

With a nod from Okoni, the scribe girl dipped her quill in the ink and began to write.

Kaia crossed her arms and leaned back against a pillar, a chestnut jackhawk peering down at her with large eyes. "The Dracour will come if I ask. I know they will."

Tekoa nodded, looking to Kaia with earnest eyes. "And we will be with you."

Klaus' shadowed eyes looked from Tekoa to Kaia and back. "But where do we call them to?"

For a moment, the group was silent as they considered the question. The first morning birds began to chirup to encourage the coming dawn, and Kaia stifled a yawn, her mind starting to cloud with exhaustion.

Okoni cracked his knuckles against his jaw. "Our latest information says Ariston has already reached the northwest Faverly battlegrounds to swell his army with fallen warriors." He snarled. "The foul bastard."

Shad leapt up onto the table. "That means he will almost certainly take Gyatan pass, if he aims to meet Nifras' army in the Deadlands." He looked east as if he could see through the miles. "Between Blackerd's canyon and the Naerami range, it's the only path for an army of that size."

Kaia nodded. "But when?"

The bench scraped against the stone floor as Klaus stood. "As soon as possible. We can't afford to be late."

A slight panic rippled through Kaia at the thought of she and Klaus leading an army alone. "What about Jago?" she whispered.

"And we will want Everard's wisdom," Okoni added. "He is a famed commander of men."

Tekoa gave Kaia's shoulder a reassuring squeeze. "An army of the dead does not move quickly. You will have time to wait for them."

His gentle smile reminded Kaia so much of Jago, she had to look away.

Shad nodded. "We will meet Jago and Everard at his Summerbanks refuge before continuing to Gyatan." His whiskers quivered. "If you should need us sooner, send a jackhawk."

Okoni slapped a palm on the grey elmcore table. "It is decided."

The girl handed him the tiny scroll she had written on before beginning a second copy. Okoni passed it to Klaus. "Ari has captured your message."

Klaus spread the page on the table and scanned the message. With a nod, he pulled a small knife from his belt and pricked his thumb. Grabbing the pen, he flicked a drop of ink on the page before smearing his bloody thumbprint over it. "Dark blood, the Shadow's mark." He passed it to Kaia.

Once again, Kaia squinted for a moment at the scrawl of letters on the page, pretending to read the words that seemed to shift before her eyes. Despite her mother's best efforts, reading had always been a struggle for her. Still, she had watched her father scrawl many a letter to the other Heirs.

Taking a deep breath, she allowed the smallest of flames to heat her thumb and forefinger, then, very carefully, she pinched the bottom of the page. With a wisp of smoke, the parchment crumbled beneath her fingers, leaving a black-ringed hole the size of her thumb. She nodded and handed it back to Okoni. "Singed with dragon fire."

She looked at the empty space at the bottom of the page—the space for the healer's mark. Kaia's brows knitted, why couldn't she remember what it looked like? She locked eyes with Klaus. Surely, Everard would find Jago in time for the battle. Without the Time Heir, they weren't whole.

Gus snorted beside her. I am here. You are here. We are whole.

Okoni rolled the tiny scroll and whistled. A golden jackhawk hopped from its pillar to the Chief's soldier with a soft chirp. The Maldibor tied the scroll to is foreleg, and then stroked its long ears as he moved out from the mews. "Dracour plains. Find Cressida."

With that, he flung his arm up, letting the jackhawk spring from his arm on its powerful hind legs before tucking them under its stomach and unfurling its long wings to climb up to the treetops. "Odriel guide your wings." He turned to the Heirs. "Four more."

***

An hour later, the five fastest messengers in Okarria had set out to carry their message across the land, with a sixth sent to Summerbanks to herald their arrival. Drained from their flight from the Terraverms, and her encounter with the Lost, Kaia would have liked to stay. But, with their task complete, they couldn't afford to waste any time. The Maldibor repacked their saddlebags with dried meat and supplies, and Tekoa led them to the western edge of the forest on a sleek black Dalteek.

He pointed up through the grassy mountain pass. "Summerbanks is through the pass and three days south from here." He smiled, his eyes gleaming. "The legends say that Odriel flies with dragons on these mountain peaks, so keep an eye out."

Klaus edged his Dalteek closer to Tekoa's and reached out a hand to grasp his forearm. "Thank you, Tekoa. We hope to see you at Gyatan."

Tekoa gripped Klaus' arm with his slender fingers. "We will be there." He looked at Shad. "Give my regards to the magus."

Shadmundar nodded solemnly from his saddle bag.

As Moonstreak walked on, Tekoa turned to Kaia next. "It was a pleasure to meet you, Guardian Dashul," he said, his words soft on the late morning gusts.

A bittersweet smile crossed Kaia's face. "Guardian Dashul." She shook her head, looking away to the snow-dusted peaks before them. "When you say that, it still makes me think you're speaking to my father."

Uncertainty creased Tekoa's forehead. "I worry for you, Kaia. I'm afraid you have a hard path to tread." He reached out and took her hand in his. He turned it over, tracing the lines on her palm, almost like he could feel the flames coursing beneath. His green eyes lit with intensity as they met hers. "If ever you need a light, just remember the one that burns within you never goes out."

For the second time that day, a bubbling warmth filled her. His compassion flowed from her fingertips to the roots of her tangled hair, wrapping her heart in a tight embrace. Her eyes dampened with gratitude and emotion.

Klaus' voice cut the moment short. "C'mon Firefly, we haven't got all day."

Ignoring the Shadow Heir, she squeezed Tekoa's smooth hands. "Thank you, Tekoa."

He squeezed back once before releasing her. "Until next we meet."

Kaia reluctantly nudged Sunflash forward, Gus already trotting ahead. "I look forward to the day."

He smiled once more, a bright, contagious grin. "Until then, remember to spoil my doe."

Looking over her shoulder, she reflected his smile back at him. "Every chance I get."

Sunflash climbed the slope as nimbly as a mountain goat, catching up to her roan companion. Klaus studied her with a strangely unreadable expression but said nothing. Kaia turned one last time to wave at her Maldibor friend, but he had already disappeared back into the forest of monsters.

CHAPTER 11
FIOLA'S

The ride to Summerbanks passed uneventfully, but on the evening of the first day, the skies opened up and dumped buckets of cold mountain rain on the travelers. Kaia and Klaus nagged at each other half-heartedly, but the fatigue of their journey sapped the sting from their barbs. The deluge continued until the skies finally relented on the afternoon of the third day. Gus shook the muddy water from his thick coat, and Kaia could feel the relief ease her tense muscles as the sun warmed her soaked bones. Almost like a dose of Jago's healing yanaa.

Jago. She thought of the white space at the bottom of their call to arms. With thoughts of her father and Nifras looming large, she had let Jago's absence hide under her other problems. She glanced at Klaus riding beside her with Shad hidden somewhere in his usual satchel. The Shadow Heir had thrown his hood back, but water still dripped onto his straight nose.

She pulled a handful of violet elcorns from a tall peakbush and threw one at him. "Hey, ink blot."

He didn't flinch as it bounced off his shoulder. "What."

Her tone softened. "Do you think Everard will really be able to find Jago?"

Klaus sighed. "No one knows the land better than that crusty magus. If anyone can find Jago, he can."

Kaia dug her thumbnail into the delicate leather reins. "And if he can't?"

He shifted in the saddle, still not looking at her. "Then we'll make do."

Far from the reassurance she was looking for, Kaia pursed her lips. If Jago were here, he would've tussled her hair with a warm laugh, teasing her fear away. Instead, she had to "make do" with the cynical Shadow Heir. "I miss him," she whispered, loud enough only for her own ears.

Klaus wiped the water from his face with an open hand. "So, while we're having this moment of civility, I never thanked you for saving my life."

Kaia raised her eyebrows, not quite trusting his sincerity. "Which time?"

He waved a scarred hand at her. "The terraverms don't actually count since you got us into that mess in the first place."

Kaia rolled her eyes.

He rubbed his stubbled chin. "And I did rescue you from the depths of self-pity. So, I think we're actually pretty even."

Kaia threw another elcorn at him, this one smoking a bit in the damp air. "You're so full of yourself."

Shad popped his head from his bag. "The rain finally stops, and then I have to listen to you two bickering again." Flicking the water droplets from his whiskers, the cat glanced around the mountain path cut into the side of the mountain. "Ah, at last, a familiar trail. The cottage should be visible at the top of the rise."

Klaus threw a wolfish grin to Kaia, and she flashed one back. With a whoop and a flick of the reins, the two Heirs rushed up the hill. They paused at the top, looking down at the orange, two-story farmhouse and matching barn nestled in an open lea of wildflowers just above the treeline. Farther below, near the base of the mountain, smoke rose from many colorful chimneys—shades of salmon, rose, and cyan—lounging in the bend of a rolling mountain stream—Summerbanks.

Shad pointed with a paw. "That orange house—"

"Last one there cleans my boots!" Klaus cut in, leaning low over Moonstreak as he bounded down the slope, nearly dislodging the yowling Shad.

Sunflash didn't wait to leap down after them. "You're cheating again!" Kaia shouted while Gus sprinted behind, barking gleefully.

A wide grin split Kaia's face as they rode towards a hot meal, a warm bath, a roof over their heads, and maybe even a little hope.

***

Before they could knock on the sky-blue door of the house, an old woman flew out of it like a mother hen and shooed them inside with a musical accent Kaia couldn't place. "Come in darlings, come in, come in! I've been waiting for you."

"Wait here, Gus," Kaia murmured to her bedraggled hound.

She and Klaus kicked out of their muddy boots and stepped over the threshold in sopping feet. Kaia took in the polished buttercedar floors, the intoxicating smell of bacon and sugar, and the crackling of a cheery hearth. To their right lay a sitting room with cushioned furniture and a neat shelf of books. To their left sprawled an enormous kitchen with a huge hearth, worn counters, a long pinkfir table, and an ornate rocking chair in the corner. A short hall split the floor with a steep staircase leading up to the bedrooms above.

Although it was not at all familiar, the house glowed with an inviting charm that felt safe and nostalgic all at once. Kaia couldn't imagine the elusive Everard ever staying in one place for more than a fortnight, but if he did choose to rest his ancient bones, she imagined this would make a perfect sanctuary.

Shad shook himself off. "Fiola—"

"Not now cat, can't you see the poor souls are exhausted." She thrust dry clothes into both of their arms and clapped her hands.

"We—" Klaus started.

She held a knobby finger up. "Not a word until you're clean, dressed, and eating at my table." She pointed towards the stairs. "Go on, go on, before the bath gets cold."

Needing no more encouragement, Klaus and Kaia tromped up the stairs as directed.

An hour later, feeling more alive than she had in weeks, Kaia pulled a chair up next to the clean-shaven Klaus at a table full of eggs, bacon, honeyed porridge, and mugs of hazel cocoa. Remembering Gus suddenly, she started to stand, when she spied him already clean and settled into a corner with a meaty bone.

Fiola handed her a plate.

"Thank—" Kaia started.

The woman held up a hand with a smile. "Not yet. Eat first. Then talk."

The Heirs shared a glance before piling their plates high with as much food as they could stack. As Kaia attacked the food, she studied the woman sitting across from them with a satisfied smile. She had long black ropes of hair with intricate patterns of silver ink lacing her dark arms and kind face. The tattoos held Kaia's eyes as she tried to decipher the words hidden among the swirls. Pryor Brigg had once told the young Heirs of soldiers from the old wars inking themselves with the names of the fallen, but she had never seen it for herself.

As their plates emptied and the Heirs let out sighs of satisfaction, Fiola leaned back, crossing her arms with a broad smile. "Now," she said. "Tell me everything."

***

They took turns telling their tale, haltingly at times, but then rushing through others. Fiola listened intently, reaching out with a patterned hand to grasp Kaia's firmly as Klaus spoke of her father's death in a soft, steady voice.

Kaia glanced up from the table to look at the old woman through swimming eyes. Fiola's amber irises reflected her sorrow, but she squeezed with strong fingers, and smiled with full, wistful lips. The understanding in her expression soothed Kaia like a balm, and she squeezed her fingers right back.

"And now, we await Jago and Everard to join our army," Shad finished.

Fiola took in a long deep breath and released it. "Evie was due back a week ago."

No one spoke. The fire cracked through the silence.

She clasped her hands on the table. "It's been a month since his last letter, but the old coot is rarely punctual."

Kaia's chest tightened. "Did he mention Jago?"

Fiola met her eyes again. "He didn't, but that doesn't mean he's not there. Evie said he needed to visit his brother in the east, but he's always stingy with the details." She looked to Shad and then Klaus, her voice low but sure. "I'm sure he'll be here before you know it." She stabbed the table with a stubby finger. "And if Ariston's army nears, you can bet we'll hear of it in Summerbanks. That town passes gossip faster than the Barker's Flu they keep spreading around."

Kaia marveled at the energy the woman radiated—almost like yanaa. Suddenly, a hopeful thought struck her—could Fiola be one of Everard's reclusive brethren? To her knowledge, except for Everard, the magi had all gone into hiding centuries ago, but maybe…. "Fiola, are you a… a magus?"

The old lady belted out a musical laugh. "Oh, goodness no, dear! I'm just an old lady. Evie and I have a… history, I guess you could say. Now, I can't seem to get rid of him or his rude cat!"

Suddenly, a young voice echoed in from the yard, "Grannnnnnnnnnnnnnyyyyyy Fiiiiooooooooooollllllllaaaaaaaaa!"

"That boy." Fiola rolled her eyes. "He knows I'm in here. I don't know why he does that."

A youngish boy with a wild auburn mop of hair and dark bruise around his eye tromped into the kitchen. A golden daycoon, round-faced and fluffy, perched on his shoulder while he cradled another furry bundle in his arms. "Hey Gran, I found this orphaned ferrefox kit in the woods…." his voice trailed away when he saw they had company. His chocolate eyes regarded them with suspicion, and the daycoon cocked its head inquisitively. "Oh—people. We don't usually have… people."

Fiola gestured at the guests around the table. "Oh, don't fret, Mackie. These are the Heirs I told you about. As for the ferrefox, isn't the barn full of needy animals as it is?"

Mackie's distrust evaporated. "Oh, of course, I completely forgot! I'm Mackie Tannen—Everard's apprentice." He turned to Granny Fiola. "And don't worry, Gran, I released the badgerret this morning, so we've got room for this one."

The Heirs greeted the boy politely, but inwardly Kaia's heart clenched. He reminded her so much of Layf it almost hurt. He couldn't have been but a year or two older.

Fiola looked at the Heirs with sparkling eyes. "Mackie has a special gift too." She tousled his hair fondly. "He speaks with flora and fauna and works wonders in my medicinal garden."

Mackie hid a blush in the ferrefox's olive fur as he nuzzled it. "Well, sort of. There aren't really any words ever, just a sort of understanding."

"And Mackie," Fiola lifted a chin at the Heirs. "They came through Odriel's pass."

Mackie's jaw dropped, and his head whipped from Klaus to Kaia, his questions falling on top of one another. "Did you see any hawks? Anything out of the ordinary? Feel any strange yanaa?"

Klaus sipped his cocoa, his eyebrows knitted. "No, why?"

Mackie leaned forward in earnest. "They say Odriel travels that pass."

Kaia tilted her head. "The Maldibor mentioned that too, but I thought he was teasing."

Fiola took the ferrefox from the excited apprentice, calmly stroking its fuzzy ears. "You haven't heard the story of Shava, the first female Dragon Heir?"

Kaia shook her head.

Mackie bounced on his toes with excitement. "They say she climbed barefoot to the top of the pass and waited all night on the highest peak without moving—no food, no sleep, no water—until Odriel finally appeared to answer her plea."

Klaus snorted. "Sounds like she hallucinated from weakness."

Kaia's wide eyes looked from Mackie to Fiola and back. "That story isn't in The Heirs' Way."

Fiola shrugged. "Some people don't believe the old legend, but it's fun to wonder." She stood. "But the day grows long. I think it's best if we all turn in early tonight."

Klaus nodded and gently kicked Kaia under the table. "Fiola's right. You should get some rest, because tomorrow"—his eyes glinted with mischief—"we train."

Kaia kicked him back, just a little harder. "You're on, Shadow."

CHAPTER 12
THE CONRADS

For the next two days, Kaia and Klaus clashed in the fields around Fiola's farmhouse, just like the old days of the Triennials. They sparred with canvas covered weapons, fists, and feet until they gasped for breath and sweat slicked their skin. Klaus still bested Kaia in nearly every bout, but she found if she dragged out the match, she could outlast him every now and then. They woke up sore and fell onto their mattresses as soon as the sun set.

Still, the exercise only seemed to enliven their squabbling pranks. Kaia curdled Klaus' milk when his head was turned, he filled her bed with stink berries, and she threw his boots into the bogswine pen.

In their brief moments of peace, Kaia welcomed Mackie's easy company as he shared his encyclopedic knowledge about every plant and creature under the sky. She watched with interest as he tended the animals in the barn and lovingly encouraged the plants to grow, as if they, too, could hear him. Meanwhile, Gus and Felix, Mackie's daycoon, playfully chased each other around the garden, and Shad took to lounging in the sun on the tiled roof of the cottage, descending only when absolutely necessary.

On the third day, sweat plastered Kaia's shirt to her chest as she ran another loop around the barn, her fists encased in fire as she pumped her arms. She couldn't see Klaus, but his labored footfalls followed not far behind. Her flames flickered as the yanaa unspooled from her core.

"Lap sixty-seven!" She puffed, reaching the farmhouse.

"Sixty-nine," Klaus said, nearly in her ear.

She threw an elbow in his direction. "You liar!"

Mackie looked up from where he kneeled in the garden, dirt streaking his face. "You've got him, Kaia!"

61

She put on another burst of speed as she rounded the house and almost ran straight into two tall, white stallions.

"Whoah!" she said, extinguishing the flames and spinning to one side.

Laughing, Klaus blinked back into sight beside her, sweat glistening on his tanned face. "I win."

Kaia ignored him as she looked up at the two immaculately dressed men on top of the spotless steeds. They had the look of a father and son. The son seemed about her age with fair curls and features while the father's square jaw and close-cropped sandy hair lent him a firmer air. The father stared at her, his eyes studying her face intently.

Glancing at his companion, the younger rider cleared his throat. "Is Lady Fiola about by chance?"

As if on command, the old woman poked her head through the front door. Her face creased into a smile. "Well if it isn't Lord Conrad and Master Valente." She wiped her hands on her flowery apron. "I see you've met our young Heirs, Klaus and Kaia."

Conrad blinked, as if breaking a trance. "Taya's daughter."

Kaia started at the mention of her mother's name.

He smiled apologetically. "Forgive me, you just look so much like her."

Fiola raised her eyebrows, and then her smile broadened. "Ah yes, I forgot you grew up in the old court."

The lord's face softened. "Yes, your mother and I were good friends."

Fiola leaned against the porch rail. "What brings you to our humble abode?"

Conrad dismounted from his ivory horse. "I'm afraid a few of our household staff have come down with that Barker's Flu, and I've run out of your potion."

Fiola nodded, her smile faltering. "Oh yes, that one spreads faster than a stink, and can be lethal if untreated." She waved a hand. "Please come in while I make you a draft."

Valente leapt from his horse and bowed before Kaia. "Guardian Dashul, it is an honor to meet the Dragon Heir."

Klaus crossed his arms and leaned against the house. His face a careful mask.

Kaia blushed, self-consciously wiping the sweat from her brow with a forearm. "Oh, no need for that."

"What were you doing running about on fire like that? If I may ask." He grinned with a soft chuckle.

She tapped the toe of her boot in the dirt. "Just training."

"And we should get back to it," Klaus added curtly, turning away and disappearing back behind the house.

Valente frowned, his eyes falling to the short sword at her belt. "Well, I'm not an Heir, but I'm decent with a rapier." He patted the hilt at his hip. "If you'd like another partner."

Kaia raised an eyebrow, taking in his willowy frame.

"Unless you're scared," he teased.

Kaia rolled her eyes with a smile, drawing her blade. "If you insist, Master Valente."

The young noble drew his sword. "To first blood?"

Kaia drew her blade and dropped back into a sparring stance. "Whenever you're ready."

As soon as the words left her lips, he was on her—beating her blade and pressing her back in an aggressively graceful onslaught.

Kaia retreated, parrying each volley and letting him set the pace until he finally fell back, panting. She kept her face carefully neutral. He was skilled, perhaps even as good as Bram. But his gentleman's technique did not include some of his strongest weapons—his elbows, fists, and feet. Compared to Klaus, this was child's play, but it was nice to have the upper hand for once.

Kaia allowed him one more offensive charge. Valente advanced with feints and lunges until his pale complexion turned red and blotchy. Tired of the show, she let the tip of his blade brush her sleeve, teasing him with victory only a fingertip away. Then she knocked the blade from his fingers with a powerful blow and raised her weapon to tickle his Adam's apple.

She smiled at his gaping mouth. "No blood needed, right?"

"Bravo!" Lord Conrad laughed as he clapped his hands together, stepping down from the porch toward his horse. "I see you have been teaching my son a most important lesson." He raised a finger. "Never underestimate a beautiful woman."

Kaia stepped back with a blush. "No—"

Valente straightened and laughed along with his father. "I would never underestimate a Dragon Heir." He bent to retrieve his rapier. "But she bested me all the same." He saluted with a flourish of the blade. "Perhaps I could come again tomorrow for another lesson."

Kaia's blush deepened. "Uh, sure, I guess."

The young noble mounted his stallion. "Tomorrow then."

Conrad nodded to her. "A pleasure to meet Taya's daughter." Then, with a click of his tongue, the two nobles cantered off through the field, towards the wood and the town below.

As they watched them ride away, Fiola winked at Kaia from the porch. "A handsome pair, no?"

Kaia wrinkled her nose as she sheathed her sword. "I guess so."

"I wouldn't trust Conrad," Shad chimed in.

Kaia looked up in surprise. She hadn't noticed the cat's perch on the edge of the brown shingled roof. "He'll point his sails where the wind blows."

Klaus blinked into sight at Kaia's side. "Agreed."

She jumped at his sudden closeness and shoved him away. "A little space, please?"

He rested a hand on his own hilt. "You almost lost that bout, letting him get so close to you."

Kaia rolled her eyes. "You should know a trap when you see one, Shadow Heir."

"I see a fetching face distracts you, is what I see."

She reared back as if struck. "Is that what you think of me? Just some wool-headed mountain girl?" She pushed past him towards the house. "I've had enough of your sour mood for one day." With that, she stomped up the porch and slammed the front door behind her.

As she climbed the stairs, she heard Fiola's sarcastic drawl. "Klaus, for the Heir with all the supposed cunning, you can be quite a fool sometimes."

***

The next day dawned with a brilliant blue sky and a perfect summer breeze. Valente arrived early with an eager smile, and Kaia jumped at the excuse to brush off Klaus' stilted silence. She ran the young noble through basic training games she had long since mastered. He laughed easily but seemed more interested in games than training. Tiring of the repetitive exercises, he showed off for her by juggling knives, and she showed him to balance a sword hilt on his forehead.

Mackie joined in with his own gymnastics—performing twisting flips off the barn loft into a hay bale. When he convinced Felix to mimic his antics with a back-flip belly flop, the trio laughed until tears ran down their cheeks.

By midmorning, the three ran out of acrobatic ideas and retreated to the meadow to relax and sip freshly squeezed Cantalime juice from a flask. They lounged on their backs among the magenta blooms with Gus stretched out happily at their feet, and Felix curled up in the hound's fur. Kaia breathed in a deep sigh, wondering at the feeling of peace that had fallen over her. Is this what it felt like to spend a day with friends?

Valente rolled on his stomach, resting his chin on his hand as he regarded her with a smile. "So, Dragon Heir." He reached out and plucked a rogue straw from her hair. "You and the Shadow are training to take on an army of dead soldiers?"

Kaia tried not to roll her eyes as the reminder broke into her moment of respite. Couldn't they just talk about something else for one day? She sighed. "Well, we've called on the Okarrian warriors to join us."

"And you think they'll come?"

She shrugged.

Mackie sat up beside her. "But the original three Heirs stood up to the Nifras all on their own."

Valente's face creased. "How did that work, exactly?"

Kaia twisted a sturdy blade of grass in her fingers. "The Dragon Heir burned the dead, the Shadow Heir dueled the necromancer, and the Time Heir healed them."

The noble glanced about the quiet farm. "So, the Time Heir is here somewhere too?"

"He's...." Kaia hesitated, tearing the grass apart with her fingers. "Traveling north with Everard to meet us."

"It'll be just like the old legend." Mackie chimed in, tickling Kaia's nose with a weed.

She sneezed and slapped Mackie's hand away with a laugh—his cheer infecting her in spite of herself. "But better!"

Valente pulled a crisp handkerchief from the pocket of his breeches and handed it to her. She sat up and wiped her face with a blush.

He flashed another brilliant smile. "Well, you're certainly the strongest fighter I've ever met." He pushed himself to his feet and dusted off his breeches. "But I'm afraid I must be going today." He whistled for his horse before looking down at Kaia once more. "Perhaps I could come again tomorrow?"

She shrugged. "Of course."

"Wonderful." He mounted and tipped his invisible hat. "Guardian Dashul, Master Tannen, until next time." With that, he clicked his tongue and rode away through the swaying field.

Mackie and Kaia shared a silent moment as they watched the white horse disappear into the wood. Kaia rubbed the silky handkerchief between her fingers. Klaus was wrong, of course—she couldn't care less about Valente's face—but, she could always use a friend.

Mackie's soft words broke into her thoughts. "You're also the bravest fighter I've ever met."

She batted him on the shoulder. "You've never seen me do anything brave."

He snorted. "You and Klaus are taking on a dead army." He stroked Gus' ears, just how he liked it. "I can't even face Ress."

Uncertainty and old memories rolled into Kaia's mind like a sudden storm. "Is that who gave you the black eye?"

"He's a local boy." Mackie sighed. "I had a bad run-in with him after I saw him kick a stray." His dusty fingers touched the yellowed bruise around his eye. "Now, I can't even bring myself to go into town." He shrugged. "It's just a black eye, but every time I think about seeing Ress again, I feel sick." He looked away, hiding a rosy blush. "I'm not brave like you."

Kaia reached over and squeezed his arm. "Anyone can be brave, Mackie." She drew back, gazing at the cloud-spotted sky. "It's a choice we make every day." The memory of Mogens' grotesque smile shadowed her face, but her voice held steady. "Sometimes, when I'm scared, I just tell myself that I'm brave, over and over." She clenched her fist. "Then, I take the first step." She smiled at him. "That's the hardest part."

He took a deep breath. "I think I could do that."

She tousled his hair. "Just give it a try the next time you're feeling afraid."

Mackie punched her arm playfully. "But who would be afraid with the Dragon Heir on their side?"

Kaia's smile fell. All too many.

CHAPTER 13
NIFRAS KNOCKS

The next morning, Kaia woke late with a tickle in her throat and an aching head. With Gus following close behind, she bypassed the kitchen and stepped out onto the porch, hoping that the clean mountain air would ease her throat. She sat on the step and picked up an old stick to throw for Gus.

She closed her eyes, willing the warm sunshine to soothe her throbbing temples. She could hear Fiola still bustling in the kitchen, Mackie crooning to the animals in the barn, and Klaus chopping wood somewhere with a repetitive thunk. Suddenly, the ground began to shake beneath her. Kaia's eyes snapped open, and she jumped to her feet.

Gus' mouth barked anxiously as he pawed at her leg. Bad! Bad! Bad!

As if a fist had closed around the sun, the sky suddenly went dark. The violent quaking surged, swaying the house and the barn on their foundations with a dangerous cracking. A cacophony of panicked bleats, neighs, and clucks erupted from the direction of the barn, and Kaia heard the doors bang open and the stampede of feet as the horses, sheep, and chickens burst out in all directions.

"Run away!" Mackie shouted as he followed after them, running crookedly as he tried to keep his balance. Kaia watched, frozen in shock, as the barn collapsed in a towering heap of dust and flying timber behind him. With another yell, Mackie fell to his hands and knees and crawled away from the wreckage.

The darkness thickened, obscuring the boy from sight, and a deafening CRACK forced her to clap her hands to her ears as she fell to her knees on the rolling ground. It sounded like thunder, louder than any she'd ever heard—as if lightning were striking, again and again—paralyzing her heart with fear.

Finally, the booming quieted, the earth stilled, and the sky returned to its beautiful blue canvas. Kaia's chest heaved as if she had sprinted a mile and Gus whined in the sudden quiet. Mackie gasped with panicked sobs in front of the wreckage of the barn. Fiola burst from the house just as Klaus ran around the side of it, the fear plain on his face as he met Kaia's eyes.

"Is everyone ok?" he yelled, looking towards the barn wreckage.

"I got the animals out, but the barn collapsed," Mackie called, his voice hitching with emotion.

Fiola crossed the yard and fell to her knees to wrap him in a hug, "Don't worry, dear, we can rebuild it."

"What was that?" Kaia asked hoarsely as Klaus offered her a hand up.

Klaus' eyes ran her up and down as if he didn't quite believe she was ok. "Nothing good."

Shad jumped down from the roof, every hair on his body erect.

"What do you think, Shadmundar?" Fiola asked.

The cat sat down slowly on the porch, but his fur still betrayed his anxiety. Fear had enlarged his pupils, so the blue irises were barely visible.

"I'm not sure," the cat said, hesitant. "But, according to legend, when the necromancer came to the land, even the golden sun grew fearful and hid from his evil, turning the sky dark." His tailed whipped furiously as he spoke. "I always thought that was an embellishment of the storyteller...."

He trailed off as the sound of cawing birds filled the air.

Kaia looked south to see a vast flock of colorful birds flying toward them, filling the sky as they fled north. The sight flooded Kaia with dread.

"I do believe," the cat said as he watched them, "Nifras has come knocking on our door."

***

They spent the rest of the morning in tense silence. Kaia helped Mackie clear the barn wreckage while Klaus and Fiola poured over Everard's texts for more information about the magi's yanai barrier that protected them. Could they afford to detour to Gyatan to meet Ariston, or did they need to run south to defend the border?

Her headache only intensifying with worry and unanswered questions; Kaia completely forgot about Valente's visit until he arrived on horseback as the afternoon slipped to evening. Firmly pressed lips replaced his usual smile when he dismounted from his stallion.

She looked up in wearied surprise from where she sorted through the debris. "Valente, I didn't think you'd come after the—"

"That's what I wanted to talk to you about," he cut in, grabbing her arm and leading her away from the rubble. "Everyone in Summerbanks is panicking. They're saying that Nifras has returned."

Kaia sighed. "Not yet." She coughed into her sleeve. "But perhaps soon."

Valente stopped suddenly and released her. He turned to stare down at the orange sunset illuminating the colorful roofs of Summerbanks far below them. For a moment, he gathered the silence, and when he finally spoke, Kaia had to lean forward to hear. "No matter how many ages pass my eyes and crowd my memory, I will never forget that sound. The very fabric of our world being torn in two with a monstrous cacophony. The land shook beneath the horse's hooves; the cliff cracked, and half of the coastal town of Soshala fell into the sea—their screams only adding to the horrific din. The early morning sun snuffed out like a weak candle. The sky turned blacker than the darkest night—a darkness that swallowed all light. The ocean churned with fury, and vast waves crashed upon the sheared village. The villagers grabbed their children and retreated inland, while the Lost materialized behind them like a rolling cloud. Their dark master—Nifras—rose up out of the sea as a massive roiling shadow, his hungry roar of triumph shaking the land. As I watched the horde approach, I remember regretting that I had only seen five lives of men. What a waste of immortality...."

Kaia coughed again, pain stabbing at her sore throat. "That's Everard's account of the first battle, from The Heirs' Way."

Valente met her eyes, gazing intensely as if to see what he might find in their depths. "My father told me the Time Heirs are both dead."

Kaia's face flushed, and her fire weakly bubbled within her. "We don't know that!"

He grabbed her shoulders. "Wake up, Kaia! You can't do this on your own. You need to combine forces with Ariston to save the land." He paused, squeezing her shoulders. "Why not fight the dead with the dead?"

Kaia knocked his arms away. "All dark magic stems from Nifras. They'll turn on us as soon as they hear their master's call." She turned away. "He can't even control them as it is. His dead soldiers roam the land, terrorizing our own people."

"You are strong, Kaia. If you helped him, you could tame his horde with fire. Like a shepherd herding sheep."

Kaia barked out a laugh. "Val, they are drawn to my yanaa like ridge wolves to a bleeding lamb." She shook her head. "But the wolves don't feed on each other."

"But—"

"If I am a shepherd," Kaia raised her voice, "it is a shepherd of death, come to collect her Lost flock." She turned to walk back to the farm.

Still, his soft words found their mark in the small of her back. "We've already lost two of the Heirs. How can you possibly protect us if you can't protect yourselves?"

Kaia paused mid-step, eyes closed as the words punctured her heart. She took another breath and walked on. "Goodbye Valente."

She didn't stop until the front door closed behind her.

She leaned against the solid oak walls of the house, feeling drained and weak. Her head throbbed, her throat felt like she had swallowed rocks, and now even her heart ached with doubt and guilt.

Gus' tail thumped from his place by the fireplace. His head cocked. *What's wrong, my girl?*

Fiola stepped out of the study. "Oh dear, what happened?"

She sagged, the words heavy on her tongue. "Valente and the rest of the town have lost faith in the Heirs."

Fiola brushed a lock of hair behind her ear. "Well, I said he was handsome, not smart."

"I don't feel so well, Gran." She smothered a cough. "I think I'm going to turn in early tonight.

She tutted as she put her worn hand to Kaia's forehead. "You're burning up, my dear." She flew into the kitchen and returned with a glass full of what looked like dirty water. "I'm afraid you'll have to take a swig."

Kaia lifted the bottle to her lips and gagged.

"*Ugh!* That's terrible stuff."

"That it is, but it'll ward off the Barker's Flu you've picked up from the village. One more sip for good measure." Kaia lifted the glass to her lips with a grimace. "And remember, three times tomorrow and the next day." She took the glass and shooed Kaia up the stairs with a flick of the wrist. "Now to bed with you child! You need your rest."

Klaus met her at the top of the stairs just as she opened the door to her bedroom. Gus brushed by her leg as he padded inside while she turned tiredly to face the Shadow Heir.

He ran his fingers through his bristly hair. "Firefly, I—"

She held up a hand. "Could we not fight tonight?" She coughed again. "I'm really not feeling up to it." She stepped into her room.

"Sure, I just—"

But Kaia closed the door before he could finish.

She arranged her aching limbs on the bed but, despite Fiola's brew, still could not ignore her burning throat. She was exhausted, yet when her eyelids mercifully shut, she was plagued with nightmares of a giant demon laughing in Mogens' scratchy voice as he crushed the house with a huge fist.

She awoke to the sound of muffled footsteps. She propped herself on an elbow, but couldn't quite get her bleary eyes to focus on the shadowy figure at her bedside. She parted her dry lips to ask Klaus what he was doing in her room when a violent hand clamped over her mouth. She struggled sluggishly with heavy limbs as she lifted her hands to defend herself, but when she took in a breath to yell, she inhaled sickly-sweet fumes instead—the distinctive smell of a *Cheralder* tree—sleeping sap.

Then there was blackness.

CHAPTER 14
KIDNAPPED

Kaia awoke in a dark carriage, coughing. In the dimness, she could discern three rough-looking men that she didn't recognize and noted with relief that Gus lay on the floor, unconscious, but seemingly unharmed. They had clad her hands in heavy metal gauntlets and bound her hands behind her. But before she could formulate any thoughts of escape, one of her captors pressed the sweet-smelling cloth to her face once again.

Each time the coughing fit woke her, the aches in her body, throat, and head only multiplied, while her strength drained. Before her captors put her down again, she noted the daylight peeking into the shadowy carriage, but she couldn't tell how much time had passed. Once, she attempted to conjure a flame from her awkward position, but to her confusion, nothing happened—as if all warmth had seeped out of her. In a moment of clarity, she realized she needed another dose of Fiola's tonic, maybe even two, but she had no idea how far away they were from the farmhouse now.

Finally, she awoke once again and discovered that she was no longer in the carriage. Instead, she was shocked to find herself in a lush bedroom full of rose-colored silks and feathered pillows. The luxury of the surroundings, however, did nothing to ease her pain. Stabbing aches wracked her body, and her muscles trembled uncontrollably as she tried to piece together what had happened.

Her muzzled ragehound lay beside her on an enormous canopied bed and yipped softly when he saw that she was awake. You smell sick. What can I do?

She raised a hand to free him, only to find it still trapped in a bulky metal glove. With a clank, she clawed at it with her other gauntleted hand, but they were somehow locked at the wrist, with a thick chain binding them together. Kaia strained against the iron links weakly, but it gave not the slightest hint of giving way.

She sat still for a moment, calming herself as she drew on her fire. The gauntlet glowed red as it swallowed the yanaa that should have ignited into flames in her palms. She had no dragon fire. A surge of panic triggered another bout of painful hacking. When the coughing finally quieted, she curled her knees up to her chest to still her shivers.

Gus whined. *Are we ok?*

A silky voice drew Kaia's eyes to the corner of the room, "How are you feeling, my dear?" Lord Conrad gazed at her intently from an armchair on the far side of the room.

"Where am I?" She meant it as an angry shout, but a hoarse whisper escaped instead.

"You are in my best guest room at my estate." The aristocrat reached into the pocket of his posh jacket, retrieved a pipe, and calmly lit it. "Welcome to Conrad Manor."

"Why?" she demanded with a strangled cough, her voice trembling along with the rest of her body.

"It's quite complicated, my dear, and I'm not sure you are in any state to hear it." His voice dripped with condescension.

Kaia struggled to sit up straighter and desperately tried to bring fire to her palms. Nothing. She'd have to bluff.

"Tell me, *now*," she ordered, hoping she sounded dangerous.

Gus echoed her growl with a low rumble, baring his teeth within the metal muzzle.

"Oh dear, please do not upset yourself so. We just want to talk to you." Conrad exhaled a puff of curling smoke. The mere smell of it wafting through the room sent Kaia into another coughing fit.

When she quieted, the lord continued, "I feel as though I owe it to your mother, after all, I loved her, you know." He studied his polished pipe thoughtfully. "Our marriage was already arranged when she ran off after your father."

Kaia's eyes narrowed, but she remained silent.

Conrad's voice strained with long-buried emotions. "But, you are such a lovely image yourself—and powerful at that. My son is quite taken with you."

Lord Conrad paused as he took another puff of his pipe. "Ariston has instructed us to deliver you to him. Which would have been simple enough, don't you think? I mean, considering how easily my men snatched you from your bed and all. But...." He swirled his pipe dramatically in the air. "We decided to give you a choice."

Kaia frowned, thinking of Shad's warning. She couldn't trust this man.

He blew another cloud of gray smoke and studied the ceiling thoughtfully.

"Lord Ariston is almost like a king—he controls everything these days. I assume you've met his mongrel, Mogens." He grimaced. "He used to be the best mercenary in the business until your father turned the dragon fire on him. The pain drove him mad after that." He tapped his fingers on the armchair. "He's willing to cut down whoever gets in his way. That means us. That means you."

He rose, pointing a bejeweled finger at her emphatically. "But, my dear Kaia, you are a bright spot. You can transform Ariston's army of Lost into a tool for good! Use it to destroy Nifras and then destroy Ariston."

Kaia shook her head. "*Transform* Ariston's Lost army? Even I can't turn water into fire."

But Conrad was not so easily dissuaded. "Just act the part, Kaia! Although you're young and inexperienced, our family has been well versed in the intrigues of the web of power for generations. We can help you navigate these treacherous waters."

Conrad turned and paced the room. "With our connections and your gift, we could be a force to be reckoned with. You and Valente might even be able to revive the monarchy." Conrad took another puff from his pipe, the smoke stinging Kaia's eyes. "But I digress!" The lord sighed and turned to her, his body rigid with intensity. "Please, if you won't do it for us—do it for the people you're sworn to protect."

Kaia kept her eyes trained on him warily but said nothing as she tried to digest the monologue. She examined her shackled hands and the elegant room that surrounded them. Although Lord Conrad had kidnapped her, he spoke with passion about saving Okarria.

I'm no good at this kind of negotiating, she thought, her mind whirling. *The Shadow Heir is the cunning one.*

She sighed tiredly. She would *not* play this game. "I will put it simply," she replied softly, her words coated in steel. "You must be out of your mind. Ariston's army will only swell Nifras' ranks. Ariston has to be stopped before the necromancer breaks through the yanai barrier." She narrowed her eyes and set her jaw in what she hoped looked like iron resolution. "For the good of the land and yourself, you will remove these gauntlets and let me leave."

Lord Conrad settled back down into his deep armchair, taking her outburst in a stride. "I do believe the fever is clouding your mind, my dear. You have no hope of defeating Ariston, much less Nifras, without the Time Heir. After Ariston bests your friends in battle, you will have no choice but to back him against the necromancer for the safety of Okarria."

"As if I could back anyone who bears responsibility for my father's murder," she spat.

"From what I heard, he killed himself," the noble commented drily. "Even your father doubted your ability to save him. If you cannot protect your father from one man, how can you expect to save your friends from an army?"

Kaia sat for a moment, stunned, as her skewered heart bled out in her chest. She blinked once… twice.

Gus nudged her arm. Breathe, my girl. You are my good person.

She nodded and took a deep breath, trying to keep her emotions from her face. She could not let this man rile her. Her mother had told her once of these kinds of politicians from her youth in the court—manipulation artists, two-faced snakes, and expert practitioners of insincerity.

She squared her shoulders. "It will begin with a wildfire and end with Ariston's army in ashes."

"You couldn't light a candle now, even if you weren't wearing the dragon claws," Conrad raised his eyebrows as Kaia lifted the gauntlets once more. "Ah, yes, those mitts were designed for your ancestor, Ulfash—gifted, but completely mad. He couldn't control his power, so he had one of the magi craft those to muzzle him." A pompous smile spread across Conrad's handsome face as he tapped his lower lip with his pipe. "How easily a fire is smothered...." His eyes glittered as they considered her, like a snake eyeing a mouse.

Kaia leaned over to mask another coughing fit.

"Poor girl," Conrad drawled with a feigned look of sympathy. "I have witnessed the brutality of the Barker's Flu with my own eyes. Without treatment, I can't say if there's much hope for you getting better."

Her words smoldered. "What are you saying?"

The man puffed smugly on his pipe. "To put it bluntly, my dear, until you help me, I do not feel inclined to help you. In fact, I think your mind might clear faster if you consider your options in the cellar." He paused as another racking spasm of coughs seized her, and then rang a small bell. "And don't count on your friends coming for you after you left that heartfelt note explaining you'd decided to seek out Ariston to find the truth for yourself."

She sagged in disbelief, his words tearing away the little mettle left that held her head high.

Two heavily muscled guards entered the room, and Lord Conrad gestured to her impatiently. They each grabbed an arm and dragged her from the bed and out the door, with Conrad's mirth trailing after them.

"Think it over carefully, my dear. I do believe you will see reason by morning. Otherwise, you may only have a few mornings left."

Kaia shook and kicked against the guards, while Gus jumped at them, clawing at their chests with his big paws. The larger guard grabbed a club from his belt and brought it cracking down on the ragehound's skull. He fell back with a yelp.

"No!" Kaia yelled as the guard raised the bludgeon against the dog again. "Stop! He'll be good." She turned to Gus, a bloody gash oozing from his head. Tears thickened her voice. "It's ok Gus, we'll be ok."

He whined. *It hurts. You're hurt. We're hurting.*

The guards led the cowed Dragon Heir and her dog down the curving stairs and through a marble hall, but they came to a sudden stop as Valente approached them.

Kaia's eyes burned with anger as they bored into the fair lordling. "I suppose you're part of this, too, Val?"

"Kaia, this isn't how I wanted it to be." He ran his fingers along the copper braid hanging down her cheek. "But, you must understand, unless we are united, Okarria will fall."

The dragon fire raged through her, snapping and crackling through her limbs, yet crashing impotently against the dam of her metal gauntlets. All of Valente's kindness had been a strategy, a tactical ploy. How could she have been so naïve?

"Lord Valente." She lifted her chin. "If you could step aside, I believe I'm wanted in the cellar."

Valente's eyes hardened as he moved to the side of the spotlessly whitewashed hall. "Think hard about this, Kaia—you'll see that we're right. You can't win on your own."

The guards hefted her through a maze of corridors lined with strange paintings and odd sculptures. They hauled her past opulent rooms filled with expensive furniture and thick rugs, her feet trailing limply across the polished floors, toward a small door at the far back of the manor. They flung open the door and unceremoniously pushed her into the dark, kicking Gus in after her with a frightened yap. The door slammed behind them and doused their only light. Blinded, Kaia took a step and found no ground beneath her foot. She flailed her bound arms as she tumbled painfully down the wooden steps, landing face flat on the rough stone floor.

Kaia groaned as she crawled to a wall and found a corner to prop herself up against. Gus followed her anxiously, and she leaned against the shaggy dog for warmth. The cellar smelled faintly of the wine that it had once housed, but with the only light flickering through the bottom of the door, she could see nothing in the dark.

She let her chin drop into her chest. How stupid she had been to be deceived by the Conrad's false smiles. Her friends were out there somewhere, looking in the wrong direction, or perhaps even cursing her name as a traitor. She choked back a sob—a friendless girl once more.

Maybe Conrad was right. If she couldn't even protect herself, how could she possibly manage to defend anyone else? Shame, despair, and fear twisted together within her, reflecting the darkness that surrounded her. Without the dragon fire, she was totally and completely helpless.

Gus licked her cheek. *Not alone. Not helpless. Together, we are strong.*

Kaia let her cheek rest against his coarse fur as her body throbbed, her inflamed throat feeling triple its normal size. All she really wanted to do was lie down on the cold floor and seek peace in unconsciousness.

Gus yipped. Not yet.

The smell of his musty fur recalled another beast to mind and his wise words: *If ever you need a light Kaia, just remember the one that burns within you never goes out.*

Kaia pressed her lips together. She couldn't see it, but that didn't mean it wasn't still there. "Right."

Using the wall for support, she forced herself to rise. Stumbling back to the staircase, she focused on putting one elbow in front of another, she crawled to the top and tested the knob. *Locked.*

She patted the stair weakly, her gauntlets clanking, and Gus ambled up to give her face a reassuring lick. She buried her face in his neck, trying to control her shakes. The only possibility for her escape lay in overpowering the next person who opened the door. But, in her weakened state, even walking out on her own power might be challenging, much less fighting the guards.

She began to cough again, the attack seizing her whole body until she could hardly draw breath. A rising panic exacerbated the fit. *Need to breathe. Can't breathe. Why can't I breathe?!* At last, the attack released her and she gulped in shallow breaths of stale air. She cupped her fevered forehead in her gauntleted hands and tried to calm herself.

Escape or die. It was that simple.

She'd wait until someone came to check on her, and then do whatever it took to overpower her captors and escape. Until then, she had to wait and try to ignore the glass in her throat, her splitting head, or the deep cold that had settled in her bones. Gus settled onto the top step, and she rested her heavy head on his flanks.

In her fevered haze, she dozed in and out of consciousness, dreaming that Mogens held her prisoner, pressing his serrated knife against her throat. She stumbled away from him towards the flaming pyre waiting to claim her. The bonfire's heat felt glorious against the cold that shook her. If she could just lie down in the flames, all the pain would go away, and she could finally be warm. Mogens pressed his knife to her back, pushing her to the fire. But her father was there, right in front of her, barring the way. Shaking his head, he shoved her away from the furnace. Mogen's knife pressed harder against her skin, piercing and cutting. The pain flooded in, the pain, the pain—

She awoke coughing again, the fits reverberating in her chest. She couldn't stop it. *No air. No air. Is this what dying feels like?* She thought as black edged her vision. Her father's face flashed in her mind again, until at last, she managed to suck in a painful breath.

She gasped raggedly as Gus looked at her with worried eyes. My poor girl.

She wouldn't be able to stop another attack like that. Is this where she would die? As a child, she had always dreamed it might be on the battlefield, a glorious hero's death or a sacrifice for the greater good. Or maybe she might have lived out a full, fruitful life, finally surrendering peacefully to old age in a quiet mountain cottage. But she never imagined the possibility of gasping for her final breath alone in a dark basement.

Voices on the other side of the cellar door interrupted her thoughts. Hurried footsteps and a loud thumping sounded from the hall. Kaia vaguely wondered if she should be worried. Perhaps the Conrads had sold her out to Ariston after all. Or worse, Mogens.

The commotion neared, and Kaia tried to wake herself from her trance, slapping her cheeks and shaking her head. *If someone opens the door, I've got to burst through with everything I've got. It may not be much, but I have to try.*

The door rattled as if something had been pushed up against it. Kaia winced—they wouldn't barricade her in, would they? Then, the familiar tinkle of keys came to her ears, and she arranged herself in a crouch, ready to spring. When the wooden door creaked open, Kaia slammed against it, flinging it wide. She raised her manacles to face her first opponent, but to her surprise, there was no one. Off balance, Kaia stumbled through the door and found herself caught in an invisible web. She struggled weakly for a moment before a mud-splattered Klaus winked into view.

"Hey, relax! It's just me!" he whispered, trying to restrain her flailing limbs.

Kaia stared at him, dumbfounded for a moment, trying to comprehend his presence in the Conrad's house of poison.

His eyes brimmed with concern beneath his dark brows. "You don't look so good, Firefly." His gaze flicked to the ragehound.

Gus whined, his ears flat against his head as he wiggled like a puppy. *Our boy!*

"Hold still, Gus." He pulled a knife from his belt and cut away the strap of the muzzle.

Finally, it dawned in Kaia's fuzzy thoughts that Klaus was there to take her home, and she threw herself into his arms in relief. "Oh, thank Odriel."

He chuckled. "I never thought you'd be that happy to see me."

She pulled away, unsteady but with renewed energy borrowed on hope. "Be quiet, and let's get out of here. Everything hurts, and I can barely breathe with all this coughing."

"It's ok, Firefly. Fiola made sure that I brought the medicine. It's outside with the Dalteek." He wrapped his long fingers around her wrists, examining the Dragon Claws. "What's this?"

"Spelled gauntlets that suppress my flames," she whispered. Klaus raised his eyebrows. "Conrad must have the keys."

"Quickly then, before the coward runs."

Klaus pulled her behind him as he led them through a maze of hallways. She tried to suppress her coughs to avoid attracting any unwanted attention. Gus' toenails clicked on the hard floor as he slinked along behind, his tail wagging furiously.

"This is why you don't talk to strangers," Klaus teased, glancing back at her.

Her eyes crinkled, too tired to banter. "How'd you know where to find me?"

He scowled. "The bastards covered their tracks well, but Mackie asked the birds to help us." He rounded a corner. "When we found out you'd been taken, we were worried Mogens had gotten to you." He paused, looking sideways at her. "I'm relieved that particular snake doesn't appear to reside in this den."

Kaia nodded, her forehead wrinkling. "But Conrad said he wrote a note in my name...."

The Shadow Heir didn't answer as he turned again into the main foyer and his muscles tensed—five hard-looking men in armor blocked the main entrance.

Conrad smiled down on them from the grand staircase, "Ah, Guardian Thane, I suppose we should have expected you, but I cannot let you just walk out with my honored guest."

Valente's blue eyes shone out from his father's shadow. "You're making a mistake, Kaia." His voice echoed in the foyer, at once grave and beseeching.

"Call off your dogs, Conrad, before they get hurt," Klaus warned. He released Kaia and drew his sword. Kaia leaned tiredly against the wall of the corridor.

"They're simply doing what they believe to be right," Lord Conrad said. "We can't have you challenging Lord Ariston as he strives to protect the land from evil."

Klaus stepped towards the men. "You can't fight evil with evil."

"Then, I'm afraid this difference in opinion will come to blows," Conrad sneered.

With a gesture from their master, the men rushed forward to meet Klaus. But just as they closed on him, he and his blade winked out of sight. The soldiers stumbled to a stop, dumbfounded.

Kaia almost smiled. It was one thing to know about the Shadow Heir's gift, and quite another to see it in action. A minute passed and then two, as the men looked nervously about them.

"Don't just stand there," Valente called from the balcony. "Find him!"

The men spread out and waved their weapons tentatively in front of them.

One of the thugs looked up at the Conrads. "Maybe he ran—"

An invisible fist smashed into his face, cutting him off. The brutes converged on the spot, brandishing their blades wildly. The clang of steel on steel rang through the hall, then a man cried out as he fell, clutching a gushing thigh. The others backed into a tight circle and slashed wildly in a desperate bid to prevent their invisible attacker from coming closer.

Even without his gift, Klaus was a skilled swordsman—unseen, he was unbeatable. Kaia and the Conrads watched as a man's sword flew out of his hand, and a bleeding stab-wound appeared in his shoulder. One of his comrades came to his aid, but only sliced through empty air in an impotent attack. In another moment, Klaus cleaved his right hand from his arm, and the man's anguished screams filled the foyer as scarlet slicked the marble floor.

The iron tang of blood filled Kaia's nose. She swallowed bile as the unwelcome image of Mogens hovering over her father's body cut through her fog of sickness. *This is different*, she reminded herself. The Shadow Heirs were Odriel's Assassins—gifted and efficient killers. Still, it was a sight to behold.

Only two of Conrad's thugs remained. Like a phantom, Klaus blinked briefly into view in front of the larger one, then disappeared again.

"There!" The brute charged at where he had last seen the Shadow Heir—exactly as Klaus intended. Devastating slashes raked the man's legs, and he collapsed to the ground, howling.

The last guardsman, learning from his comrades' mistakes, remained still and strained to hear the footsteps of his invisible opponent. With a smile, he made one sure powerful cut to his right. Kaia held her breath as the man's smile turned into a frown. He put a hand to his gut, and it came away red.

He crumpled to the manor floor as Klaus appeared behind him.

Kaia looked up from the battle's aftermath to the Conrad's balcony, only to find that they had fled.

"Just a distraction to cover their escape," Klaus spat as he sheathed his sword. "The cowards."

Fear rose in Kaia as she lifted her gauntleted hands. "What'll we do without the keys to manacles?"

"And you don't think I thought of that?" Klaus smirked as he produced a key ring from his pocket.

Kaia smothered a coughing fit, trying to force the words out. "How did you…?"

The Shadow Heir shrugged as he briskly crossed the room to her. "They were expecting me to attack right away, so I searched Conrad's pockets instead. It just took a minute to scale the balcony." He unlocked Kaia's shackles and pulled the gauntlets from her stiff fingers.

"The Heir of cleverness…" she breathed with ragged relief, her hands tingling with renewed sensation.

"We'll ask Everard if he can remove the enchantment from these," Klaus hooked the shackles onto his belt and grabbed her hand. "Come on, let's go before any more guards come running."

As Klaus and Kaia stepped out of the mansion into the cool night air, the Conrads' alabaster stallions galloped by them in a blur towards the gate. Lord

Conrad pulled up sharply at the end of the drive, the moonlight illuminating his face.

"Before you go," he called out toward them. "I'd like to remind Guardian Dashul that my offer stands." He winked at her, and Kaia found herself wishing she had the strength to set his great mansion on fire. "And do be careful on the way home," he added in his slimy voice. "The road can be quite dangerous, you know."

With a smirk, he kicked his mount into a gallop and disappeared into the night.

Klaus snarled an ugly string of curses under his breath.

Kaia tried to keep her eyes focused. "Dangerous...?"

"He's mocking us." Klaus laced his fingers with hers and began to lead her across the lawn with Gus following closely at their heels. "What did he mean about an offer though?"

Another coughing fit shook Kaia as she tried to explain. It sounded even more ridiculous coming out of her mouth.

"Hmm...." Klaus glanced at her out of the corner of his eye. "We'll have to ask Fiola and Shad more about him when we get back." He paused as he thought. "If he is Ariston's ally, I doubt we've seen the last of him."

Kaia nodded. At the moment, it was difficult just putting one foot in front of the other, much less trying to out-strategize an oily noble.

Nudging her with his nose, Gus whined sympathetically. *We go home now.*

By the time they reached the tree-lined path out of the estate, the chills had returned, and she began to tremble. She almost fell, but Klaus caught her.

"Earth below," he mumbled before scooping her up like a small child.

"No," she protested, "Put me down. I can walk."

"You're falling behind." He shifted her weight in his arms. "Is being carried so bad?"

"It'd be just like you to drop me in the mud," she whispered hoarsely.

"I don't see any suitable puddles nearby." He laughed.

Too tired to struggle, Kaia abandoned her protests. Still shaking, she leaned her head against his chest, his warmth helping to relieve her chills.

He bowed his head and pressed his cheek against her forehead. "How're you trembling when your forehead is burning up?"

The rocking of his steps made her eyelids heavy again. "It's called a fever."

"Don't worry. I'll get you the draught."

Waiting outside the estate gates, the Dalteek whickered as they approached. Kaia greeted Sunflash with a small smile, but something still tickled her heavy head.

"Did Conrad leave a note in my name?" She closed her eyes. "I was so worried you would think I was a traitor."

"Oh, Firefly." He clutched her tighter to him. "I know you better than that." The weighted words fell deliberately from his tongue, his steps slowing. "I've noticed your trouble with letters."

Boiling shame flooded Kaia, scalding her heart. Her eyes snapped open, and she pushed away from Klaus as she struggled to get down. "I can walk."

Klaus released her, and she took four steps to bury her burning face in Sunflash's soft mane. For a moment the Heirs listened to the chorus of crickets gossiping with the crescent owls.

Gus yipped and pawed at her leg. Do not be sad, my girl. You don't need to be sad.

A cough punctuated Kaia's sigh. "I *can* write." She tried to scrub the blush from her face with a sleeve. "It's just difficult."

Klaus laced his fingers in hers, pulling her away from the huge mount. He looked into her face with strangely earnest eyes. "Firefly, I couldn't care less if you've never written a letter in your life." He tucked her side-braid behind her ear. "You're enough just as you are."

An avalanche of gratitude shocked Kaia to her core, filling a void she had hidden so long, she had forgotten what wholeness might feel like. She nodded and looked away, but couldn't order her feelings into the words that could capture this new sensation.

Klaus looked up at Sunflash and squeezed her hands. "Now, I don't think you're in any condition to ride."

"But I have to," she murmured, struggling to keep her eyes open.

"No." He led her to his roan Dalteek. "I don't want you falling off your doe. Moonstreak is strong. He can bear both of us for now."

Klaus moved his hands to her waist to help her into Moonstreak's saddle. Kaia's head spun with the sudden motion, while the Shadow Heir fetched blanket and flask from Sunflash's saddle. Kaia shivered and swayed in the saddle as he swung up behind her. He wrapped the blanket around her shoulders and held the flask to her lips. "Fiola said to drink all of it."

As the bitter, gritty liquid grated down her burning throat, Kaia grimaced. She gagged and took another breath before choking it down.

"Yuck," she groaned.

She could feel the rumble of Klaus' chuckle against her back

"You're enjoying this way too much," she spluttered.

"Oh, I just like saving your life." Another snicker shook his chest. "Again." He stuffed the flask in a saddle bag and reached around her to grab the reins with both hands, spurring Moonstreak into a walk and clicking his tongue to urge Sunflash and Gus to follow. Kaia still trembled, but between the blanket and the warm circle of Klaus' arms, she let herself relax.

"Hey, it's still two to one," Kaia protested.

When he spoke, she could feel his hot breath tickling her ear. "One to two, but I think we'll have to keep a running tally."

She opened her mouth to deny it but reflected that he was being incredibly kind. For him, anyway. She fell into a fit of coughs and managed a small shrug. When she finally stilled, they rode for a while just listening to the trill of insects in the dark. The rhythmic, rocking steps of the Dalteek made her eyelids droop again.

Klaus's deep voice resonated in her ear, "You can sleep now, Firefly, I've got you."

Despite her chills, the fuzzy warmth of trust bloomed in her stomach with velvet petals. "Thank you," she whispered, laying her head against his arm.

As she drifted off, she inhaled his scent of soap and leather, letting the comfort of the smell sink into her bones. She could never have guessed that she would fall asleep in the Shadow Heir's arms and feel completely safe.

CHAPTER 15
RETURN

Raindrops peppered the gray morning as Kaia awoke. The cold drizzle sapped what little heat she had managed to maintain, and she shook violently. Klaus hugged her close to share his body warmth, but soaked as he was, could do little. He offered to stop and find them some shelter, but Kaia shook her head. She wanted to get back to Fiola's warm fire as soon as possible, so they pressed on through the mud and rain, stopping only to switch Dalteek. With shaking hands, Kaia accepted water but couldn't manage any food with her swollen throat.

Klaus' forehead creased with worry. "I'm sorry, Firefly."

She shrugged and tried to reassure him with a weak smile, since talking hurt too much. If Shad had been there, he probably would've said something sassy about the longest the two of them had ever been together without arguing. Kaia savored the pleasant change, and by dusk, she recognized a ridge that she knew lay no more than a day's easy ride from Summerbanks. The sight gave her hope, and she tried to sit up straighter in the saddle.

Oblivious to this good news, Klaus' breathing grew heavy and even, and his right arm twitched. Before long, his head sagged onto her shoulder. Kaia smiled. He probably hadn't slept since he left to find her. She took the reins from his limp hands and tried to muffle her coughs so as not to wake him.

As they rode, a half-forgotten memory from her first Triennial bobbed to the surface of Kaia's thoughts. She remembered herself as a little girl, hopelessly lost in the darkening mountain wood and out of breath from chasing an invisible Klaus through the underbrush.

She looked around desperately, her breath coming faster as she realized she recognized nothing. Pellie, her ragehound, whined and nosed at her ear. The lights of the house had vanished behind the fat tree trunks as the thick bracken turned to shadows in the creeping dusk. Her eyes squeezed shut as she tried to call fire to her palm, but her hand shook with growing panic. The scratching of the waking night creatures grew monstrous in her five-year imagination, destroying the calm she needed to draw her gift.

"Be brave," she whispered to herself as she wiped her eyes and started in the direction she had come.

"That's the wrong way, you know," the eight-year-old Klaus taunted from thin air.

"Klaus! I don't know the way back!" Her voice trembled as she knotted her fingers into Pellie's thick fur.

An exaggerated sigh tickled the back of Kaia's neck, and she turned to find Klaus with his hands on his hips. "I guess I could let you follow me back," he drawled. "But could you at least make yourself useful and light the way?"

Kaia's lower lip trembled as she once again closed her eyes and fought for the composure to produce a flame. She opened her eyes and looked to her open palm—nothing. Her arm dropped, and she shook her head. Klaus grimaced before snatching her still quivering hand.

"C'mon then, we'll just have to find our way in the dark," he grumbled, looking back at her damp face. "And dry your tears—it's not like I'd ever leave you out here on your own."

Kaia smiled to herself, it was nice to know that not everything changed.

She drew her collar closer to her neck as cold rainwater trickled down her shirt. As Sunflash picked her way down a narrow deer trail, Kaia listened to the tapping of the raindrops on the broad tree leaves above her and looked up at the dark sky. There would be no moon or stars tonight, but she wished fervently that the drizzle would stop.

Klaus murmured something unintelligible in his sleep and twitched again. Kaia smiled tiredly into the dark, but it wasn't long before the Shadow Heir's rhythmic breathing, and the hypnotic rocking of Sunflash's steps had her eyelashes drooping once again. If she went to sleep, perhaps she would wake up in a warm bed, swathed in blankets. Her head nodded, and she jerked it up suddenly, rubbing her eyes with a damp, icy palm. *One of us has to keep watch.*

She gazed into the pitch black surrounding them, and she suppressed a shudder, her skin prickling. The Dragon Heir strained her ears for any unusual sounds but heard nothing. Even so, her instincts had escalated from an unsettled murmur to a silent scream.

Gus smelled it first. He whined insistently. *Bad. The badness is here!*

Then, Kaia heard an unwelcome sound that she remembered distinctly, the creaking of rotten bones.

She shrugged Klaus' face roughly from her shoulder. "Wake up!"

"What?" he protested groggily, trying to rub the sleep out of his eyes.

"I think we're about to have company of the worst kind," she answered, her teeth chattering—from nerves or fever, she wasn't sure.

Klaus' muscles tensed behind her. "Can you light a fire?"

His voice had a hard edge to it now. For a heartbeat, Kaia was five years old again, lost in the dark and unsure. She shook the thought away but couldn't still her knocking teeth. "The rain isn't a problem, but I don't have a lot of yanaa. Klaus, if there are a lot—" Her heart turned cold as the smell of decay reached them. "This might be difficult."

"Do what you can." Klaus' body jerked as he scanned the dark forest. "In any case, we need the light."

With a deep breath, Kaia closed her eyes, reaching for the calm at her center. She was no longer five and afraid. She was the Dragon Heir—with power at her fingertips. She let a small fire grow in the palm of her hand, making it burn tall, hot, and bright.

It revealed a nightmare.

Countless pairs of coal black eyes stared at them from the trees. These were worse than the ones that she had encountered at the castle or in Carceroc—these were old bodies. A film of green smoke curled around bones barely knit together by strips of flesh. The black pits of their eyes were framed only by skulls. Any semblance of humanity had been stripped away with most of their bodies, leaving skeletal marionettes driven with a thick shroud of dark yanaa.

The Dragon Heir recognized an ambush when she saw one.

She could feel Klaus' heartbeat accelerate behind her. There had to be over a hundred advancing through the trees on both sides. The Heirs didn't have much time to mount a defense.

"Stay on the doe," Klaus ordered as he dismounted. "If you lose your dragon fire, ride to Fiola's for help. I'll be fine." He drew his sword for the second time that night. "Take care of those on your right first. I'll start on the left. Listen for the switch."

Kaia nodded wordlessly as the Heir blinked out of sight. She looked to the fifty or so that approached from her side and let her flame grow. She could only hope that Sunflash didn't shy at the fire. In her weakened state, creating the flame was a slow process, and beads of sweat rolled down her forehead, stinging her eyes. At last, she directed a jet of liquid fire at the first wave of dead, a dozen perhaps.

Sunflash flinched at the blast but somehow managed not to panic. She pawed at the ground nervously, but Kaia ran a quick hand through her mane to steady her. The flames enveloped the approaching Lost, illuminating the wood as it fed on their shroud of yanaa. But instead of crumbling right away, they screamed in protest, railing against the onslaught as they continued their advance. Kaia's heart flared with fear. The green radiance of their yanaa resisted her flames, proving them tougher than any she had faced before— Ariston had grown stronger.

More wails spiked the air as she prepared the second inferno. Klaus could only pick them off one at a time, but he made fast work. An invisible executioner, he whirled through the mob, decapitating one after the other, their bodies returning to useless heaps of marrow and rot.

She flung the second fireball and watched with satisfaction as it exploded against the shambling Lost, blowing them into flaming bits.

"Kaia! Switch! *Now!*" Klaus shouted.

She wheeled Sunflash to the left. There were perhaps thirty Lost before her. She tried to conjure another fireball, but she had no heat in her body to draw upon. The flames built sluggishly, but the relentless Lost drew ever nearer. Their long, claw-like fingers stretched out to her, and she could see maggots writhing in their arms. Finally, she could wait no longer, and with her spare hand she hurled a volley of small fireballs at the closest attackers. They hit the targets, but didn't have the heat to incinerate them. A nightmarish battle cry arose from the Lost as they flung their flaming bodies at her.

Sunflash's quick hooves danced back as the Lost's raking fingers grabbed for her. Kaia screamed, kicking out as one brushed her boot. Fueled by panic, Kaia held both arms out and yelled in desperation—a river of fire forced of pure adrenaline erupted from her palms, engulfing the front line. Her eyes watched the burning Lost as she sucked in deep breaths, letting her body gradually crumple beneath her until she lay limp on Sunflash's neck.

When she felt sure her lungs weren't going to burst, she managed to gather a small hand-sized flame to tally the remaining Lost on her side. She counted a dozen still stalking the dark. She looked on Klaus' side and saw a crowd of ten gathered around a patch of air that she hoped didn't hold the Shadow Heir.

She sat up and tried to will her small flame into a weapon, but to no avail. Her heart sank. "Klaus," she called hoarsely into the dark, "I have no more fire."

His weary voice echoed back at her from closer than she expected. "Take Sunflash and Gus and leave for Fiola's."

Kaia could hear his ragged breathing, and another head flew from a body. She drew her sword, letting the blade borrow a weak glow from her remaining flame.

"Gus, stay!" she commanded the steadfast dog as she urged Sunflash towards the dozen on the left.

The doe leapt forward, and when they reached the first of the Lost, she reared, puncturing its skull with one of her sharp hooves. Kaia clung desperately to Sunflash's mane and just barely managed to remain in the saddle.

Another wailing Lost rushed them from the side, and Kaia sliced cleanly through its rotting neck with her sword. A second made the mistake of grabbing Sunflash by the tail and disappeared in a flash of kicking hooves. Sunflash threw her head to crush the ribcage of a third while a fourth scrabbled at her bridle from the right. Kaia hacked at it with sloppy blows. On the fifth slash from the heavy sword, the corpse fell apart in a mass of splintered bone.

Kaia sagged in the saddle. Seven left. The glow of her blade had faded. The logical part of her brain insisted that she was spent and that she should ride for Fiola's, but abandoning Klaus to these monsters was unfathomable. Her sword growing heavier by the second, Kaia grabbed a hunting knife from the saddle and flung it at the nearest Lost in exhausted desperation. The abomination screamed in dismay as the knife skewered its nose cavity. But before Kaia could straighten, skeletal fingers seized her left thigh and tried to drag her from Sunflash. She stared into the creature's maggoty, eyeless face as it clawed at her, gouging her flesh. Kaia grunted with pain as she raised her sword with both hands.

Abruptly, her tormentor's head rolled off its shoulders. Kaia gasped in relief, dropping the sword. Her body wilted as terror drained from her tense muscles.

"I told you to run." Klaus' voice smoldered from the dark.

"The Dragon Heir..." Kaia panted "...does not run."

She stuck her tongue out in the direction of his voice before falling, letting herself once again collapse onto Sunflash's neck. Stifling a cough, she heard Klaus stumble around in the underbrush, taking care of the last scattered Lost before blinking back into sight and returning to her. Kaia held a candle-sized flame out to look at him. Sweat dripped from his face, and his head drooped. The battle had sapped him as well.

She smiled wearily. "I don't think you're in any condition to ride."

"Maybe." He smiled as he leaned against Sunflash and gave Kaia's boot a tug. "We'll go a little farther and stop for a few hours while we both get our strength back." He whistled for Moonstreak and Gus before leading Sunflash back down to the little trail.

As the adrenaline abandoned her, the wounds in Kaia's leg began to ache. She swayed dizzily in the saddle. "Conrad didn't think we could, but we did it—sick, tired, and all."

The Shadow Heir rubbed a hand through his sweaty hair. "How could Conrad send the dead after us?"

Kaia shrugged with heavy shoulders. "Maybe Ariston was with him after all?"

"But why would Ariston know we were here? We only just arrived, so he would've had to already be here...." Klaus straightened, his eyes widening. "Firefly, Conrad *is* Ariston."

Too tired to register shock, Kaia's head dipped as she struggled to keep up. "But if that's true—why isn't he with his army?"

"He must've come ahead of his army to spy on Everard." He knocked a fist against his head as he thought. "That's the only explanation."

She glanced at the dark path in front of them, bone fragments of the Lost still scattered across it. "So, what do we do now?" She yawned hugely.

He chuckled and shook her boot again. "Now, we need to get back to Fiola's and regroup."

Kaia opened her mouth to say something else, but the words slipped from her tongue as she slid from her saddle into oblivion.

***

When she awoke, she was warm and dry, and the burning in her throat had faded considerably. She opened her eyes to find herself back in Fiola's farmhouse—a warm afternoon sun streamed in through the open window, and a soft breeze toyed with her hair.

She wondered for a moment if the whole episode had been a dream, before realizing that something heavy lay across her stomach. She looked down, thinking it was Gus, and found a dozing Klaus draped across the bed sideways, with a colorful quilt draped over both of them. Fiola sat in her armchair in the corner of the room with a voluminous treatise on medicinal herbs in her lap. She noticed Kaia's curious look and smiled.

"You made it in this morning," she whispered. "He managed to carry you up to the bed before he collapsed." The old woman giggled to herself and shrugged. "You two looked so worn out, I just decided to cover you up and let you be. I think you were still half asleep, but I did manage to clean your leg and get some medicine in you earlier."

Kaia merely nodded. Fiola rose to tuck the blanket around her like a child, and Kaia let her head sink back into the soft pillow.

***

Gus' happy barking woke her the next morning. She sat up to see Mackie laughing as Felix and Gus chased each other in the field just outside her window. She looked to the bedside table for her medicine and found a bowl of steaming liquid sitting next to it. She took a swig of the bitter draught before she reached hungrily for the bowl, but after she inhaled the stew, her belly still grumbled for more.

Kaia coughed to ease her still itching throat as she swung her stocking feet to the floor. Dressed in an oversized nightshirt, she looked around the room for fresh clothes or even the muddied ones from the day before, but found nothing. Kaia padded across the room and opened the door. She spied Fiola bustling by the foot of the stair.

"Fiola, do you know where my clothes are?" she called.

Fiola glanced up at her, dismissing her with a wave. "Dear, you should still be in bed! You won't be properly well until tomorrow."

"But I've already been in bed for a full day!"

Before Fiola could answer, Klaus emerged from the room next to hers with an oblong periapple in his hand. "Why is it," he began as he took a bite out of the periapple and walked toward her, "that when your friends give you good advice—don't trust the Conrads, go back to Fiola's, stay in bed—you resist?"

He leaned so close to her that their noses almost touched. His breath smelled sweetly of the fruit, and his hazel eyes glinted.

Her stomach fluttered at his closeness. "Can't I just go down and get something to eat?"

"No," he said flatly. "If you are hungry, we will *bring* you something to eat. Go back to bed." With a gentle hand, he pushed her back into the room and closed the door in her face.

***

The next day, Kaia woke before the sun, bursting with energy. The birds trilled ringing melodies in the predawn air, encouraging the sun to awaken from its slumber. She threw off the nightshirt and dressed in the clothes hanging from a nearby chair. She reached down to ruffle Gus' fur and bounded out the door and down the stairs, breathing in the heavenly scent of sizzling sausage.

"Good morning!" she chimed as she bounced into the kitchen. Shad sat at his usual place on the window sill, Fiola smiled at her brightly from the hearth where she tended the pan, and Klaus glanced at her from where he leaned against the wall, but it wasn't any of their voices that answered her.

"Good morning, Guardian Dashul."

Kaia turned in surprise to see a man regarding her from the rocking chair. He looked exactly the same as when she had last seen him four years ago. He wore the same long black cloak and still kept his gleaming white hair and beard short and neatly trimmed. Only the crow's feet edging his onyx eyes hinted at his years.

Everard had returned.

CHAPTER 16
PREPARATIONS

Everard had arrived before the sun, and Fiola and Klaus had wasted no time in filling him in. He confirmed that a state of abject terror reigned in the wake of Nifras' recent attempt to break the magi's *yanai* barrier, and nodded in approval at their efforts to gather the army at Gyatan, but his unblinking night eyes gave away nothing as they related their revelation of Conrad's identity.

Suddenly, he slammed his hand against the arm of the chair. "I can't believe I didn't see it." He rose and paced back and forth, cloak sweeping the cobbles as he muttered to himself. "He was always trying to win you. The abduction of Tam and Klaus, Valente's kindness, and one last desperate ultimatum—an alliance against Ariston or death." The magus stopped and shook his head. "Make an obstacle an asset or destroy it." He harrumphed and resumed his pacing. "The man is clever. If not for Tam's sacrifice, he might have succeeded."

"But why not send the whole army after her?" Shad interrupted.

"Perhaps he underestimated her. Perhaps that's all he had to send." Everard turned his gaze to the Dragon Heir. "We are lucky the bulk of his army is still to the north, or the Heirs may not have survived the night."

Kaia sat at the table, impatiently tapping the rosy wood with a finger, only one question on her mind. "But what about Jago?"

A long sigh seemed to bend the stiff magus, forcing his head back down. "Unfortunately, despite an exhaustive search, I've found no trace of the Time Heir." He pressed his lips together. "Nor has his pregnant wife seen him since Pryor Brigg's death."

The room went still. Even the breeze from the window died. For a long moment, only the popping of the sausage filled the tense kitchen.

The words cracked down on Kaia like a hammer. Jago was dead—smiling, kind, joyful Jago. And he would never meet his child. She could only imagine the oceanic depth of his wife's sorrow.

Gus nosed her foot beneath the table, looking up at her with big eyes. *I am sad with you.*

Lost in Everard's news, Kaia nearly forgot Klaus leaning against the doorway until he spoke. "We will mourn him." He brushed by Kaia as he moved to sit next to her at the table. "And adapt."

Sadness glistened in Fiola's eyes as she crossed her tattooed arms in front of the fire. "How long do we have before Conrad reaches Gyatan?"

"One week," Everard braced his hands against the table. "We'll have to leave at once to meet them." His hard eyes bored into each person in turn. "Then, it is only a matter of time before Nifras breaks the *yanai* barrier." He paused and closed his eyes, as if recalling a distant memory. "When he steps foot upon the land, the sky will not grow light again."

No one spoke as they absorbed Everard's words.

Klaus was the only one who seemed unperturbed as he grabbed a biscuit from the center bowl. "Sooner than we thought."

Fiola rose silently to pile eggs and sausage onto plates, setting one before Kaia, and then giving her shoulder a reassuring squeeze.

The magus stroked his neat beard. "Besides the trading town, the region is arid and quite desolate. He paused. It will make the perfect battleground."

Klaus swallowed a mouthful of biscuit. "How many does Ariston have?"

Folding his hands behind his back, Everard gazed out the window at the mountain peaks. "My ears in the north say two thousand dead and perhaps four hundred deluded villagers," Everard said in a clipped voice.

Kaia and Klaus exchanged an incredulous glance. Kaia's mouth fell open as she looked to Klaus. He pressed his lips together and raised his eyebrows at her.

Her head swiveled back to the old magus. "Everard…."

"It really should not be a difficult battle," the magus snapped, turning back to them. "Five hundred seasoned warriors, a magus, and two legendary Heirs against villagers with pitchforks and a horde of clumsy corpses that Conrad cannot control."

"And an Heir killer," Kaia grumbled as she picked at a plump egg.

She jumped as the magus slammed his palms heavily on the table and fixed his black eyes onto hers. The biting words cut through her skin like an icy wind. "Nifras and his army will be much worse."

With that, the magus strode out of the room. Kaia blushed scarlet at his sharp reprimand and studied the cherry whorls of the table, remembering why she never liked the magus. He had always been brusque with her, even before she had accidentally set his cloak on fire as a girl.

Fiola glided around the table and rubbed her back with a strong hand. "Don't you mind that grumpy old magus, dear. His anger is merely a poor attempt to hide the shame he feels at the cowardice of his own kind." Kaia nodded once, but said nothing. "And he forgot to mention, you'll have Mackie and me there too! How could we lose?"

Klaus looked up from his plate, his eyebrows raised. "You're going to be fighting with us, Fiola?"

"And Mackie, too?" Kaia's eyebrows knitted. "But he's so young."

"Well," Fiola shrugged with a chuckle, "we won't exactly be fighting. I could handle myself in my younger days, but now my old bones just can't do it anymore. Medicine, though, I've still got. Mackie and I will be on the field to aid the fallen." She plucked up a sausage, chewing it thoughtfully. "And Mackie says he's also recruited a different kind of help for you."

Kaia tried to think of who she could mean. "Who's that?"

"He says the predators of the wood are willing and able. He's been out in the forest since Everard returned, sending the animals to Gyatan."

The Dragon Heir smiled, thinking back to their talk of bravery. Mackie had a good heart.

Klaus slapped the table and turned to face Kaia. "In any case, if we are going to be fighting in a week, we have to make sure that you fill up and get your rest, Firefly. Two thousand Lost is a lot of bodies to torch." He grabbed her plate and piled it high with eggs, sausages, biscuits, and gravy. "You can start with that." He slid the mountain of food in front of her with a grin.

She rolled her eyes. "You need to stop telling me what to do."

She pushed the plate back at him. Her belly felt so tight with unease, she wasn't sure she could fit food in it. The world was crashing down again, and it was up to them to put it back together. She sighed.

Klaus nudged her with his shoulder. "It'll be fine! The original Heirs took on ten thousand. You and I can definitely handle two." His smile widened. "I'll take on the first nineteen hundred, and I guess I can let you have the stragglers."

Shaking her head, Kaia let her tense muscles relax. She shouldered him back and picked up her fork. "Oh, my dear Shadow Heir, how I would love to see you try."

***

Everard and the Heirs rode westward on their Dalteek, while Mackie and Fiola followed with a wagon of food and medical supplies. At dusk on the eve of Conrad's expected arrival, the company descended from the Naerami mountains toward the town of Gyatus, snuggled up against Blackerd's canyon in the heart of the Gyatan Plain.

As they descended from the mountains, Kaia gaped at the strange landscape from a craggy outcrop. Before them the vast gorge of Blackerd's canyon split the earth like an ugly scar, dividing the wilderness of west

Okarria from the civilized east. On the eastern edge, the squat dwellings of Gyatus cropped out of the dusty plain like hardy weeds. Squinting, her eyes trailed to the north, where she spied canvas tents flapping on the sea of scrubby golden grass and a camp bustling with men, Dracours, and Maldibor.

She exhaled and a tangle in her stomach unraveled. The warriors of Okarria had answered their call and made it in time. The Dracour must have practically flown to reach them. From the camp, she let her eyes continue their crawl northward to scan the blue horizon. Empty. For now.

As they drew closer to the tents, Kaia could smell the musk of the Maldibor and looked for Tekoa as a hail echoed through the field: "The Heirs have arrived!"

A volley of voices of different timbres echoed the call, and the clamor increased tenfold as the warriors dropped what they were doing and rushed to see the honored travelers. Before the Dalteek even reached the first tent, the army had assembled impatiently at the edge of the encampment. As the Heirs trotted closer, three riders—a Dracour, a Maldibor and a man—rode out from the mob to meet them.

Kaia's childhood teacher, Cressida, rode out in front of the others. The Dracour matriarch was impossible to miss with her long reptilian body and muscular human torso. Ram horns curled around her head, and she wore her long, gray-streaked hair in the typical Dracourian braid. Covered in shining metal from neck to flanks and bristling with weapons, she glimmered in the sun as she ran toward Kaia, smiling with sharp teeth.

Kaia slowed Sunflash to a walk to give her the traditional Dracour greeting. "We hunt together again."

The Dracour walked forward to meet her and touched her forehead to hers with the usual reply. "May the killing be swift." She drew back, and her gaze hardened. "Your father is mourned, Guardian Dashul."

Kaia inclined her head soberly. "Thank you, Cressida."

She nudged Sunflash to greet the silver Maldibor in his leather armor. It took Kaia a moment, but she recognized the fierce-faced, straight-backed beast must be Chief Okoni. She reached out to clasp his thick arm. "It is an honor to have you here with us."

He bared his teeth at her in their way of smiling. "It was an honor to have been invited."

Finally, she turned to the armored man on the end, who had already dismounted and knelt to pat a wriggling Gus. When he stood and removed his helmet, Kaia almost fell from her Dalteek.

"Bram! What're you doing here?" She leapt from her horse and barreled into him with a hug. "It's so good to see you!"

"I've been training with you for the last seventeen years, Kaia," he said, releasing her. "When the Dracour got your letter, I asked Mother if I could come as well." They turned together to watch Everard and Klaus trot ahead with Cressida and the Maldibor chief.

"But—" Kaia started to protest.

His eyes cut sideways to her. "I'm as old as you are."

"O-of course." She tugged her copper braid as she looked him over. He wore his wavy coffee hair shorter than usual, and the armor made him look much larger than she remembered, even though he had always been nearly a full head taller than she. *With his helmet on, I thought he was a warrior,* she reminded herself, *and he's proven himself against the Lost before.*

She grabbed Sunflash's reins to lead her towards the camp. "How's Mama, Layf, and Eleni?"

Bram walked with measured steps beside her, leading his own dun horse. "Layf was disappointed that you missed his birthday, but they are all safe back in the mountains."

Kaia winced at that. It had been over a month since she'd seen her family, and she couldn't foresee a return any time soon.

"We heard about Father," Bram murmured. Kaia nodded but said nothing. "Eleni and Layf took it hard, but Mother already seemed to know." He glanced sideways at her. "Now they worry about you."

"I see." Kaia exhaled slowly. "They should be worried about you as well. This will be a difficult battle."

Bram shrugged, and then flashed a cocky smile. "I'm sure they are, but I'm confident."

Kaia rolled her eyes at him.

"Someone has to avenge Father after all," he said matter-of-factly. "I mean after you let —"

Before he could finish the sentence, Kaia turned and slapped a hand across his chest, halting him mid-step.

"Don't. You. Dare." She hissed through gritted teeth, a storm of buried sadness roiling within her.

His gray eyes turned to steel. "Did it happen differently?"

"You don't know the first thing about what happened," she growled, tears welling in her eyes as she mounted Sunflash.

He stood tense, unwavering. "If I had been the Heir—"

"You don't think I've thought that a million times?" A tear trickled down her cheek. "That I wouldn't gladly have given you the fire if it meant we could get Papa back?" She shook her head. "I wish you Odriel's wings in the battle tomorrow, but if that's all you have to say," she turned and mounted Sunflash, "I don't want to see you until it's over." With that, she spurred Sunflash after the others.

She scrubbed her face and tried to even her breathing before she caught up to Klaus. She watched the chieftains talking earnestly ahead as she rode just behind them, refusing to meet anyone's eyes and struggling to keep her countenance impassive. Klaus tried to catch her eye as they entered the camp, but the cheer of the crowd pulled his attention away.

With another roar, the men, Maldibor, and Dracours rolled up to them in a large wave. Many had known her father and wanted to give their condolences. Others just wanted to cross arms and express their gratitude for her protection. Snatches of conversation floated around her.

What an honor it will be to fight with you! Now we'll see some real yanaa!

She looks skinny—can she even swing a sword?

I thought there were supposed to be three Heirs.

I didn't realize the new Dragon Heir is a girl.

She greeted each and every warrior, but as soon as the crowd cleared, she excused herself and trotted off for the edge of camp. There, she dismounted near a small scrubby tree a short way from the rest of the tents. She leaned her saddle against its trunk to claim it and fed Sunflash a handful of dried periapple before leading her back to the nearest trough.

The warriors of the camp clamored around Everard and Klaus as they explained their strategy for the morrow, but Kaia sat in the dirt and hugged Gus, enjoying the momentary quiet. A pressure pulsed in her forehead from pent up tears, but even now she refused to release them. This was not the time for tears, even if her twin brother was a brute.

"Still spoiling my doe?" a voice called from behind her.

"Tekoa!" Kaia jumped up and turned around.

The burnt umber beast bared his teeth, and his green eyes glinted cheerfully. He wore a hulking broadsword across his back, but other than that, he looked exactly as she had first seen him. She rushed into his big furry arms, trying to hold her breath as she did so. "How are you?"

"I'm well, my lady, and you?" His voice reverberated in Kaia's chest, resonating with an empathy that soothed her skinned heart.

She pulled away with a wistful smile. "Sunflash and I are well enough." Almost as though adding her agreement, Sunflash turned to nuzzle the great Maldibor. "There's a boy in camp that can speak to animals, and he assures me Sunflash is contented."

Tekoa stroked Sunflash's thick mane with a huge paw. "I can see that."

A thought brightened Kaia's face. "Oh! And she even saved my life."

His paw moved to scratch her between the twisting antlers. "Did she now? She was always a clever fawn."

Kaia patted Sunflash's flank. "She's skilled in the art of killing the Lost."

"As are you, it is said," rumbled Tekoa with a fond glance.

She winced. Kaia had already gathered that the camp warriors expected the Heirs to end the battle in minutes. "I suppose we'll find out tomorrow."

"Do not worry, young Kaia," Tekoa said as he fed Sunflash a crust of bread from his pocket. "You are a strong girl, and victory is in your blood. You'll see."

Kaia looked away. That was easy to say when the lives of all these brave people and her friends—her only friends—didn't depend on him. To make it worse, her brother had just reminded her that she had already suffered a wretched defeat.

Tekoa put a hand to her back. "Come." He gently guided her towards the center of the camp. "They'll worry if you don't join them for dinner."

For the second time that summer, Tekoa passed her a heaping plate of food as they sat around the fire. Kaia smiled grimly to herself—she'd rather walk through Carceroc a dozen times than face tomorrow's battle. There would be no drinking or dancing this night, just the sharpening of blades and the oiling of armor.

She ate mechanically as Mackie regaled the others of Klaus and Kaia's adventures with the griegals and the recent ambush. His enthusiasm was so misplaced in the tense atmosphere that it was hard not to grin. He turned to the Heirs now and then for details, and they would just shake their heads with a smile. When he told of Kaia's rescue from the Conrads, she looked to Klaus at her right elbow and blushed when his steady eyes met her gaze.

Kaia glanced around the fire. Everard and Fiola sat close together, Mackie gamely told stories with the round-faced Felix on his shoulder, and Gus lay at her feet. She saw Cressida, Tekoa, and other smiling faces milling about the camp. Even Shad sat nearby, flicking his tail back and forth.

She was surrounded by friends, but in her heart, she felt a hole.

Tomorrow, they wouldn't be able to help her. Tomorrow, in the heat of battle, the eyes of the army would be on Kaia—looking for hope and strength. If the Heirs won, it would be everyone's victory, but if they lost, the failure would be theirs alone.

A clear soprano pierced through her thoughts, and she looked up to see Mackie singing.

> *The Dragon Heir is strongest they all say,*
> *But watch out if you know what's good for you,*
> *He will turn you into ashes of gray,*
> *So be careful what you say and do.*

> *The Shadow Heir is smartest they all say,*
> *But you'll never see him coming for you,*
> *He walks unseen even on sunny days,*
> *So you must speak kindly of that one, too.*

> *The Time Heir is the kindest by far,*
> *Unlike the others, you don't have to fear,*
> *He'll fix you up and won't leave a scar,*
> *When he comes to town, it's cause for cheer.*

Kaia threw a small pebble at the boy. "Mackie, I hate that song." It was an old tune that children chanted when they played. Bram had often teased her with it when they were young. "The dragon sounds awful!" she groused.

Mackie laughed. "But, it's not bad, Kaia. It's just part of the legend of the Dragon Heir."

Felix chirped, as if to second the statement.

Klaus leaned towards Kaia. "Yeah, Firefly, it's part of your *legend*."

"Father's legend, perhaps," Bram murmured from behind them, just loud enough for her ears only. Kaia turned from the fire to see her brother staring at her through the darkness.

Kaia rose and took a step towards him, "I seemed to have fared well enough."

"Will you be able to deliver justice for our father, then?" The shadows of the fire played across his face.

Kaia snarled, her fists clenching as she tried to control her temper. "I will use my gifts to burn the Lost—as is its purpose." She jerked her head at Klaus. "The Shadow Heir is best with the blade—he'll take the leaders."

Bram's eyebrows raised as he snapped a stick in his hands before throwing it into the fire. "The Shadow Heir to the rescue again." His eyes flicked back to her. "You're not *scared*, are you, sister?"

Kaia opened her mouth to respond when Klaus came between them, putting a hand on their shoulders, "This doesn't look like a loving repartee between siblings on the eve of battle."

Bram shrugged. "Just making sure The Dragon Heir is ready, that's all."

Kaia straightened. "I am the first-born of Tamsin Dashul, the Dragon Heir by birthright, blessed with courage and the gift of fire. I have been trained for this battle since I could walk. Best worry about yourself, instead, *little* brother,"

With that, she knocked Klaus' hand off her shoulder and stalked off back to her pack on the far side of camp.

Gus yipped at her as they walked. Calm, my girl. Calm. Breathe.

Kaia sucked in deep breaths as she fought the urge to flame. She yanked her saddle out from under the tree and hurled it out into the open. With a cry of frustration, she hammered her fists into the ground, grabbing fistfuls of dirt in her fingers.

Gus snuffled at her ear. You will be ok. I am here.

She gently pushed his nose away and sat back, looking at the clear, star-filled sky. She pulled her knees to her chest and closed her eyes as she let the emotions beat against her in furious gusts. She inhaled the night air and exhaled fear, rage, and sorrow—expelling it from her body.

Gus curled up by her feet and breathed his own canine sigh. We are safe. We are ok.

The luminous, crescent moon sparkled above Kaia, but it couldn't cheer her this night. She pressed the palms of her hands into her eyes. Okarria's army had asked her for protection, but she couldn't even save her father from one man. Bram, though infuriating, was right. She was just an untried girl…but she was also the Dragon Heir. The dragon wasn't supposed to hesitate, wasn't supposed to feel fear.

The pressure in her forehead returned. She looked up to the velvet navy sky and thought of Mogens and the Arimoke villagers that had exiled her.

They said she was a killer of men, which she wasn't…yet. Is that what she would become tomorrow? An Heir the townsfolk could rightfully fear? Her father had turned the dragon fire upon a man and created a monster. Would she do the same?

The uncertainty made her muscles tighten and her head ache. Her father was supposed to be here to help her, to answer her questions. She was too young to be Guardian Dashul, too young to fight this war. She didn't even have Jago's guidance. Her eyes grew damp, and she squeezed them shut, reaching out for Gus' reassuring bulk.

She glanced up sharply as footsteps approached.

"They have a tent for you, you know," Klaus teased.

Her muscles relaxed—not Bram. She closed her eyes again without answering. If no one else knew about her doubts, she could be the fearless Dragon Heir they expected her to be.

He kicked the dirt. "You know, I never liked Bram. He's always been a profound ass."

Kaia opened her damp eyes, but looked away, not trusting her voice to be steady.

"Kaia." Klaus sat in the dirt next to her, stretching his legs out and leaning back on his hands to look at the sky.

She cleared her throat. "It's fine."

"Your brother's a jealous fool. It's not your fault."

"I know that."

"But do you believe it?"

She looked at the stars, pinpricks of light in the darkness. "My father should be here," she murmured. "And Jago, too."

"Yes." Klaus edged closer to her in the dark. "But that doesn't mean we can't do this." He nudged her shoulder with his own. The gesture was simple, and yet this simple show of fellowship—of kind compassion—rocked Kaia to her core. She rested her head on her forearms, and the pressure in her temples eased as tears escaped down her cheeks.

"I'm scared," she whispered. The confession burned her throat.

"I'm glad to see you have some sense, after all."

She let out a shaky breath and slapped his leg. He grabbed her hand and squeezed it, leaning his head towards her as if whispering a secret. "I'll be right there with you, Firefly."

Kaia returned his steady gaze, feeling his confidence course from his fingers to hers. Her shoulders relaxed as he rubbed his calloused thumb across hers. Kaia nudged him with her shoulder and looked back toward the sky. "I'm counting on it."

CHAPTER 17
ARISTON'S ARMY

Kaia awoke to paws on her chest and Shad's sapphire eyes staring at her in the dark morning. "It is time."

She rose quietly as Gus yawned beside her, showing his long shepherd's teeth. She strapped her father's hand-me-down sword around her waist, her last resort in this battle. The camp was already bustling with activity as the warriors made last-minute preparations—shining shields, limbering exercises, and discussing formations.

Kaia followed Shad to a tent where they had set aside an extra set of armor for her. She tried on the shoulder plates, gauntlets, and a helmet she could barely see out of, but the oversized gear made her limbs feel clumsy and slow. Finally, she discarded most of it and walked out with only a mail vest, reasoning that no one should be able to get close to her in any case.

As Kaia walked over to the fire to grab a hasty breakfast, she passed Fiola preparing her tent to tend to the inevitable wounded. She arranged bandages, basins of water, and many, many pallets. She directed others to help her with a voice that rang with the air of command. *She's a tough old woman,* Kaia thought with a smile.

She spotted Felix curled up on a stack of blankets as Mackie scurried about obeying Fiola's orders. She was glad to see the cheerful boy was out of harm's way.

Seeing Kaia's glance, Mackie waved at her and pointed to the edge of the camp. There, lounging some distance away from the rest, gathered a pack of bears, lions, and wolves, all of them still as though patiently waiting for the call to battle. Kaia's brows shot up at the strange sight.

Mackie laughed at her surprise and gave her a wink for luck. She gladly returned it before continuing on her way.

She walked over to a cooking fire in the center of camp, not sure exactly where to be. Lost in her thoughts, she jumped when Klaus appeared at her elbow. As befitting a Shadow Heir, he was clad only in black leather armor muffled with cloth wrappings to ensure speed and stealth. The armor seemed to accent his muscular arms and tall frame—just like Odriel's Assassins of old. Kaia could only imagine the fear he would inspire with his sudden appearance on the battlefield. Klaus' lips quirked briefly in greeting, but his eyes glinted humorlessly. As Kaia glanced around the camp, she saw his expression reflected on many of the warriors.

Scooping porridge from the pot over the fire, they finished their small breakfast standing up just before the horns began to blow. At first, only one bellowed through the pre-dawn darkness, then it was joined by another and another until the entire camp echoed with the rumbling battle call. Adrenaline raised the hair on the back of Kaia's neck as she jammed the last bite of food in her mouth and strode over to the assembling army in the fields north of the camp.

She gazed across the golden grass and managed to make out a long dark line on the horizon stretching from the canyon to the base of the mountain. Ahead of the line, a single rider approached them. Klaus and Cressida stood beside her while Everard and the Maldibor chief sat upon their magnificent Naerami mounts.

Cressida's powerful tail pounded the ground. "It's a messenger."

Everard folded his hands behind his back. "To negotiate terms of peace."

The rider halted before them and puffed out his shining chest plate, his mouth twitching with a nervous tic. "Lord Ariston has sent me to command you to cease your foolish resistance. Nifras is our true enemy. We should not divide our strength."

"We refuse to trade a demon necromancer for a human one," Okoni growled.

"He cannot even keep his dead soldiers from attacking the innocent," Cressida added.

Klaus stepped forward. "Unless you bear the terms of Ariston's surrender, you may leave." His hard voice rang with authority across the dusty field. "We will eradicate this abomination he calls an army, and none that stand with him will be spared."

The messenger sneered as he turned his mount. "You are a fool to stand against us. Ariston is more powerful than your pathetic Heirs combined."

Feeling the rage bubble within her at his arrogance, Kaia let a gust of flames billow out of her palms in a bright flash. The quick burst didn't touch him or his mount, but his horse took fright and reared. The silly man lost hold and fell flat on his back as his horse took off running towards the mountains, away from both armies. The Heirs and chiefs let out a low chuckle, but Everard glared sharply at Kaia. She smirked with a shrug.

"Looks like your horse has more sense than you," Klaus taunted the messenger as he got to his feet. "I suppose you'll have to *run* back to Ariston."

"Have your laugh now," spat the man. "The Lost will soon be gnawing on your bones." With that, the emissary turned tail and stalked back to the safety of Conrad's horde.

Everard sighed and turned to the small party. "Remember, Dracours on the right flank. Humans and Maldibor on the left. Klaus will find and eliminate Ariston as soon as possible."

Kaia nodded absently through all of this as the dark line grew larger on the dusty plain, like ink spilled across yellowed parchment. "And Kaia." The magus leaned toward her, lowering his voice. "Let the boy take Gus."

Kaia turned to Mackie, who had quietly stepped up beside her. She looked back to Everard with her jaw hanging open. Gus had been by her side for the last four years, and before that, she had Pellie. She had hardly walked a step without a big, shaggy dog beside her. The gravity of the battle dawned on her.

Mackie met her eyes briefly before looking away. "I'll take good care of him, Kaia."

Kaia nodded numbly, crouching down to give Gus a final pat and a kiss on his wet nose. "You two stay out of trouble."

Mackie clicked his tongue, and Gus wavered, his wet canine eyes beseeching Kaia, trying to tell her something she could not quite decipher. Mackie clicked his tongue again, and Gus shifted his gaze.

Something unheard and unseen passed between them that Kaia longed to be a part of. With one last whine, Gus reluctantly followed the boy as they weaved their way back through the army. Kaia put a hand to her chest in a vain attempt to quell her stuttering heart as she watched them go. It was as if she had awoken to find a limb had gone missing in the night. Loneliness tightened its grip on her chest.

She closed her eyes. *Courage*, her father's words echoed in her thoughts. *To win on the battlefield you must first conquer the fear within.*

With a sharp breath out, Kaia opened her eyes and trained her gaze forward again, her brows drawn low over a steeled stare.

The enemy host approached over the dry, grassy plain in a ragged line that stretched across the horizon. The Lost were armed this time, something she had not seen before, and their condition ranged widely. Some looked almost human while others stood on yellowed bones, but all shambled jerkily forward at a quick pace.

"Ariston has stolen these creatures from the ancient battleground graveyards to the west," Everard reminded them. "They will be more skilled than those you have faced before."

Kaia swallowed as she watched the dead's human shepherds on horseback to the right and left of them, sporting rusting armor and moving with skittish steps much like the pretend soldiers she had seen at Butterdelf. Further proof that Ariston could not control his brood. From her place on the ground, she could not see beyond the first few lines, but she imagined that Conrad led them from behind, with Mogens beside him and a shield of unnatural dead flesh between her and them. A wall that Klaus would have to cut through to get his sword across their throats

"Steady," Everard called. "Wait for my signal." The chiefs had spread out to their respective flanks, each one holding up a hand to still the impatient warriors. When the overwhelming stench of the dead reached Kaia's nose, the line of horses shuffled nervously behind her.

The collective sound of hundreds of dead feet dragging through the dusty grass filled the tense air, and she looked up at Klaus. Confidence, she reminded herself, giving him a sure smile—but she was surprised to see his dark brows lower in worry.

"Reeeeeeeeaaaaaaady," Everard called.

His eyes still locked on hers, Klaus closed the gap between them in three steps. He moved as if to embrace her, but seized her arms instead. He leaned down so that his rough cheek pressed against hers, and his lips brushed her ear.

"If you only listen to me once in your life, listen to me now," he whispered, his arms slipping to shoulders and squeezing them tightly. "Be safe, Firefly."

A blush heated Kaia's face. "Klaus…" She wanted to reassure him—to lend him confidence as he had for her, but before she could voice her feelings, he released her. His eyes held hers for another heartbeat, a gaze with a message that Kaia couldn't read. Then, the Shadow Heir vanished.

Conflicting emotions buzzed through her, leaving her spine tingling and her stomach aflutter. It occurred to her then that something had changed between the Heirs in the last few weeks. The thought thickened the blush on her cheeks, but foreboding kept her rooted to the earth. *Why did that feel like a farewell?*

Before Kaia could dwell on it further, Everard shouted to her.

"Kaia, bring the fire!"

Kaia tossed her head to clear it and raised her hands above her head. Her first task was to inspire their small, outnumbered army while striking fear into those of their enemy that had hearts to feel it—to make the largest fire she could possibly control. She took a deep breath and called the inferno. Her nervous energy caused the flames to billow up in a swirling elmcore-sized tower of searing flame, unlike anything she had ever created. The sight of it filled even her with excitement. It stretched in the air so high that she imagined it might burn away the clouds. Ariston's warriors shielded their faces from the bright column, but the corpses only shuffled faster, eager jaws snapping at the yanaa's lure.

"Release!" Everard bellowed.

Kaia brought the blaze down in front of her as if she held the tail of a tornado of fire, twisting it from left to right in front of her. As it fell upon the heads of Conrad's puppets, it took on a life of its own—roaring into a crackling wall of flame from which nothing could escape. But when the dead keened in the throes of a second death, Kaia heard no anguish—only a rallying war cry to spur their brethren.

Catching her breath, Kaia released her river of flame, letting it run over the front lines, and signaled to Everard with a closed fist.

The commanding magus' voice boomed over the lines of warriors. "FORRRRRRRWARRDDDDD!"

The chiefs on the right and left released their own battle cries and howls, angling around the burning dead as they aimed for Conrad's living fighters while Everard stayed by Kaia's side to face the dead alongside her. She winced as the armies clashed in front of them.

The Dracours on the right flank seamlessly cut through the clumsy opposition like a scythe through wheat. The bears, lions, and wolves—wild and roaring—ran out in front of the Maldibor and human riders. Ariston's soldiers balked at the sight of the charging predators, allowing them to easily break through their lines, with the riders charging in close behind. Kaia's chest swelled with pride as she watched their allies at work. There may have been few, but they were warriors, indeed.

"Now, you must conserve your yanaa," Everard said, raising his voice above the din of battle. "Wait until you can see the next line advancing into your blaze before you release another blast."

"I can see them now." Her fingers twitched nervously as she watched shadows appear through the quickly collapsing flame wall. It took more yanaa to project the dragon fire further, but she didn't want to let them get any closer. The sudden image of her body being torn apart by the rotting, jagged teeth of the Lost sent a chill through her bones. She winced. *Don't get distracted. Concentrate on victory.*

"Go ahead." Everard gestured with a hand. "When you tire, I can push them back until you catch your breath."

The Dragon Heir gathered her yanaa again, but this time she did not bother with a flamboyant column of fire. She spread her hands before her and created a man-sized fireball in each. With a *whoosh* of flame, she created two beams of fire that cut across the field and into the line in front of her. Steadily she drew her hands apart until the flames reached the edge of the line of Lost. Their shrieking cries pierced the air.

She let the rays of fire fade and paused to catch her breath. Her skin already prickled with sweat. She scanned the army for any sign of Klaus weaving his way to the leaders—heads mysteriously falling off bodies, a random path appearing in the crowd—but saw nothing.

Part of her was glad. She knew the clever Shadow Heir would never betray his movements, but she wished she could know that he was well. The din of battle rattled her nerves and overwhelmed her senses. The cacophony of cries, shouts, and grunts from both living and dead, the ringing of steel on steel and clashing of armor, the whinnies, snorts and hoof beats of frantic horses. Deafened and disoriented, Kaia could not perceive any order to the madness, much less determine the tide of the battle.

Everard's sorrel Dalteek pawed the ground and tossed its expansive rack of antlers. "Again, Kaia!" the magus shouted.

Once again, fire flew out of Kaia's palms like a boiling river, halting the advancing dead in their tracks. Beads of sweat trickled down her temples, and it took her a moment to catch her breath. "How many do you think I've torched so far, Everard?"

"Three hundred, perhaps." The magi's sharp eyes scanned the battlefield. "You are doing well."

Despite Everard's reassurance, Kaia's heart fluttered. Seventeen hundred seemed like a lot left when the intense exertion had already depleted her yanaa supply significantly.

"Another!" Everard urged.

Mechanically, Kaia repeated the process while trying to watch the right flank. The Dracours had already made short work of the hundred or so would-be human warriors and were pressing in on the ranks of the Lost. Everard had strictly instructed them to keep their formation tight and clear and attack only the middle ranks of dead to avoid being seared by Kaia's blaze. Even so, she kept a sharp eye on them. Injuring or killing even one of her friends with her fire would be a thousand times worse than losing one of them to the enemy.

She could already see wounded and dead of all kinds: Maldibor, Dracour, beast, and man lay crumpled on the field in the wake of the charge. As she replenished another flame wall, she saw something moving quickly out of the corner of her eye. Her eyes widened as she realized it was Granny Fiola and Mackie leading mules burdened with injured warriors back to the safety of the sick tents.

I thought they would stay in the rear. Odriel protect them, Kaia thought. Biting her lip, she turned her eyes back to the dead. She couldn't afford to get distracted.

Kaia burned wave after endless wave—the never-ending cry of the Lost echoing in her ears. The howl of the Maldibor, the shouts of man and Dracour, and even the roars of bears and wildcats faded as she gradually became less aware of anything outside her immediate line of sight. Her vision narrowed to the line of Lost directly ahead of her, and her ears attuned only to Everard's commands. She still held the line well ahead of them, but her arms grew heavier with each barrage. She lost count of her fire blasts at ten, and they began to take longer to conjure. A few more volleys and she fell to her knees, gasping for air. Sweat dripped from her chin and nose and soaked her clothes, while the dusty ground greedily drank up the moisture.

"Everard," she panted, "How... many... more?"

Both flanks had defeated the human portions of the army and now sandwiched the dead on the right and left, but the friendly ranks seemed much smaller than Kaia remembered. Wounded trickled back to the camp—limping, crawling, or carried by one of Mackie's mules. *Granny Fiola must be busy in her tent.*

Everard looked at her, his dark eyes unreadable. "At least a thousand."

Kaia balked. She had estimated perhaps six hundred and had hoped for less.

"Rest for a moment." The magus dismounted. "I can relieve you for a time." He took a step forward and faced the army. Kaia watched him intently, the secretive magi rarely exposed their yanaa to outsiders, much less revealed it in battle. He laced his hands in front of his chest with his index fingers pointing at the sky. His body tensed as if laden with a sudden load and he shook with effort, a vein bulging in his forehead. At first, nothing happened, and Kaia got to her feet, expecting to be called on again to throw back the dead approaching through her dying flames.

But as she looked at her enemies, she noticed a small ball of light hovering in the air just above their heads, as if the sun had been moved out of its place high in the sky and lowered down to the battle. Suddenly, streaks of silent light burst out of the ball to strike the bodies below. Instead of screaming, the dead gurgled as they convulsed under the rays. They folded in on themselves as if a great weight threatened to crush them. Arms, heads, and legs bent towards their torsos as they jerked and gagged in pain. The process progressed with agonizing deliberation, each limb curling individually. Ten minutes, an eternity in the midst of battle, elapsed before the bodies finally collapsed to the ground.

When their spasms finally ceased, they lay on their backs with their limbs curled at odd angles, like spiders that had been swatted in the kitchen. The ball of light had struck almost two complete lines of dead. Kaia's jaw dropped, and her heart filled with hope. With Everard's powerful yanaa, they could take care of the remaining dead in no time.

The thought had scarcely crossed her mind when the light faded, and Everard staggered against his Dalteek.

Kaia reached out to steady him.

"I am fine, girl." He waved her away. "I am simply not made to send the dead back to their graves." He turned a sharp eye to her. "Have you recovered?"

Kaia's heart fell. She had expected more stamina from a legendary magus.

But with the dead still coming, she didn't have the time to humor disappointment. Her joints creaked as she turned away, stiff from the yanaa's toll. She licked her salty lips and raised her leaden arms in front of her once again, muscles burning. She decimated another two lines before her legs jellied with exhaustion. The fire sapped strength from every muscle in her body. Everything hurt. Her back, her abdomen, neck, legs, and arms all screamed at her to stop. Yet, she saw no end to the relentless onslaught of dead.

"Everard!" she cried over the clamor of the battle. "Didn't you say there were only two thousand?!"

The magus didn't look at her. "I estimated."

She sat on the dusty ground, trying to regain some strength just as a shadow fell over her from behind. She leapt up with wild eyes, startled and ready to fight, but it was only Mackie, looking dusty and tired. Something about his dark chocolate eyes looked different, then Kaia realized what it was—he looked older than he had that morning.

"Sorry!" He bobbed his head. "Granny sent me with this." He held up a flask. "Figured yours was empty."

"Thanks, Mack." She took the drink, and Mackie nodded once more before running off again. She emptied the flask in seconds. The cool, tangy liquid seemed to linger on her tongue, and she imagined she could feel its reinvigorating juices flowing through her veins. The next flame came easier to her palms. Instead of a continuous wave, she pulsed the blasts throughout the line now, willing it to spread from shoulder to shoulder to close the gaps and save her a little yanaa.

As she worked, she stole a quick glance at the wider battle spread wide across the field. Their left flank had spread precariously thin, and she imagined their warriors must be as weary as she was. The Dracours still rode in tight, agile pods, but even so, it didn't seem like they were making much of a dent in the corpse army. There were just too many, and the dead never tired. While the Okarrians' strength faded, the Lost only grew more frantic in their attacks, as if they could smell weakness like blood in the water.

After another two waves of flame, Kaia's exhaustion returned, and she noticed that the frontline of Lost had slowly but steadily shrank the distance between them. The rotting stench of the dead combined with the drain from the flame blitz threatened to overwhelm her with nausea. She bent over with her hands on her knees as she tried to catch her breath. Sweat slicked every inch of her.

"Do you think you could throw another one of those light balls for me, Everard?" She said between heaving breaths—her lungs fit to burst. She didn't even feel like she had enough energy to lift her head.

"Take heart girl, I can see the army's rear."

She jerked herself up to scan the battlefield, and her heart jumped. Behind the last four lines of Lost, she saw warriors in gleaming armor atop horses, perhaps a hundred spread across the field, engaged in fierce battle with their own riders. *Everard never mentioned trained soldiers*, Kaia thought distantly. Behind that line of cavalry, Kaia saw something that made her heart stop.

"Everard," she gasped, "Those are giants!"

"No," Everard shook his head. "Those are the corpses of giants. Conrad's personal retinue."

The giants fought with their backs to the steep ravine, cornered by the Dracours' ruthless flanking actions. Even as the Dracour bombarded them with spears and arrows, the tree-sized monsters looked elsewhere, swinging their arms and stomping their legs wildly, as if trying to squash a biting ant. Only one thing could draw them that way.

"They must be looking for Klaus!" Kaia yelled.

Her panic gave her renewed energy. Even in her fervor, the flames took some time to build, and when she threw them, the frontline of dead were almost within distance for a quick dashing attack. Their army matched the trained warriors well enough, but three hundred Lost still stood between her and Klaus, only a quarter mile away.

"Kaia," Everard warned, "They are getting too close."

Exhaustion and growing desperation strained her voice. "I'm trying, Everard!"

She directed another blaze at the howling Lost, but it burned much too weak. It encompassed only fifty at most, and still they stumbled on.

Everard brought his hands to his chest again, and a tiny dot of light appeared above them. Twenty of the nearest dead began to curl, but more marched closer.

"Kaia!" Everard grunted through gritted teeth.

Kaia panted too heavily to answer, but she was already trying to build more fire in her palms. The bulk of their army, less than two hundred souls now, clashed against the tangle of soldiers and giants dispersed across the field. Kaia and Everard were on their own.

The young Dragon Heir discharged another arc of fire into the Lost, then looked across the field to the giants. She thought she could see Klaus blinking in and out of sight, too drained to maintain his invisibility. One of the giants brought a foot crashing down on the edge of the gorge. His great arms windmilled as the dry earth crumbled beneath his feet. In a blink, the edge of the canyon gave way, and the giant crashed down into the river far below. Kaia felt a surge of triumph. Klaus purposely lured the huge creatures to the canyon edge—the shrewd Shadow Heir certainly lived up to his reputation.

Kaia directed another long streak of fire against the advancing line and glimpsed Klaus halfway across the field, drawing four shiny soldiers away from the dangerous limbs of the three remaining giants. She could see him whirling and dodging, blinking out of sight for only seconds at a time, while the trained soldiers pressed their attacks with relentless professionalism. *That doesn't look good. He can only take so many.* Then, Kaia saw an odd-looking corpse making for the small circular battle. *It's too fast to be dead*, Kaia thought, *but it doesn't look like a man either....*

A cold knife of ice pierced Kaia's heart. *Mogens.*

By this time, the dead had encircled Kaia and Everard, pressing in ever tighter. She whirled and cast a weak arc of fire to keep them back. Although her own position grew increasingly dire, her eyes stuck to Klaus as he moved slower and slower, desperately parrying the attacking soldiers with a blade broken just a hand's length from the hilt.

Then, everything in Kaia's world seemed to still. In her mind, at that moment, the battle stopped—the howling, the clanging, the yelling, Everard's warning of the encroaching circle—all of it silenced in her mind's eye. Although Klaus battled half a battlefield away, it seemed to her as if she was not ten feet from him, watching him desperately claw for his life.

The Shadow Heir dove out of the way as the unexpected, oversized foot of one of the giants stomped down. Rolling to his feet, he parried the blade of one of the soldiers while he kicked another that stood behind him. Then he winked out of sight for just a second, reappeared to slash at a third soldier, and grabbed the forearm of the fourth to protect himself from his strike.

Lurking unseen behind him, Mogens rushed, his sword raised. Sensing danger, Klaus released the soldier and whirled to parry the blade whistling down on his head. He flickered ever so slightly in an exhausted attempt to disappear, while the soldier behind grabbed Klaus around the chest, holding him steady. A wicked dagger flashed in Mogens' off hand as he thrust the blade forward into Klaus' unprotected gut.

The Shadow Heir crumpled to the ground.

Kaia screamed, a tortured, hideous sound as all sensation left her body. The Lost had closed to within five feet of her, and one of them slashed at her arm, but she did not feel it, nor did she care. The Lost were no longer her concern. Her body filled with an uncontrollable primal heat, a heat that she could not and did not want to control. A cyclone of flame whipped around the Dragon Heir's body, and her rage grew with exponential speed, as did the pressure of the howling heat within her.

And Kaia exploded.

The whirling flames encasing her body burst from her in a deafening blast that incinerated the ring of dead surrounding her and knocked the living into the dirt. With no ragehound to stop her, Kaia propelled herself on a column of fire at incredible speed across the field.

Tasting the enormous surge of yanaa, the Lost giants stepped forward to cut short her rampage. With a snap of her arm, she dispatched a slashing flame at the creatures. The ground shook as the aberrations collapsed to their knees, their deep voices lamenting their end. Mogens darted towards the canyon's brink as Kaia, cloaked in flame, sped towards him. In a desperate attempt to escape, he leapt from the canyon wall, his lipless mouth sneering as he fell. Kaia's body flared to engulf the living demon but closed on nothing as he splashed into the roiling river.

Her revenge stymied, Kaia howled, her rage only burning hotter. In a fury, her blazing eyes whipped around, spying her next target—a flashy armored figure flanked by guards and fleeing on an immaculate white horse that Kaia recognized instantly. With a rush of fire, Kaia knocked the rider from his mount. In another beat, her flaming hand burned at Lord Conrad's throat.

He screamed as the star-hot flame that had incinerated his army of Lost and visions of glory devoured him, as well. His cries echoed across the stunned plain as Ariston, the would-be savior of Okarria, burned alive at the hands of a seventeen-year-old girl.

PART THREE

A LEGEND REMEMBERED

CHAPTER 18
BURNED OUT

The Dragon Heir reluctantly woke to the chaotic clamor of the sick tent: groans of pain, calls for bandages, and the soft roar of many trying to keep their voices down all at once. A lantern flickered next to her, casting a small glow around her bed in the dimness. She felt a heavy weight lying on her stomach and, seized with a desperate hope that Klaus' sleeping head rested on her once again, she craned her neck to look down.

But she found only her shaggy red shepherd looking anxiously back at her. With a choked sob of disappointment, she let her aching head drop back to the pallet.

Her body throbbed as she tried to piece together the battle's end. She remembered her rage as one remembers a vivid nightmare; as if she had merely been a spectator of the events that had taken place, and yet the memories filled her with relentless grief. She had lost control. How many of their own had been unintentionally caught in her inferno? Her eyes widened in horror as she recalled the sounds of Conrad's bloodcurdling shrieks as he burned to ash at her hand. Kaia jammed a fist into her mouth to stifle her own cry. *Now, I'm truly a monster. The people of Arimoke were right to fear me.*

Gus whined and scratched at her with a paw. No. You are my girl. Always my girl.

Kaia closed her eyes and tried to slow her breathing. She could not rest before she discovered how many living had been consumed in her blaze.

She strained to sit up, biting down on her lip to choke back a cry of pain. Her muscles cramped with an agony that squeezed her bones, but only her left arm was wrapped in bandages—a memento of the Lost's final attack. The needles of pain that coursed through her body paid testimony to the fact that the Dragon Rage had taken more from her than she had to give. Gus gave her right hand a sympathetic lick, and Kaia patted him absently as she looked around.

Sheets hung neatly on a line around her corner of the tent, creating a semblance of privacy. She looked to the mat beside her and the resolve holding her tears at bay dissolved. Dimly illuminated by the glow of the lantern, Klaus' still, pale body lay next to her. Frantically, she shifted Gus' head from her stomach and crawled on throbbing hands and knees to Klaus' rigid form. She gazed for only a moment before she jerked her eyes away. *Gone.*

"Klaus, you idiot! You can't just tell me to be safe and then get yourself killed. You're supposed to be smarter than that." She huddled on her knees, choking on her sobs as they wracked her tender muscles. Her head sank to the floor and her body caved in on itself. Neither her spirit nor her muscles could support her anymore. Her pain morphed into a flood of surging grief. "I'll hate you for leaving me here alone."

"Just when we were starting to get along...."

Kaia's eyes widened.

"Really, you couldn't think of anything sweeter to say on my deathbed?" he murmured, sitting up on his elbows to look at her with tired hazel eyes. For a breathless moment, Kaia was shocked into stillness. "And do you really have to talk so loudly? People are trying to sleep around here. I—"

But Kaia didn't let him finish the thought. She threw her arms around his neck, pushing him back onto his thin pallet. "Klaus," she choked, his name heavy with emotion.

"Ow, ow, ow, careful," he hissed with a wince. Kaia released him gently, shifting herself from his chest to lie by his side. She couldn't still her gasping to say anything, so she just pressed closer, trying to smother her sobs against his chest. He stroked her hair with a soothing hand.

"What's the matter, Firefly?" he chuckled. "I'm still in one piece." Klaus lifted the blanket so she could see the bandages wrapping his chest, his right arm, and his right leg. "He tried to gut me, but my armor was tougher than he counted on. I got away with an ugly gash."

"Klaus," she whispered, as the tears only flowed faster, "I thought you'd left me." She buried her soggy face into his bandaged chest.

"I know," he murmured, tossing the blanket across them. "It's ok now." He gently brushed her braid from her cheek and tucked it back behind her ear. "Just relax."

"I lost control," she sobbed. "How many of our own did I...." Kaia couldn't finish the question.

"None." Klaus squeezed her shoulder. "The only one near enough to you to be caught in the Dragon Rage was Everard, and he was prepared with a yanaa shield."

Kaia exhaled a rush of air, and her heart unclenched. "It would have been unforgivable," she whispered.

Klaus rolled to his side with a wince. "But it didn't happen."

"What if Everard hadn't protected himself?"

"Kaia," Klaus locked his stern eyes on hers. "We needed it to happen. That's why you and Everard were kept behind, away from the rest of us. Everard was ready."

"But Conrad!" she protested. "I used the dragon fire on the living...."

"Stop this, Kaia," Klaus warned, bristling. "War is an ugly thing. Do you think you're the only one who killed yesterday?"

Kaia turned her tear-streaked face away from him. Klaus spoke the truth, of course. The Shadow Heir was known as a skilled assassin, but she hadn't been prepared to take another's life.

The Shadow Heir exhaled, deflating. "Kaia," he murmured, rubbing his thumb along her arm, "I'm sorry. It was my task to deal with Mogens and Conrad, and I failed."

Tears budded in Kaia's eyes again as she turned back to Klaus.

"But, those two hewed their own paths. They chose evil." He squeezed her arm. "If it hadn't been for you, we wouldn't have survived the day." He reached out a hand to wipe away one of her tears. "Thank Odriel for you, Firefly."

***

Kaia woke just before dawn to find the tent still dark and Klaus' pallet empty. Gus' feathery tail swished through the dirt as she stirred. Her body had stiffened, only intensifying her aches, but Kaia could not abide being in the confined space a moment longer. She pulled a privacy sheet aside to find rows upon rows of pallets filled with the injured. The sides of the tent were open and she could see that some even lay in the yellowed grass surrounding them.

In the early morning gloom, the able-bodied glided like ghosts among the wounded, passing out bandages, food, and water. Hot jets of pain shot through Kaia's limbs as she forced herself to stand, sucking air through her teeth. She hissed as she took stumbling steps through the prone forms of men, Dracours, and Maldibor to the open air outside the tent.

Kaia limped through the camp, anonymous in the dark, unsure of her destination. She hadn't gone far before a hand grasped her uninjured arm.

Klaus sighed. "And just what are you doing up?"

She glanced at him out of the corner of her eye. "I could ask you the same thing."

In the approaching dawn light, she could see his dark hair sticking up and the charcoal circles framing his hazel eyes. He held on to her elbow as he walked with her, but Kaia couldn't tell if it was to steady her or himself. She looked away from him and spotted Fiola's obsidian ropes of hair to the far right of the pallets.

Kaia's heart quailed as she gazed beyond the old woman to see the fallen gathered at the edge of camp. There were almost as many dead as wounded. Granny Fiola's voice rang through the still dawn as she appointed gravediggers and ordered the bodies to be arranged for identification. Her movements were quick and her commands sharp, but her normally lively amber eyes betrayed a tired dullness. She had obviously worked through the night.

As Kaia watched, Everard approached the old woman. When Fiola saw him, she seemed to shrink as she crumbled into his arms. Kaia could see her shaking slightly from a distance, but she only allowed herself a moment of weakness before pulling away from Everard to direct another soldier. Seeing the crotchety magus comforting someone was a disconcerting spectacle. Kaia wondered briefly again about their bond as she and Klaus limped over to them.

When Fiola saw them, she rushed over. Her tattooed arms crushed Kaia and Klaus against her chest in a fierce embrace, and Kaia tried not to wince.

"Oh, my dears, my dears!" Fiola exclaimed. "I'm so glad you're all right." She released them and wiped her dewy eyes.

Kaia turned to Everard. "How bad was it?"

The magus sighed deeply, "It was a costly battle." He paused as he looked over the rows of dead.

"How many?" Kaia pressed. She wanted to know how many lives she had lost. How many she had failed. Her conscience needed to know.

"We began with five hundred, and we will be burying more than five score," Everard said, not looking at her.

Kaia gasped at the number. So many. "Were any of them..." her voice shook, "...burned?"

"No," Klaus, Fiola, and Everard said at once.

"Ours were safely out of your path," Everard reassured her, his tone strangely gentle.

"But..." Granny Fiola began, her voice uncharacteristically weak as she turned her gaze downward. Kaia looked up sharply as a tear trickled down Fiola's wrinkled cheek. "Your brother wanted to explain," she finished, shuffling away before Kaia could respond.

Kaia's heart fluttered in panic, and she looked to Klaus for explanation, only to see her own confusion mirrored in his face. Klaus squeezed her elbow, and they followed Fiola through the rows and rows of dead. As they passed Maldibor, Dracour, man, woman, and beast, each step felt more difficult. Kaia's guts tightened with dread as she searched for familiar faces among the mangled bodies. Ahead of them, Fiola stopped next to a man standing over a body that Kaia could not see. As they drew closer, Kaia realized it was no warrior, but Bram standing beside Fiola. With trepidation, she stepped up beside Fiola and Bram, her whole body pounding along with her throbbing heart.

Bram turned his dirty face to her. His blank eyes blinked slowly as if he had forgotten why he was there at all. "Kaia…."

Kaia looked down, and nausea washed over her in a tidal wave. She fell to her knees with a hand to her open mouth and spewed the contents of the stomach on the ground. Little Mackie Tannen lay in the grass, his body sliced from neck to navel. Felix pawed at his still shoulder with small brown hands, cooing softly. Fiola bent down to scoop the animal up, her tears falling silently into his golden fur. Kaia drew gasping breaths as tears cascaded down well-worn paths on her cheeks.

"What happened?" she whispered, looking to Bram. Reading the guilt on his face, she rose to her feet. Kaia grabbed his shirt with a shrill scream. "WHAT HAPPENED?!"

Bram turned his face away from her, avoiding her eyes. When he finally spoke, his words were stunned and flat. "At the end, there were only a few of us left. I was so tired. Mackie was there, just running in and out, helping the injured and handing out flasks. When he passed me one, I was so thirsty I drank it right there in front of him. Then, a squad of soldiers came out of nowhere. Mackie caught one coming up behind me. I would have been gutted like a fish, but…Mackie just shoved me out of the way." Bram looked back to her with pleading eyes. "It all happened so fast, there was nothing I could do! He didn't have to do it! He didn't even know me!"

Kaia was looking at Bram, but her mind was back in Summerbanks. *I'm not brave like you.* Mackie had said with adoring eyes. *Anyone can be brave, Mackie,* she had told him.

And of course, he had been.

Kaia glared at her brother with disgust as she shook with grief and rage. She wanted to shout and curse in his face. Bram, who was only there to avenge Papa and blame her for his death. *It was your damned jealousy that killed Mackie! You aren't worth it!*

Instead of shouting, she shoved him as hard as she could. Bram fell to the ground, and Kaia brought her balled fists to her sides. But when Bram kept his head bowed, Kaia could only sag as her surging anger melted away into grief. Mackie's sacrifice had not been Bram's decision, just like Papa's had not been hers.

Why do the best of us have to die?

She stared at her filthy brother crouching in the field of bodies and spoke low. "Now you know what it is like to watch someone better than you trade their life for yours."

Then, kneeling stiffly before Mackie's torn body, she touched her fingers to her lips before pressing them against his cold forehead. She said a silent prayer to Odriel to guide him safely to the other side, rose to her feet, and turned away.

***

At sunset, those that could still stand gathered to recognize the dead. First, a warrior with heavy bandages wrapped around his forehead and right eye stepped forward over the row of graves to speak for the fallen humans.

"Odriel, these people fought bravely to protect your beloved land against corruption. May you guide their noble souls to the other side."

Then, he read the names of the dead. As he read each one, another warrior stepped forward to speak in memory of the lost soul. Eighty-seven souls had fallen—eighty-seven warriors whose families waited anxiously for a return that would never come. When the man called out Mackie's name, it felt like a stab to Kaia's battered heart. Fiola stepped forward, Felix at her feet.

"Mackie brought tooth and claw to aid us in battle," Her voice rang loud and clear. "Then sacrificed himself for another. He died innocent, but courageous as any warrior." She suppressed a sob. "May Odriel guide his sweet soul."

As Fiola stepped back to her place in line with the Heirs, Everard put his arm around her shoulder and leaned his cheek against her brow.

Kaia tangled her fingers in Gus' fur beside her, and he pressed against her. *We are sad, but I am with you.*

After the last human's name was called, Cressida stepped forward to honor the twenty-three Dracours who now lay in fresh graves. She pulled her sword from its sheath and rested the flat of the blade against her nose and forehead, its tip pointed to the sky. The Dracours gathered behind her followed suit.

"Great warriors." She closed her eyes. "Though you may have fallen in battle, your spirits join the wind on our faces, the air in our lungs, and together, we fight as one for eternity."

The Dracour warriors raised their blades to the sky before slowly, silently lowering them back to their sheaths. A soft breeze whistled around them in answer to their elegy.

Lastly, the small Maldibor clan stepped forward. Out of the thirty-six that had joined their battle, only twenty-eight remained. Eight family members had sacrificed themselves to a cause that concerned man much more than beast. *Blessed be to Odriel, Tekoa survived*, Kaia thought. She didn't think she could have borne his loss along with Mackie's.

The shaggy beasts made two tight circles around the graves. They stood there for a moment in silence before Okoni lifted his head to the sky with a heart-rending howl. One by one, each lent his voice to the chorus—twenty-eight souls howling with grief in a dirge that was both beautiful and unbearable. Kaia took an involuntary step backward as their raw emotion seized her. Klaus' hard chest steadied her, and she leaned into him. She had no more tears to shed, but her heart ached with their grief all the same

Finally, the last voice dissolved into the still summer dusk.

All of the Maldibor returned to the crowd except for one. Sensing the burial was over, the remainder of the army dispersed back into the camp in silence.

Kaia watched the last beast standing stiffly over the grave. "What about him?" she whispered.

"The Maldibor clan will share a vigil through the night," Everard said, as he turned to head back to the tents.

As everyone left, Kaia stayed, regarding the one-hundred and eighteen souls that she had failed. She looked past them to gaze at the dry field where they had taken their last breaths. Her rage had scorched the land in an ashy, black circle.

When Nifras had been defeated in the south, the once fertile land of the battleground had turned to desert and became known merely as the Deadlands. Kaia knew that this plain, watered with the blood of so many and scarred by her own hand, would also bear the name of the atrocious battle. She wondered vaguely what the field would be called. *Dragon's Lea? Ariston's Stand?*

Klaus, waiting patiently beside her, interrupted her thoughts. "Kaia—"

The ground trembled beneath their feet, cutting him off.

Kaia flailed her arms as she tried to keep her balance and stumbled a few steps before falling to her knees. The pink sky turned dark as night, and once again she brought her hands to her ears as the crashing of thunderclaps filled the air. This episode dragged on longer than the last, and Kaia counted the booms. On the nineteenth, a tremendous *crack* sundered the air.

Kaia searched for Klaus in the near dark with eyes wide with alarm. The Shadow Heir scowled at the sky, waiting anxiously for the light to return. He released a tense breath when the sky finally lightened, and the ground ceased to shake. As the sky turned from a charcoal gray back to orange, Kaia realized that something was wrong. The south remained in shadow.

"Klaus," she whispered, raising her hand to the sky. "Look at the sun."

Klaus followed her trembling finger. Although the sun still hung above the horizon, the right half of the great orb burned an angry red while the left half remained eclipsed in darkness.

***

The Heirs and other leaders gathered around the fire that night to discuss Nifras' attack on the barrier. Kaia, still exhausted from the previous day and stunned by the new turn of events, only half-heartedly listened to the conversation. She could already guess the course of the talk. It exhausted her to even contemplate the possibility of facing the necromancer's army. She and Klaus had barely survived against two thousand. How in the land and sky would they face ten?

"There is the matter of Nifras himself," Everard said, his gaze drifting to the darkness surrounding them.

Cressida tossed her ram horns toward Klaus. "The Shadow Heir is gifted to battle him."

"Yes," Shad agreed, his round eyes glowing in the firelight. "But with what weapon? He cannot use that common blade he snapped in two yesterday."

Okoni, the Maldibor chief, nodded his great head. "To kill a demon god, a blessed edge is surely needed."

"Does such a relic even exist?" asked the warrior that had replaced the fallen Gyatus leader.

Only the crackling of the fire answered his question. Kaia looked from face to face, each shadowed by more than flames.

"Yes," Everard said simply. "It does."

"Well then, where is it?" Cressida demanded in the curt Dracourian manner.

Everard's black eyes stared into the distance, and he did not answer the question immediately. "The weapon that Kallar, the first Shadow Heir, used to defeat Nifras. It is said to be indestructible."

"*Odriel's Tooth*," Klaus murmured just loud enough for Kaia to hear. "I've heard that it's made of shadows, but my father said it was just a legend."

Everard crossed his arms. "Unfortunately, through the years, it has been lost."

Okoni growled at this news while the other chiefs hissed in audible disappointment.

"However," Everard went on, "there is one who knows its location. He lives east of the mountains, in the marshes of Tazgar."

"Why haven't we heard of this before?" Klaus asked, bristling at the thought of his ancestor's inheritance kept hidden from him.

"Because," Everard muttered, his eyebrows arched in annoyance, "when I demanded the blade's return, Dorinar refused to disclose its location."

"And who is this Dorinar?" rumbled Okoni.

Shad answered the beast. "He is Everard's brother."

This news spurred a chorus of comments from the circle:

"Another magus?"

"Well, then we must try again."

"Is there no other way?"

"We have no choice."

"Who can we send?"

Everard's voice rose over the urgent murmurs. "Dorinar will only bestow the weapon upon its rightful owner." Six pairs of eyes turned to Klaus.

Klaus straightened and spoke formally. "I'll retrieve the blade."

Everard gestured to his feline emissary, flicking his tail at the edge of the fire's glow. "Shadmundar will show you the way."

Kaia raised her voice. "I'm going, too." She set her jaw firmly as the council turned their glinting eyes to her. "I'll not allow the remaining Heirs to be separated." Her voice softened, and she met Klaus' stare. "No good has come of that recently."

The words were met with nods and mumbles of assent.

"You must leave with the dawn and hasten on your journey," Everard faced south. "We will regroup and meet you in the Deadlands."

"What happens if they fail to retrieve the sword?" the Gyatan asked. Once again, the council fell silent. Kaia could hear the wind whistling through the plain beyond.

Finally, Okoni's deep voice echoed in the night. "Then we shall have to pray."

***

An hour later, exhausted with the ceaseless talk of strategy and supplies, Kaia slipped away. She felt rather than heard the Shadow Heir rise to follow her.

As soon as they were out of earshot, Kaia let her thoughts spill out. "Everard said it would be easy."

Klaus put a hand on her shoulder, gently turning her to face him. "What do you mean?"

"The battle with Conrad." She heaved an impatient sigh, as the anxiety that had churned within her for the last hour boiled to the surface. "It was supposed to be easy! But we only barely survived. Now, what are we going to do against the necromancer?"

"Shh... calm down, Firefly." Klaus spoke softly, as if to calm a wild horse. "It's going to be ok."

"NO! It's NOT, Klaus!" she shouted, backing away from him. "Without Jago to heal us, we tire much too quickly! We're not going to survive the next one." Her voice trembled. "And nor will anyone else. I can't protect them."

She stared into his hazel eyes, unbidden memories surging into her mind. Klaus lying unmoving next to her. Felix crying piteously as he pawed at Mackie's cold corpse. Her father's mangled body surrounded by a pool of blood.

"Nifras will kill them all."

"Kaia!" Klaus barked, grabbing her wrists. "Calm down. You cannot panic." He paused as he let her catch her breath. He brought his hands to her arms and locked eyes with her. "This is a terrible war, and people are going

121

to die, but you can't just shut down again. Don't let your emotions control you."

"Klaus, we buried the dead an *hour* ago." Kaia jerked away but couldn't control her voice as it pitched. "And the sun will not dawn whole tomorrow."

Klaus's words hardened. "It's time for you to grow up, Kaia. We don't have time for these childish hysterics! The Dragon Heir has to be stronger than that."

Kaia reared back, stung.

Klaus continued, softer. "Kaia, if your grief overtakes you, I don't know if I'll be able to save you again." He tugged softly on her arms to bring her into an embrace.

Kaia's skin paled beneath her freckles. *Is that what he saw? An emotional child always in need of rescue?* She knocked his hands away and stepped out of his reach. "I'm sorry if I've disappointed you, Guardian Thane, but we can't all be as callous as the cold-blooded Shadow Heir."

Klaus winced as though she had flung stones instead of words. But before he could open his mouth to respond, Kaia turned away, and she stalked into the night.

***

When the maimed sun finally crested the horizon the next morning, Kaia, Klaus, and Shad gathered to depart. Kaia watched the sun with a measure of relief. She had not been confident that it would rise at all.

As she cinched Sunflash's saddle, she cocked her head at the dappled gray Dalteek with a tall rack of velvet antlers saddled beside her doe instead of the elegant Moonstreak.

Shad, already tucked into one of the saddlebags, answered her unspoken question. "Moonstreak was cut down in the battle, and Stormshade lost her rider." He paused. "She will be useful when we need to fly south."

Klaus didn't meet her eyes as he stepped up to the gray and stroked her neck reassuringly. Stormshade's dark eyes seemed heavy with sadness as they regarded the Shadow Heir. For a moment, Kaia thought to ask Mackie about Stormshade, then she caught herself. Kaia squeezed her eyes shut as an involuntary shudder wracked her body. With a lump in her throat and her fingers trembling, she turned to say her goodbyes to the small group that had gathered to say their farewells.

Bram nodded stiffly. "See you in the Deadlands."

"Take care," she returned, not quite able to keep the chill from her voice.

Fiola, with Felix on her shoulder, embraced Kaia tightly with her strong arms. "Be safe, my love."

"Thanks, Fiola," Kaia whispered, giving Felix a pat. Remembering Klaus' reproof, she struggled to keep her emotions hidden.

With a deep breath, she looked up to see Tekoa step forward. A wistful smile crossed her lips as she barreled into the Maldibor, not even bothering to hold her breath this time. His smell seemed almost comforting now.

"My dear Guardian Dashul," he rumbled. "The doubt you carry with you is heavy. If you don't leave it behind, this journey will be arduous."

Kaia looked at the great beast, "How can you...?"

He chuckled and tapped his muzzle. "This nose smells more than you would believe."

Kaia turned to Sunflash and fiddled with her saddlebags. "Everything is so different now, Tekoa."

"Yes, the world is always changing, as are the people in it. But make no mistake, Guardian Dashul, you are and have always been the Dragon Heir. It does not mean you have lost yourself."

Kaia bit her lip as she looked back at the hulking warrior. "I wish I had your certainty."

Tekoa gave her a leg up into the saddle, and Kaia grimaced as she tried to arrange her sore limbs. "It's there, dear Kaia," he assured her. "You must only find it again."

Lastly, Kaia looked to Everard. He nodded brusquely, his coal eyes revealing nothing. "You have till the next full moon. Rendezvous on the westernmost point of the Deadlands."

Kaia straightened, returned his nod, and turned Sunflash to the east. Klaus and Shad sat astride Stormshade just ahead of her. Kaia kept her face blank as Klaus' shrewd gaze assessed her, determined to prove she was just as strong as he.

"Ready?" she asked, her voice icy.

"After you," he clipped. With no more to be said, Kaia urged Sunflash into a canter, and they began their journey into the wounded dawn.

***

The Heirs took to the well-traveled roads at the base of the mountains to speed their journey. With Conrad gone, they no longer had to worry about attracting the wrong sort of attention. Even so, they were surprised to find villagers and tradesmen shy away from them as they passed. The news of Ariston's fall at the hands of a merciless Dragon Heir had shot across the land like an arrow, and the Heirs could no longer go unnoticed.

Kaia watched eyes widen with fear as they spotted the monstrous ragehound and the girl he preceded. She maintained a mask of indifference as travelers left the road to avoid them or held up talismans to ward her away. Klaus observed her with careful eyes but said nothing as they kept to their brisk pace.

The reactions to their presence only grew more extreme as they arrived at the first sizeable town to the east of Gyatus. The noise and bustle ceased as their Dalteek slowed to a walk on the cobbled streets. The unnatural silence grew eerie as the villagers parted before the Heirs on their strange mounts like wheat in the wind. They kept their eyes forward as whispers rose behind them. With the Heir's backs to the crowd, they buzzed with more boldness. Kaia began to pick out words from the hiss of the crowd.

"That's the Dragon Heir?"

"She destroyed our only hope."

"How could she?"

"They say she's a demon."

"She has no chance against Nifras."

Before Kaia realized the spectators had turned into a mob, Klaus had ridden too far ahead of her and the villagers filled in behind Stormshade, cutting her off. Before she could even blink, the first stone slammed into her head. In a flash, Kaia was five again and attending her first, and last, day of school.

A group of older children pushed her back and forth, calling her names, daring her to show them her powers. One of them tripped her, and Kaia fell to the ground, skinning her knees. Another snatched her by the hair and tried to drag her backwards, while a third a threw a rock at her head.

The sharp pain snapped Kaia's control. Hands glowing hot, she grabbed her captor's wrist, causing him to cry out and release her. She turned into a whirlwind of fists and feet as she rammed herself against her attackers, lashing out at whoever was near. The teacher rushed out of the schoolhouse in panic. She gathered the children in a group behind her, as if it was they who needed protection, not Kaia.

That day, they banished Kaia from Arimoke and told her never to come back.

Hot blood oozed from the wound on the back of her head as another rock whistled by her ear. Sunflash pulled back as men grabbed for her halter.

"Let me pass!" Kaia growled, but the mob only pressed closer, grabbing at her boots. Kaia heard Gus' sharp yelp as a gangly boy grabbed the gentle dog roughly by the neck, and another pulled his tail.

"Let him go!" she thundered.

Kaia cleared her mind and held up a hand, willing heat to flow from her core to her fingertips. To her dismay, nothing happened. Sweat beaded at her temple as she tried again. Her palm remained empty. A cold knot of fear curled in her belly as Gus yelped at a rangy oaf trying to loop a chain around his furry neck.

Anxiety flooding her thoughts, she searched for Klaus, but he continued up the street, oblivious to their struggle.

"I SAID *STOP!*" Kaia bellowed savagely, drawing her blade. Sunflash reared with a whinny, echoing the sentiment, and her menacing hooves raked the air. The disgruntled villagers rumbled louder but backed away from the

Dalteek and her lowered antlers. Kaia urged the doe towards Gus and slapped his attacker with the flat of her sword. She whistled, and Gus fell in close behind Sunflash as she galloped down the road past the stunned Shadow Heir and away from the Okarrians she was sworn to protect.

***

The light was already ebbing when Klaus caught up with her. Shad sat up, ears pricked and alert in his saddle bag.

"What was that about?" Klaus exclaimed, almost accusingly.

Kaia touched the back of her head. Her fingers came away smeared with scarlet. She sighed.

"Oh, come now Klaus, it's like you used to tell me when you were young." She flicked her eyes to him, "No one likes the Dragon Heir."

Kaia was surprised and perversely pleased to see a hint of color rise to Klaus' cheeks. "I've never seen anything like *that*!"

"Lucky you, Shadow Heir," she muttered, her voice flat. "Lucky you."

"But, why didn't you frighten them away with your flames," Shad prodded from his perch. "I've seen you do it before."

Now it was Kaia's turn to blush. She cast her eyes to the dirt road. "I don't know."

"What do you mean you don't know?" Klaus pressed, his tone still sharp.

The unfair edge to his voice grated on Kaia. "It means *I don't know*," she spat. "It means 'I tried, and nothing happened,' ok!"

Her outburst was met by stunned silence from both cat and man. She looked ahead stubbornly as they walked on in the advancing dusk, insects trilling around them in the tall grass.

"It's because you're tired, of course," the cat said at last. "The battle yesterday must have drained you."

"Or perhaps you're just overwhelmed," Klaus muttered.

"I am not *overwhelmed*, Klaus Thane," Kaia snarled. "We lost over a hundred souls yesterday, I burned a man alive, watched you die, and the people I'm fighting to defend thanked me by throwing stones and hurting my dog." She turned to him, a challenge glinting in her hard eyes. "I think I'm managing *just fine*."

For once, the clever Shadow Heir was at a loss for words.

CHAPTER 19
DORINAR

That night, Kaia wrapped her cloak tightly around her shoulders to ward off the late summer chill. Klaus bent over a pile of kindling and struck the pommel of his dagger against a flint stone. He blew gently on the sparks, and under his encouragement, a flame caught and grew. Shame coated Kaia's cheeks. The vaunted Dragon Heir couldn't even start a campfire.

As the blaze cackled to life, Shad disappeared under a blanket.

Gus cocked his head with questioning eyes from where he lay at her side. What's wrong, my girl?

For the tenth time that evening, she held out a palm and let her mind empty. She could feel the heat deep at her center, as always, but when she tried to coax it to her waiting fingers, nothing happened. Kaia brought her clammy hand to her forehead and squeezed her temples, silently sending a prayer to Odriel to return her gift.

Klaus rose from the catching fire and leaned against the boulder next to her. "Still nothing?"

She looked up with tired eyes and shook her head, burying her fingers in Gus' thick fur.

"Maybe you should give it a rest for a few days. Give yourself some time to recover," Klaus suggested.

Kaia shrugged. This new complication had thawed the tension between the Heirs, but she was still careful to hold herself in check while his eyes were on her.

"I feel naked without it," she muttered, grinding a hole in the dirt with her boot heel.

"Well, it's a good thing you have me here to look after you, then," Klaus joked, a smirk curving his mouth.

"Am I so much like a child that I need a minder?" she snapped.

Klaus sighed as he rubbed the scar in his brow. His gaze bored into the crackling fire. When he finally addressed her, his words came slowly, as if drawn out of him by force. "I spoke harshly yesterday. I'm sorry."

Kaia faced him with a raised eyebrow. A week ago, she would have thought the proud Shadow Heir incapable of apologies. Yet, here was his second in as many days.

Klaus met her eyes. "I just couldn't bear to see you torture yourself again."

His earnest words toppled the flimsy wall between them. A knot in her stomach loosened. "It wouldn't have stung so much if it hadn't hit so close to the mark," Kaia admitted. She pressed her heel into the small hole she had made in the dirt. "I'm not a master of my emotions, as you are."

"To be honest, I hope you never learn." Klaus' hazel eyes crinkled with a smile Kaia could not help but return. "When you grieve, the sun does not shine, and when your heart is light, the whole world smiles with you."

A crimson blush burned from the base of Kaia's neck to the roots of her hair. "Except for the stoic, Guardian Thane," she mumbled with a nudge.

"Ha," he scoffed and tossed his head, his eyes shining. "The Shadow Heir gives away nothing."

"I wouldn't be able to breathe if I contained myself like that."

Klaus nodded. "As it should be. The dragon and shadow—two different beasts."

Kaia yanked sharply at a loose thread on her sleeve. "Only the dragon is a beast, the shadow is just a mystery."

A silent moment stretched between them as the leaves whispered to each other in the wind above their heads. "Kaia, those villagers—"

"Are not worth talking about," Kaia interrupted as she laid back on her blanket roll. She blew air slowly out of her puffed cheeks. "I've been dealing with it as long as I can remember." She looked up at the stars glittering fiercely above them, a bright rebellion against the oppressive night. "It's like they say, '*The Dragon Heir walks through fire alone.*'"

"Except when you walk with me," Klaus countered, the corner of his mouth quirking up again as he lay back onto his own pallet. Kaia nodded into the dark. As she slipped into slumber, Kaia was acutely aware of Klaus' sleeping form, deeply breathing only inches away, and she drifted off with the shadow of a smile still on her face.

***

In her dreams, Kaia walked the battlefield once again. Mogens and Klaus dueled before her, but as Kaia surged towards them, her legs were sluggish. She looked down to find herself wading through a bog of blood littered with the bloated corpses of the fallen. Mogens' wicked knife plunged into Klaus again and again. Kaia screamed, trying to call her gift, but no flames appeared. Before she could inch her way to them, Klaus' lifeless body sank into the lake of red.

She sat up sharply, sweat cold on her brow. With Mogens' twisted face still burning in her mind, her frantic eyes searched the darkness around them. Fingers grazed her shoulder, and she flinched back with a small cry. Shad's triangular ears popped out of his blanket in alarm.

"Firefly, it's just me," Klaus mumbled, his voice thick with sleep. "What's the matter?"

Kaia grabbed tightly to his wrist, her knuckles turning white. "Mogens is still out there."

Klaus blinked slowly, his eyelids heavy with sleep. "He fell in the gorge," he shrugged. "There's no way he would've survived that fall."

"But did we find his body?"

"The river would've carried it away."

Kaia locked eyes with Shad's luminescent gaze peering out from a wadded blanket across the smoldering fire, and her heart sank. "So, we don't know," she whispered.

Kaia turned away, but she didn't go back to sleep.

***

The days passed listlessly after that. They circumvented any villages in their path, and Kaia's flame remained untouchable. The misshapen sun continued to haunt the sky, while ghastly nightmares plagued her nights. Just the thought of Mogens still living rattled her bones. To survive the dragon fire twice, dark magic had to be behind it somehow.

Klaus tried bantering with her to keep her spirits up, but he could not break through her brooding thoughts. Though Klaus swore Mogens died in the ravine, Kaia knew that Shad felt differently. He slept through the day, but at night, while she thrashed away in a cold sweat, his luminous blue eyes kept watch. To add to the growing gloom of the trio, the midsummer rains arrived in force, making fires difficult to kindle and turning the road to a thick muck.

On the seventh day, the forest surrendered to marsh, and the road all but disappeared into a muddy, overgrown trail. The Heirs were forced to dismount from the Dalteek and pick their way through the treacherous mire. On the ninth day, the trail disappeared altogether.

"Which way now, Shad?" Kaia sighed as she tried to shift her hood to keep out the inescapable drizzle. Gus shook out his fur uselessly beside her. "I can't see the trail anymore."

Wiping the dripping water from her nose, Kaia could just barely make out Shadmundar's peevish cat eyes peering out from Klaus' saddle bag. She wondered briefly if the cat had hated the wet as a human, or if the distaste had come with the transformation.

He wiggled his whiskers. "That's because we have arrived."

"At Dorinar's cottage?" Kaia looked around in confusion. An ankle-deep bog surrounded them.

"Where?" Klaus didn't bother to hide his annoyance as he ruffled his soaked hair.

"Just past that copse of trees, there. It's well hidden. As you know, the magi typically don't welcome visitors."

"Fantastic," Klaus drawled.

"Shad," Kaia stifled a yawn as they slogged through the swamp, "What is this magus like anyway?"

The cat's muffled voice emanated from his dry pouch. "He is both a hermit and scholar."

"Aren't all the magi hermits?"

"If you ever meet them, you can let me know."

"But, this one has Kallar's blade."

"That is what Everard believes."

"He doesn't know?"

"Do not fear. Dorinar will know where the sword is, even if he doesn't have it. But I doubt he would let such a precious artifact fall into clumsy human hands."

When they finally reached the small grove, Kaia could just barely discern a ramshackle dwelling cunningly hidden among the trees. Moss coated the roof and vines hung over the grimy windows. Creeping ivy obscured the walls, camouflaging it perfectly among the trunks that crowded around it. Kaia could barely make out the outline of a door hidden behind a low-lying branch.

Kaia shifted in the saddle. "Are you sure he still lives here?"

Before Shad could respond, Klaus hammered a fist on the green-streaked everoak door. They paused and listened for movement in the house, but only heard the patter of raindrops on leaves.

Klaus rolled his neck to the side with a crack. "My name is Klaus Thane, the Shadow Heir of Okarria, and I have come to ask for the council of the magus, Dorinar."

Once again, they paused, but the quiet sound of rain filled the silence again.

"Open up, Dorn," Shad called. "You know why we're here."

"Go away," a reedy voice grumbled from behind the door.

"Guardian Thane has come to claim what is rightfully his."

"Rightfully his?" the indignant voice squeaked. The door cracked open, and a curly haired young man peered out from the gloom within. "Obviously, his ancestors couldn't be trusted with it, since it is no longer in the Heir's possession."

Kaia was taken aback by how young the magus looked. Surely, he was just as old as Everard, and yet he looked perhaps only a decade older than she. His stained clothing was as shabby as the cottage and hung from his thin frame. A mop of curly brown hair fell untidily into his suspicious black eyes, and his skin looked like it had never seen the sun.

Shadmundar sighed audibly. "You know it was stolen, Dorn."

"Humans always have excuses!" the man snapped.

"It's wet out here and we're coming in, whether you like it or not," Klaus growled, pushing past the magus through the cracked doorway.

The magus stalked after the Heir. "I most certainly do not like it!"

Shad leapt from his perch, shook his fur in the doorway and padded silently after them.

Kaia looked around for a barn to house the Dalteek and the smelly, mud-coated ragehound, but could see nothing amidst the thick greenery. "I won't be long, Gussy." She stepped out of her muck-caked boots and closed the door behind her.

Her eyes widened as she took in the dimly lit room. Stacks of books, papers, and scrolls littered every available surface–table, floor, chairs. Various mugs and plates lay scattered among the documents. The room had absorbed the chill of the rain that fell outside, while the fireplace lay ashy and unused. Cobwebs hung from the corners of the ceilings and a layer of dust coated assorted piles of paper and cloth. A gray tabby hissed at Shad as he delicately picked his way through the piles. Kaia tiptoed after the black cat towards the raised voices emanating from down the corridor.

She followed Shad into a narrow, candle-lit hall. Kaia's curiosity grew as they passed room after room in the deceptively large house. At the end of the corridor, they finally came into a cramped study lined with overflowing bookcases and a small fire burning in the hearth.

Klaus scowled and stalked across the floor, eyes raking over the heaps of odds and ends as water dripped from his cloak to the stone floor. "Where is it?"

The magus crossed his arms. "As if I would keep it here."

Kaia's eyes flicked from Klaus back to the magus. "But you know where it is?"

"I am a historian. I know where most things are," Dorinar retorted.

"Tell us where it is!" Klaus slammed a fist against the wall. "Have you looked at the sun lately? We don't have time for this! We need it to stop Nifras!"

"Just the two of you?" Dorinar seized the fire poker and stabbed at the flames. "You'll need a lot more than that."

Kaia rubbed her forehead with a clammy palm, trying to ward off her exasperation. "Then help us, Dorinar."

"Not my affair," the magus sniffed as he put the poker down and shuffled the papers on the desk by the clouded window.

"Dorinar," Shadmundar said sternly. "The sword belongs to Guardian Thane."

Dorinar paused in his puttering's. "As if such things can be trusted to humans."

"Dorn…" Shad had a note of warning in his voice.

The strange man threw up his hands, scattering the papers he had been straightening. "Well, what if I don't remember? How about THAT, Shadmundar?"

Shad's tail flicking from side to side. "You must be joking."

"I'm an old man, cat. I can't be expected to remember every minute detail of human existence." The bookish magus, who looked nothing like an old man, glanced at them suspiciously from the sides of his eyes before seizing a book and opening it to a random page. "So sorry to inconvenience you. Best of luck with the battle. Goodbye."

"We're not leaving until you tell us where the blade is," Klaus rumbled darkly.

"And what are you going to do? Threaten me?" Dorinar scoffed, his voice cracking. "How original! Humans are all the same!"

"We'll simply stay here until your memory is jogged." Klaus brushed a stack of papers off one of the frayed chairs and unceremoniously collapsed into it. A small cloud of dust puffed into the air as he sank into the cushions.

"No!" Dorinar shrieked. "You must leave this instant! I do *not* entertain visitors. I'm a very busy man! I don't have time for this nonsense."

"The sooner you tell us where the blade is, the sooner you can get back to your solitary, pathetic existence," Klaus said, his hazel eyes meeting Dorinar's ink-black ones.

Color flooded Dorinar's cheeks as he snapped the book shut. "Senseless, stubborn humans!" He pointed an accusing finger at the Shadow Heir. "Wait as long as you want, you hopeless fool. *I* am not the one running out of time!" With that, the magus stormed out of the room, the slam of a door punctuating his exit.

For a long moment, the trio listened to the rain tapping its cold fingers against the glass window as the flames slowly died. With a sigh, Klaus grabbed the poker to prod the failing fire. Kaia let out a breath she didn't know she was holding and let her tense body sag against the wall. Shad leapt onto the great chair facing Klaus.

"Well?" Klaus ground his fists into his eyes.

Shad pawed at the papers on the cushion. "This was not unexpected."

Kaia shrugged. "But what do we do now?"

Shad's eyes combed the books that surrounded them. "Well, Dorn is a fastidious historian. The location of the sword is bound to be documented in one of these tomes. Perhaps we can find it."

Kaia looked at the hundreds of books that surrounded them, puffing out her cheeks as she exhaled. "...Right...."

Klaus picked up one of the books he had thrown to the floor, wiped the grime from the cover, and opened it to the first page. "Might as well get started."

Kaia took another look at the rows of books and excused herself to care for Gus and the Dalteek. After stumbling around the house's walls in the wet, she managed to find a derelict barn that held a milking cow, a chicken coop, a rabbit hutch, and a bored, fat gelding. There wasn't much room for the Naerami does, but it was the best she could do for them. After watering and feeding the Dalteek, she dried off Gus as best she could with a horse blanket and returned to find Klaus and Shad exactly where she had left them, surrounded by stacks of volumes piled high around their chairs.

"The dog smells," Shad muttered, his eyes glued to yellowed pages as he flipped busily through the texts. Gus settled into a damp lump by the fire.

Kaia didn't bother to respond as she bent down to dislodge a book from its hiding place behind the nearest bookcase. She perched on a nearby chair and opened the book to the first page: *An Account of the Royal Court in the Reign of King Wayrcham, the Noble, written by Teraeza Jamette,* followed by lists of names, dates, and accounts of different councils, debates, and edicts that made Kaia's eyes glaze over with boredom.

Her eyes blurred as she painstakingly deciphered the spidery text that referenced events and people she'd never hear of. She looked up as Klaus thumped a thick book closed and began to flip through another one, his eyes darting back and forth across the pages. Even Shadmundar moved faster than she, methodically clawing through page after page. It would take her an age to get through even one page, much less understand what any of it meant.

Perhaps if they hadn't banished her from the schoolhouse, the teachers could have helped with her word troubles. Kaia's cheeks heated with the sting of her exile once again. She tossed the book back onto the floor in frustration. Klaus' hazel eyes and Shad's blue ones briefly flicked up to her and then to each other. A blush crawled down Kaia's neck. To see them quietly acknowledge her ignorance humiliated her more than if they had teased her.

She stood and strode from the room, only to find the next room over—the kitchen—as disorderly as the rest of the house, with dishes strewn about the counters, stained documents littering the table, and half a loaf of bread sitting forlornly next to the water basin. Fidgeting restlessly, Kaia picked her way over to the pantry. The door opened on creaking hinges, and several small creatures scuttled for cover as she revealed their refuge. But, in addition to the provisions and herbs she expected to see, Kaia found yet more books stashed haphazardly on the shelves. There was a small stack shoved beside the flour sack, a few more pushed behind a bottle of wine, and another underneath a round of cheese.

Kaia collected the volumes on the table and glanced at one of the titles, *A List of Odriel's Blessings in the Age of King Roggitt, written by Teraeza Jamette*. Kaia scratched her head as she glanced around the room again. There was a book on one of the chairs, one on the mantle, and even one under a table leg. She sighed in exasperation. The record Klaus and Shad were looking for, if it even existed, could be anywhere. With a roll of her eyes, she gathered up the texts and all the other crumpled papers she could find in a haphazard, food-encrusted stack and made her way back to the study. She said nothing as she dropped the tower of pages next to Klaus' armchair and went back out to look for more.

In the next room, a bedchamber by the looks of it, she found books squirreled away under the mattress, stacks of papers in the dresser drawers, and even a scroll hidden in the pillowcase. This was not simple absentmindedness, Kaia thought, as she felt the other pillowcases for hidden works. Teraeza Jamette had authored every text she found. The magus had hidden her works deliberately. But why? She looked at another title, *The Account of the Dragon Heir, Shava, in the Second Age, by Teraeza Jamette*.

Kaia stilled. *Shava*. Mackie had told her about Shava. She flipped through the looping words, and a loose sheet escaped from the pages. She picked up the wrinkled parchment and found a detailed ink sketch: a barefoot young woman, hair cropped short, eyes closed, sitting on top of a mountain, with a brown hawk circling above—Odriel's preferred form.

As Kaia ran her fingers over the grave face of her ancestor, she remembered Mackie's words, *"They say she climbed barefoot to the top of the pass and waited all night on the highest peak without moving—no food, no sleep, no water—until Odriel finally appeared to answer her plea."*

A rustling in the hall interrupted Kaia's reverie, and she hastily folded the sketch before stuffing it into her breeches pocket.

She spent the next hour going over every inch of the room to ensure she hadn't missed anything. She barely noticed when the magus whisked into the dusty bedchamber, stared for a moment, and then left the way he came.

When she turned her search to the spacious sitting room they had come in through, she found the magus tucked sullenly into an armchair in the corner. He snuck peeks at her as she checked under the rug and rifled through his desk. Though Kaia could feel his dark eyes lingering on her, she refused to return his gaze. When she found a bundle of pages beneath a loose flagstone, she glared at the magus accusingly, but his face studiously pressed into yet another book.

This is useless, she thought furiously. *Dorinar is completely mad.*

The Heirs spent the night in the cottage, and the next day started much the same. The rain continued to fall while Gus stretched by the fire and Kaia combed the premises for hidden manuscripts. While Shad and Klaus sorted through Dorinar's never-ending collection of texts, the magus bustled about, glaring whenever they saw him. More than once, Kaia overhead Klaus confronting Dorinar—their voices rising to shouts and then sudden silence as one of them stormed away.

In the midmorning, Kaia had turned to rummaging through yet another repurposed bedchamber when under the bed, her fingers encountered a long, smooth surface among the usual clutter. Curious, she reached another arm under to grasp the edges and extract the object from its hiding place. It was a portrait, its colors swirling under the shining glass of an ornate frame. Kaia got to her feet. Upright, the painting almost reached her chest. She leaned it against the bed and backed up to the wall to regard the whole picture.

Kaia brought a hand to her mouth. Mountain girl as she was, she had not laid eyes on many pieces of artwork, but anyone could tell the painting was beautiful. Thousands of minute brushstrokes came together to form a woman with long red hair and a half smile as she peered over a bare shoulder at the artist. Projecting an aura of confidence, her stunning green eyes crinkled mischievously from under a cocked eyebrow.

The portrait spilled life, bringing light into a room that had been dour a moment before. Who was she? And why was this magnificent piece under the bed? The girl had a spark, that much was obvious, and whoever had painted the portrait had clearly worshiped her. *Could it have been Dorinar?* That didn't seem possible.

After another moment spent considering this, Kaia seized the portrait and shuffled into the common room for better lighting. She shooed the house tabby from the mantle and placed the girl's image above the fireplace. When she took a step back to get a better look, she trod right onto Dorinar's slippered foot.

"Oh, sorry..." Kaia started, stepping away from the magus. He seemed to hardly notice her as his dark eyes stared at the painting, transfixed.

"Where did you find that?" he whispered.

Something in his gaze made Kaia uneasy. She had been rummaging through *his* cottage after all. "It was under the bed."

"I'd prefer if you didn't display that painting," he said stiffly.

"Why?"

"I don't have to explain myself to you." The magus turned back to his armchair.

"How can you not love this painting?" Kaia protested, gazing at the portrait. "She looks like she knows all your secrets. She has such spirit."

"She did." Dorinar's voice was gruff.

Kaia glanced at him. His wistful eyes shimmered beneath his curls, and suddenly she could see the weight of his years churning there despite his youthful features.

When he spoke, he articulated his words slowly, as if each one recalled a memory. "She was doting and joyful, but fierce. And stubborn. So very, very stubborn...."

Kaia smiled at his description. "She sounds like a kindred spirit."

"*Ha!*" Dorinar barked. "There was *no one* like her. She was astoundingly intelligent—even now, her writing haunts me."

Kaia raised her eyebrows. Could this be Teraeza Jamette? Is that why he hid her works?

"How can you say humans are all the same if she was unique?"

"Even the strictest of rules have their exceptions," the magus grumbled.

"What happened to her?"

"What happened to her is what happens to *all* mortals. She died," Dorinar said curtly, opening a book in front of his face to end the conversation.

Kaia grimaced as she looked back at the painting. All people died one day, but that was all the more reason to treasure their memory—not hide it away. The stilted silence was broken only by the listless rain drumming on the thatched roof and the fire sizzling below the mantle.

She looked at the shelves of books that surrounded them both and imagined a time when this girl sat at a desk, maybe in this very room, her head bent, pen scratching away at parchment. She was sure the cottage had been much different then, and Dorinar, too. Kaia's thoughts twisted and turned. *That* Dorinar would have helped them. Maybe he was still in there somewhere.

Kaia crossed her arms and looked hard at the magus, curled up in the corner of the room as far away from her as possible. "Why do you study history anyway?"

The magus sighed in annoyance. "By establishing patterns in humanity's history, you can effectively predict the future."

"But why do you bother studying humanity if you refuse to live among them?"

"I've witnessed generations of human lives—the same short, meaningless lives over and over. I can hardly bear your presence anymore."

"Maybe we wouldn't be so predictable if you deigned to share your knowledge," Kaia snapped.

"So that humanity can use it to sow death and destruction?" The magus lowered his book to peer over it at her. "I think not."

Kaia clenched her fists. "Knowledge can deliver us from the darkness."

"Or send you deeper?"

She growled in frustration. Klaus should be playing these word games with the magus, not her. Her voice rose in timber. "If you let Nifras destroy us, there will be no more history for you to study."

"How vain...." Dorinar smirked, placing the book gingerly in his lap. "There was history before humans, and there will be history after. In fact, I look forward to studying something new."

Kaia's voice cracked. "You don't relate to humans at all?"

"No." The magus turned his head away to the rain-streaked window.

Kaia studied the girl's portrait again—the dozens of shades of green that composed her eyes, the perfect tilt of her smile, the way the light shone from her face. Someone had spent hours upon hours perfecting it.

Her voice gentled when she spoke again. "Our connections to people in life and death, grief and love...they're what make us human." The magus turned his unreadable coal black eyes to meet hers. "You won't admit it, but it's something you've experienced."

The magus rose suddenly, his book falling to the floor. He stalked up to Kaia, his face only inches from hers. Kaia felt the yanaa in the room charge around them.

"I've had enough of you and your infantile attempts at wisdom," he spat. "You have walked this earth what, two decades? A pittance."

Kaia returned his glare as he seethed. The moment stretched on as anger swirled in the air between them. A wet nose nudged her palm. She looked down in surprise; she hadn't heard Gus come in. With a frustrated sigh, Kaia turned away from the intransigent magus and stepped towards the hall.

"It's the best I can do," she murmured. If Everard and Klaus couldn't convince the magus to help them, why had she thought that she could do better?

"Take down that picture before you go," the magus snapped. "I told you I don't want it displayed."

Hearing the catch in his voice, Kaia turned to him with a sad smile. "And yet you keep it," she said softly.

"It pains me every second I must be reminded of her." The magus' words shuddered as he looked up at the painting. He passed a hand over his eyes. "If I can't fill my thoughts every second of every day, she'll find me...." his voice lowered to a whisper. "Gliding silently into my mind, tempting me towards a wonderful madness." He lifted his accusing onyx eyes to Kaia once again. "Even the sight of *you,* the poorest comparison, is enough to send me sliding back." The words were coated with venom, and yet Kaia couldn't suppress the smallest of grins. "It's that cheeky insolence!"

She shrugged. "Memories are to be cherished."

"They are torture." The magus' voice thickened with emotion. "When I remember her light, living without her in this darkness becomes unbearable." He stalked to the window once again, gripping his hands tightly behind his back. "If I had never met her, I could have been content."

Kaia's heart swelled, and she walked over to gaze out the window beside him. For a moment they stood, not a hair's breadth away from one another, and watched rain fall through the tangled trees around the cottage.

"I knew bliss, and now grief consumes me," he whispered.

Hesitantly, Kaia reached out a hand and rested it on Dorinar's shoulder. She wasn't sure how long they stood like that. The magus trapped in reverie, with Kaia as his anchor—a silent reminder that he did not have to grieve alone. After what felt like an age, the magus blinked and turned his night-dark eyes to her, as if surprised to find her there. He took her hand in one of his and turned it over once as if considering it.

Abruptly he stiffened, his eyes flinty once more as he dropped her hand and turned back to the room.

"You must go." Dorinar strode away from her, suddenly determined to put as much space between them as possible. "You *have* to go. I cannot stand it anymore!"

As he brought his hands to his head, clenching fistfuls of unruly hair, books began to fly off the shelves and documents swirled from their stacks on the desk.

Kaia's eyes widened at the spontaneous whirlwind. She swallowed, feeling the yanaa prickling her skin, but she could not leave yet. "We need the blade," she said hesitantly, looking at the portrait once more. "Teraeza would have helped us."

Dorinar turned his crazed black eyes to her, "Don't claim to know who she was!" he seized the frame and hurled it from the mantle. The glass shattered on the stone floor, but Teraeza's expression remained unchanged as it smirked up at them. A vase fell off the shelf and crashed next to it, and chairs scooted across the floor. Gus yipped uncertainly and brushed up against the back of Kaia's legs. The door blew open wildly to the rain and slammed shut again.

Kaia held his gaze steadily and lifted her chin. "We are her people."

With a small cry, Dorinar turned away from her and the room stilled. The man's heaving breaths were unnaturally loud in the silence. Errant pages fluttered to the floor like autumn leaves.

Just as Kaia turned to leave, Dorinar's shaky voice rang through the room. "Enough!" he blustered, bracing himself on a chair. "So be it. I hid the sword in the Tazgari caves for safekeeping, not five miles to the northeast as the crow flies. When you cross the brook, follow the current to find the cave entrance. The scabbard hangs in the back of the second chamber." His voice flattened. "Invisibility means nothing to the *cobalan* that lives there, and he does not take fondly to trespassers."

Kaia nodded. She moved to leave but then paused. Turning, she picked up the shattered frame from the puddle of glass and set it against the wall. "I'm sorry that your memories pain you," she murmured. "But I believe you were lucky to know her." With that, Kaia stood again to go out.

"Wait" Dorinar rushed to his desk, yanked out drawers and overturned them, spilling the contents on the floor. He dug through the pile on the floor and retrieved a small trinket—a silver armlet with a black swirling pattern.

The magus grabbed her hand and thrust the band into it. "Forged from star silver by Ikrid, the third Time Heir. A poor replacement for a healer, but it does have minor restorative properties." Kaia gaped, speechless, as the magus stared down at her, her hand enclosed in his. "Now leave me in peace child, and do not return."

With those parting words, the magus stalked out of the cottage and into the rain.

CHAPTER 20
ODRIEL'S TOOTH

"Shad, have you ever heard of the Tazgari caves?" Kaia said as their party followed the babbling brook the magus had indicated. The downpour had slowed to a fine mist as the misshapen sun neared its peak.

"No," the cat said peevishly, trying to shake the raindrops from his whiskers. "I know it's hard to believe, but I do not know everything."

Klaus tapped his thumbs on his saddle. "What about cobalans?"

"Little. I have heard of a subterranean goblin-like race that fears the sun, but only in passing."

Kaia fingered the hard armlet beneath her shirt sleeve. She opened her mouth to wonder aloud if they had missed the cave, when Klaus suddenly pulled Stormshade to a halt in front of her. Ahead of him, the banks ended in a mossy ledge. "Good thing I snitched supplies from Dorinar's barn," he said, dismounting. "We'll have to use the rope to climb down."

Kaia descended from Sunflash's saddle and moved to stand beside Klaus. She looked over the slippery drop-off. "Earth below."

The stream fell into a gaping wound in the swamp, a dark cave large enough for a horse to follow the trickling water and hanging vines straight down to its death. Kaia imagined slipping over the edge and plunging into blackness, and she took an involuntary step back.

We'll need the lanterns, she thought, peering into the dark throat of the underworld. Tingles of trepidation buzzed in her fingertips as she scanned the rocky rim of the hole. The marsh trees leaned into the abyss as if being sucked into the navel of the bog.

"Why does Dorinar have to make everything so difficult?" Shad grumbled to himself.

Klaus tied a rope around a sturdy trunk. "Shad, you and Gus stay here with the does," He yanked on the knot. "I don't know how deep the stream will be down there." After throwing the heavy coil of rope into the cavern, Klaus knelt to light the lanterns with the matches he had found in Dorinar's barn. The stink of burning oil filled Kaia's nose as he straightened, lamp in hand, and held one out to her. Kaia accepted the handle uncertainly. She couldn't remember the last time she'd held one.

Reading her thoughts, Klaus gave her a reassuring smile. "Don't worry, as long as we don't get them wet, these lanterns will do just fine." He hooked the light onto his belt and picked up the rope.

"Try to be quiet and quick," Shad warned. "Who knows what kinds of creatures live in that pit."

Klaus nodded and looked to Kaia. "Wait for the rope to go slack before you follow." With that, he disappeared over the ledge. Kaia looked down to see him descending the slick cave wall with enviable grace until all she could see was his fragile lantern glow bobbing along in the dark. It only took a few moments more before the line went slack and Kaia followed suit.

The cavern wall wasn't as sheer as she had first thought, and she too descended rapidly, the circle of cloudy sky shrinking above her. In minutes, she splashed down in the thigh-deep water next to Klaus. Taking the lantern from her belt, she held it up to get a better feel for her surroundings. The shallow water cut through a wide chamber with sharp rocks protruding from ceiling and floor, like a toothy maw. On the far side, she could just make out a narrow tunnel. Besides the gentle murmuring and dripping of the water, a muted silence filled the cave.

"Dorinar said the blade would be in the back of the second chamber," Kaia whispered.

Klaus drew his blade and gestured towards the far tunnel. "Let's go, then."

The dark water hid jagged outcroppings and loose rocks, making footing treacherous as the pair stumbled through the cold water. Their splashing seemed deafening as it echoed. Kaia's eyes flicked, looking for any sign of life. She flinched when the lanterns cast ominous shadows on the cavern walls behind them.

"Easy, Firefly," Klaus breathed.

They had to stoop to enter the tunnel, but it was only a few paces before it opened into another room, even larger than the first. With no natural light, their lanterns did little to dispel the oppressive cavern darkness. Smooth rock formations grew up out of the ground like trees, and thick pillars of stone stretched from ceiling to ground.

The Heirs climbed out of the stream onto the loose shale floor of the chamber, the thin layers of loose rock grating together under their feet. Kaia stayed close to Klaus, drawing her blade as they weaved in between mounds of rock. In the smothering darkness of the cave, Kaia silently cursed Dorinar for hiding it in such a dreadful place, and then doubly cursed herself for not being able to light their way.

"There," Klaus whispered, "On the back wall. I see it."

Not far ahead on their right, Kaia could see the glint of a gold-encrusted scabbard hanging from a rock, jutting out from the cave wall like a thorn. Klaus strode towards it purposefully, but before he reached it, Kaia saw there was a problem—the scabbard was empty.

Klaus scowled as he swung the empty sheath across his back and held up his lantern, casting about for the lost relic. "Dorinar tricked us," he seethed.

"But then why is—"

A ghastly howl echoed through the chamber, cutting off Kaia's thought. *"Who trespasses on the Xar's den?"*

Klaus shifted his grip on his blade. "It is the Shadow Heir, Guardian Klaus Thane, come to claim Odriel's Tooth." His voice resounded in the enclosed space.

"You come to steal from the Xar?" the voice growled, a sound like metal scraping on metal.

"The blade is rightfully mine!" Klaus called, casting about for the source of the voice.

"But, the Xar has it. It belongs to the Xar." Every time the creature spoke, the words seemed to be coming from a different location. Kaia strained her eyes against the dark but could see nothing. She heard a faint shuffling coming from the direction they had come and wheeled around.

"We need it to defeat the evil that threatens our land," Kaia called.

"The one that slays the sun," the creature said knowingly.

Klaus scanned the darkness, his stance tense. "Yes, Nifras brings darkness and death."

"The Xar likes the dark. When the sun is dead, the Xar will walk the land."

A shudder ran down Kaia's spine as the dire words echoed about the cavern.

Klaus smacked his blade on the stone floor. "The Lost will rule the land!"

"But the Xar has the strong sword," the grating voice hissed.

Face darkening in anger, the Shadow Heir opened his mouth to yell something else.

Kaia shook her head. "There's no reasoning with it, Klaus."

"Stay in the light. I'm going to try to find it," he snarled, his features bunched with anger. He put his lantern down and blinked out of sight. Kaia's gaze swiveled around the cave as she strained her ears for the slightest noise.

"The tricks don't work on the Xar. You smell of the warm flesh, your footsteps sound like the prey."

Kaia heard quick footsteps and then Klaus' scream in the dark, a struggle, and the earsplitting howl of the creature.

"Klaus!" she yelled, running in the direction of the scuffle, only to spin around again at the sound of a crash behind her. Kaia raised her light to see that something had dashed Klaus' lantern against the rocks.

A hand grabbed her shoulder from behind. Kaia leapt away with a twist, holding her blade at the ready.

"It's just me!" Klaus said, holding up his empty hand. His shoulder oozed blood, but he looked otherwise unharmed. "One of those things bit me." He eyed his injury. "But I think I managed to catch it with my edge."

As if to confirm Klaus' words, Xar's voice echoed around them, "*You have wounded the Xar. Now you will not escape.*" The sounds of sliding shale surrounded them.

"How many are there?" Kaia tried to keep her voice calm. For the thousandth time, she tried to call the flames to her fingers. Still nothing.

"I don't know." Klaus turned to put his back to hers. "I didn't even catch a glimpse. It's just too dark."

The shuffling got louder as the predators encircled them. Kaia could now see flashes of white flesh darting from rock to rock.

"We need to get out of here," she whispered. "We only have one lamp left."

"Not without the sword."

Kaia turned to talk sense into Klaus, but her words froze on her tongue as her lantern illuminated a nightmarish creature crouched on the boulder in front of them. The cobalan was roughly man-shaped, with long ears and nearly translucent skin. It had snake-like nostrils instead of a nose, and hollows covered with white flesh where its eyes should've been. It stood shorter than her, but its thin, spider-like limbs ended in long, needle fingers. In one of its hands, it gripped a magnificent sword. The blade stretched the length of the creature's body. Wicked spikes edged the hilt and pommel, and the sleek double-edged blade glistened black, polished to a mirror-like shine.

Kaia heard Klaus' breath catch in his throat.

In a blink, the Shadow Heir launched himself towards the cobalan with a shout. Just as he reached the creature, two more of the pale-bodied cave dwellers leapt upon him from the dark. He knocked one away and slashed at another.

Kaia heard something approach her from behind and ducked instinctively. A screeching cobalan dived over her head, then wheeled and lunged at her again. Kaia rolled away and slashed deep into the cobalan's back, but was caught off guard as another fell upon her. The creature's swift attack slammed her to the ground and smashed her lantern against the rocks.

Complete darkness swallowed them.

Kaia thrashed, kicking the creature off her and slashing blindly with her sword. With a shriek, the injured cobalan released her and fled.

Kaia leapt to her feet in the pitch black. She forced herself to focus despite the icy fingers gripping her chest. She had the power to light this place, to save them.

She concentrated on her ragged breathing, blocking out her surroundings and looking inward to her soul, the essence of her being, of her gift, just as her father had taught her. The dragon fire burned there—she could feel it within her, as familiar as her reflection. She summoned the flames up from her heart to her fingertips.

Nothing.

The sounds of the screeching creatures pierced Kaia's concentration.

Klaus grunted somewhere nearby. "Kaia, call the flames! I know you can do it!"

"I'm trying," she snapped, her voice cracking. A guttural growl grew around them.

"*Prepare yourselves prey. The Xar comes for you,*" hissed the cobalan, as the gurgling of its clan buzzed to a fever pitch.

"Kaia, if you don't light the way—" Klaus' voice was cut off by the clang of sword on sword. Kaia turned towards the noise, just as one of the creatures leapt on her back, clawing and biting. She shouted as three more tackled her from different directions, bringing her to the ground. Kaia heard Klaus cry out in pain as she lashed out at her attackers. In desperation, she tried to call her gift once more, and suddenly, the cave burst with light. A small sun had breached the cave and now hovered over the Heirs.

The light revealed a cave crawling with cobalans. They scuttled on the ceiling like spiders, perched on every boulder, and formed a ring around the Heirs. The new light fully illuminated the Xar as he stood over Klaus, Odriel's Tooth raised high.

"*Burning sun!*" the Xar cried, lifting his arms to shield his face. Without a second of hesitation, the Shadow Heir cut down the cobalan and relieved him of the relic, sliding the great blade into the sheath on his back. The mob around Kaia writhed in agony as they crawled for the shadows. Deafening screeches of indignant pain from scores of cobalans echoed around the cave.

Klaus looked to Kaia for the source of the light, but she shook her head at him. It hadn't come from her.

"Hurry, you senseless humans, I can't hold them for long!" Dorinar yelled in his reedy voice from the tunnel entrance they had entered from.

Needing no further encouragement, the Heirs raced for the exit. Just as Kaia caught sight of the magus, Dorinar's sun charm failed, and darkness swathed them once again. In comparison to the blinding spell, Dorinar's lantern seemed as flimsy as a candle in a storm. Still, the Heirs blundered towards it. In mere seconds, the cobalan clan had recovered and bellowed a war cry.

The creatures fell on them from all directions. Three sets of fingers clawed at Kaia's arms and legs. She hacked at them without slowing her momentum, only to feel another two fall on her from above. She looked over to see Klaus besieged by his own throng of assailants. Kaia locked eyes with Dorinar, not fifteen paces away.

"There are too many!" she called, felling two more cobalans with a slash of her blade and throwing another off her shoulder with the other hand. "We're not going to make it."

Dorinar rolled his eyes dramatically and pressed his hands together. His brow furrowed in concentration, and a barrier of light formed in front of him. The magus extended his hands with a grunt, and the barrier moved forward. He lunged a leg forward, and the barrier came within five paces of the Heirs. "Get behind the barricade!"

With a spin and a wide sweep of her blade, Kaia managed to fling the eyeless beasts from her body and take three paces before another group tried to pull her back. She chopped at them with her blade and took a step before another one locked its arms around her neck. With one more stumbling lunge she passed through Dorinar's defense. Screeching, the cobalan on her back slammed into the light barrier as if it were made of brick. More white-skinned cobalans piled up against the yanaa shield, breaking against it like a rough sea on the rocks.

Kaia turned, breathing hard, to see Klaus already in front of her.

Dorinar lifted his chin, his teeth gritted together. "In the tunnel! Quickly!"

The Heirs disappeared into the stone corridor, and Dorinar followed close behind, his barrier moving with him as the cobalans hammered against it. Dorinar stepped through the passage and clenched his outspread hands into fists, collapsing the tunnel behind them.

***

Above ground, the magus and the Heirs stood, scratched and bleeding, at the entrance to the cave. Gus nosed Kaia from her boots to her neck, reveling in the new smells that covered her, and Shad's bright eyes regarded them curiously from his perch on Stormshade's saddle.

Klaus spoke first, "I thought you said *a* cobalan."

Dorinar sniffed. "Well, that was a century ago. I didn't conduct a census."

Kaia put a hand to her chest as if to steady her still thrumming heart. "Why'd you come after us?"

He turned his ancient eyes to her, "I wanted to know why a Dragon Heir would need a lantern."

Kaia turned her face away.

Shad's ears flicked as he answered for her. "After the last battle, she seems to have lost the ability to summon fire."

"Interesting." The magus held his chin thoughtfully. "I have never heard of such a thing. I'll have to make an annotation in the annals...." Mumbling to himself in thought, Dorinar shuffled away in the direction of his cottage.

144

Klaus threw up his arms. "Aren't you even the slightest bit concerned?"

"Still not my affair," the magus returned distractedly, still walking. "Besides, I helped you get the Tooth." Dorinar gestured vaguely at the massive sword hanging from Klaus' back. "You can stop pestering me now and be on your way."

Kaia's voice pitched as she called after him. "What will we do without the dragon fire?"

Dorinar paused and glanced at her over his shoulder. Kaia could see a gamut of emotions spinning in his midnight eyes. "Find a way." He shrugged. "Heirs always do." With that, the magus strode away into the marsh.

***

That night, the Heirs made camp in the forested foothills of the Naerami range, just west of the Tazgar swamp. Klaus couldn't take his hands off his new weapon. He drilled and exercised endlessly in the glow of their campfire, and when he finally tired of slashes and parries, he admired the shadow sword as he reclined against his pack.

"It's impossibly light," he exclaimed, fingering the whorls along the deadly sharp pommel. "And the workmanship is flawless." He ran a hand along the flat of the blade, "To think, this is the very blade Kallar used to defeat a demon god...."

Kaia managed a half smile at the Shadow Heir's wonderment, but her heart felt cold. At last, Klaus put the blade aside and sat back with a contented sigh. Gus stretched out between the Heirs with his own canine huff, his feathered tail sweeping the ground lazily. As Kaia stared into their dying fire, Klaus reached out to brush her bruised elbow.

"It's ok, Firefly. I'm sure you'll be back to normal by the time we reach the Deadlands in a week." He withdrew his hand, and his eyelids drooped. "Get some rest. We've still got miles to go." He closed his eyes and slept soundly within seconds.

Kaia waited a few moments to be sure Klaus was asleep before pulling the folded parchment from her pocket. Shadmundar stalked silently out of the darkness to sit at her side.

Kaia traced the inked image of the hawk above the Dragon Heir's serene countenance. "Shad, we would have died in that cave if Dorinar hadn't been there to save us." Kaia looked back to the fire. "If I don't reclaim the dragon fire, we'll all die." She shook her head. "I have to find answers."

He flicked his tail. "But where will you find them?"

Kaia showed him the page. "Do you know the story of Shava?"

"Ah," Shad inclined his head. "Little more than we heard at Fiola's hearth I'm afraid." His eyes poured over the page. "A desperate girl who entreated Odriel for help—alone, barefoot, and heart bared."

"She found Odriel in these peaks." Kaia nodded to the mountains rising in the dark in front of them. "I'm going to find him."

"Do you believe you can?"

"I have to." Kaia folded the parchment carefully and slid it back into her pocket. "I'll follow in Shava's footsteps." She pulled off her boots and stockings. "Alone, barefoot, and heart bared." She got to her feet, feeling the chill, damp grass between her toes. "You and Klaus need to ride south in case I don't make it in time."

Shad nodded. "You must move quickly. Your army awaits you in the Deadlands."

An unexpected surge of hope coursed through Kaia. "I will not fail them." In silence, she gathered her things, roused Gus with a nudge, and collected Sunflash. The night sky had cleared, and a bright half-moon smiled down on them to light their way.

Kaia turned as she walked her doe towards the towering mountains. "My thanks, Shadmundar."

He bowed his head, "Good luck, Guardian Dashul."

CHAPTER 21
THE SEARCH FOR ODRIEL

Feeling a bit unsettled, Kaia reached the steep slopes of the snow-speckled Naerami Mountains the next morning. Based on a desperate feeling deep in her gut, she had left Klaus in the middle of the night to ride into the mountains alone without her boots. Now, she questioned the wisdom of that choice.

I'm just going to walk up into these mountains and scare up Odriel himself? By the light of the day, the notion sounded preposterous. But she had come too far to turn back now. She looked up at the peak rising above her. Short wisps of grass grew here and there, but boulders of orange, salmon, and grey hues dominated the steep incline—much too steep for even a nimble Dalteek to bear her weight.

Sighing, she dismounted and gingerly set her bare feet on the cold, jagged slope.

Gus nudged her leg with his wet nose and looked up at her with his wet brown eyes. Wherever you lead, I will follow, my girl.

Kaia ran her fingers through his coat. "We're going up, Gus."

Sunflash whickered her encouragement, and with tentative feet, Kaia climbed.

She gritted her teeth as the sharp rocks cut into her soles, bending down on all fours to let her hands share her weight. As she scaled the bleak landscape, she inspected every scurrying stone squirrel and shadow for a sign of the legendary being. She looked up to the grey sky. *Odriel, please hear my call. I might be the first Dragon Heir to lose the fire, but don't punish the people of Okarria for my failings.* She squeezed her eyes shut, trying to propel her prayers out into the surrounding mountains through sheer force of will. *Odriel, we need your help.*

As she ascended, the air turned chilly in the high altitude, and patches of snow hid in the shade. Kaia hugged her cloak tightly around her and pressed on, hunger and thirst beginning to claw at her. Gus and Sunflash trailed along gamely, the thick-coated beasts unaffected by the harsh mountain clime.

Hand over hand, she climbed, with the events of her journey spinning through her head in a never-ending loop of faces—Layf hugging her goodbye, her father's swollen face, Mogen's grotesque grin, the rotting dead, Conrad pleading for mercy, Mackie's still face among fallen heroes, and the eyeless Xar. As the images swirled and eddied, another memory washed up from the last Triennial: *"Next time, I'll be strong enough,"* she had told Klaus.

Kaia flinched, scuffing her toes on a rock. How wrong she had been. At every turn, with every face and memory, she had let her loved ones down. She had proved herself to be nothing but a naïve, tender-footed young girl. Now, her whole world hung on this one last desperate hope, and it was no brighter than a match burning down to her fingers.

***

At last, Kaia reached the peak, just as the crimson half-sun sank into the soft gauzy clouds blanketing the land below her, taking its meager offering of warmth with it. She set her back against a boulder and Sunflash settled carefully beside her with a soft nicker, eager to offer her body heat. Kaia ran her scratched fingers through Sunflash's velvety fur and hugged Gus close to her.

Feet sore, belly empty, and mouth dry, she thought of Klaus with a pang, wondering how he had taken her sudden disappearance. He probably thought she had stormed off in a childish fit, but he would never have understood if she had tried to explain. She frowned. It had felt so right in that moment, but now, alone among the silent mountain peaks, doubt needled her.

As darkness deepened, she wondered wearily how much longer she could afford to spend on the mountain before looking for help elsewhere. She dreaded returning to the army empty-handed and explaining, shamefaced, that she could no longer conjure fire—that, for all practical purposes, she was no longer the Dragon Heir, but merely a gloomy harbinger of certain death and despair. Without her gift, the people of Okarria, from the greatest warrior to the smallest babe, would be slaughtered—or worse.

She straightened. No.

Remembering the calm image of Shava, she folded her dirty, scraped feet under her and sat tall. She rested her hands on her knees and took a deep breath in, closing her eyes to look within for the essence at her core. She may not be able to draw out the heat, but the yanaa still writhed beneath her skin.

She called to it, bending it to her will, and then, with a conscious effort, projected it out around her—an invisible beacon. With it, she sent out her most fervent prayer: *Odriel, guide me.*

***

The gray morning found Kaia exhausted, stiff, and half-mad with thirst. As the first fingers of light stretched from the horizon, the Dragon Heir let herself sag against her golden Dalteek. No hawk circled the sky, no words of wisdom had reached her ears. She was no legendary Dragon Heir of old. She was just a girl, cold and alone, and she had failed.

Kaia imagined the accusing eyes and acid tongues of Bram, Everard, and the people of Okarria—all thinking the same thing: if only she had been born six minutes later.

Bleak thoughts tearing through her mind, she stared blankly at the clear sky and saw what looked like a ruby thread weaving through it, like a strand of the sun that had been cut and now drifted to the earth. She blinked, trying to clear the hallucination from her vision. But as the sun ray dove towards her, she could make out its serpentine body, rivaling the girth of a Carceroc tree, ending in a massive head framed in a curly orange mane. Flight seemed impossible from its wingless body, but there it was, curling and drifting in the clear air as if swimming sedately through a mountain stream—a dragon.

The drake spat a small gush of fire harmlessly into the air, as if mocking her. Drawing closer at incredible speed, Kaia could see its yellow eyes and the ridge of spikes along its sinuous spine. Sweat prickled on her brow as the creature aimed straight for her.

She grabbed Gus and shifted her body in a futile effort to shield him from the glistening white teeth, but just as she thought it would swallow them in its cavernous jaws, it banked sharply to one side. As the giant body looped around the peak, the whoosh of air from its flight hit her like a gale, whipping her brown locks wildly behind her. Kaia felt as if time stopped as she watched ruby red scales flash past her eyes, inches from her nose. Entranced, she reached out to touch the dragon, her fingers just skimming the smooth, supple armor as it rippled by.

The tip of its feathered tail flicked by her as the great creature weaved joyously back up into the air. Kaia watched it, breathless as the dragon spiraled upward and shrank once again to a mysterious red line in the sky. When the thread had faded into a dot, Kaia realized her jaw hung open and snapped it shut with a click.

As a child, her mother had told her stories of the mischievous caelidrakes. Mysterious as the magi, they slumbered for hundreds of years at a time, waking for only a few hours every century to taste the air and dance across the sky. Her mother had said catching a glimpse of one was rumored to grace you with good health and fortune.

Kaia looked at Gus with wide eyes. "Did I dream that?"

Unperturbed by the passing of the inconceivable dragon, Gus sniffed curiously at a small turtle hiding among the rocks. *This does not smell like a turtle.*

Kaia sighed and lay back into Sunflash in a daze, replaying the image again and again in her mind as she tried to commit every detail to memory. She looked up at the ominous half circle of the sun and wondered how the world could at once be filled with so much wonder and so much terror at the same time.

It is a thought I often dwell upon myself.

Kaia sat up with a start. The thought had not been her own.

She glanced around wildly for her mind's intruder. "H-hello?"

Down here, my Heir. Kaia turned her eyes to the rocks. The only other living creature besides Sunflash and Gus was the small turtle.

She blinked, wondering if the altitude and deprivation had sent her over the edge of her sanity. "Um... you're the turtle?"

Would you prefer me to take another form?

"N-no that's fine." She looked down on the brown, craggy shell of the turtle. His tiny head only protruded slightly, but he looked up at her with dark, intelligent eyes. Kaia sat in shock for a moment, trying to convince herself that this turtle might indeed be the magnificent Odriel of the old legend.

You have called me. The deep voice resonating through her mind startled her out of her silence.

"Y-yes, Odriel, we need your help. Nifras is attacking, and the Time Heir is missing, and I've lost the dragon fire...." The words tumbled over each other in their haste to rush out. The turtle blinked languidly at her outburst.

I've gone mad. Kaia thought. *And now I'm ranting to a turtle.*

Allow me to reassure you. The thought had scarcely alighted on her mind before the turtle transformed in front of her eyes. He glowed blue as he grew in all directions.

Gus stepped away from the former turtle and fell back into a bow with a yip. *Not-turtle is big now!*

The glowing mass unfolded itself into a hulking brown bear. Kaia drew her knees to her chest, leaning back apprehensively from the towering beast.

To answer your question, you have not lost your gift.

Kaia's teeth chattered as she tried to calm the stormy ocean of feelings that threatened to capsize her. "Then why can't I call it forth anymore?" she said hesitantly, not wanting to sound impertinent.

Your fear stops you.

"But I'm not afraid!" she contradicted him before she could stop herself. The bear lay down on a great slab of speckled rock and calmly regarded her with his great brown eyes. She opened her mouth to say something else when her mind filled with vivid images like a sudden dream.

She saw the sun go dark and the forbidding shadow of the necromancer loom over an endless Lost army. She watched as the bony claws of the dead ripped apart Fiola, Everard, Shad, and Tekoa, one by one. She stood helplessly, unable to call out or run to them—unable to protect them. Finally, she watched Klaus step in front of her protectively before the dark demon god grabbed him at the throat. She beat desperately at Nifras' black boned legs as the life drained out of the struggling Shadow Heir. Finally, his limbs went still, and his open eyes stared blindly at nothing. With a deafening laugh, Nifras threw the Heir's limp body to the hungry army of the Lost. The dead tore at his flesh with rotting teeth and yellowed nails while Kaia could do nothing but look on in horror.

As Kaia's eyes refocused on the great bear and the reality before her, screams echoed across the mountain range. It took her a moment before she recognized the screams as her own. She clapped a hand on her mouth and looked up into the soft eyes of the bear.

Kaia. The deep voice vibrated through here, clearing the nightmare. **You must let go of your fear.**

"How?" she whispered, her voice trembling.

You must find the strength within you.

"But I can't save them!" she insisted.

Yes, you can. Odriel pressed the image of Kaia releasing the Dragon's Rage on Gyatan plain into her mind.

She hid her forehead with her palms. "That only happens when I lose control."

You are wrong, and that is why you cannot find your gift. You are looking for rage, but the greater power comes from love. He pushed the images of the limp bodies of her father and Klaus into her thoughts. **Try.**

Kaia attempted to focus, but thoughts of Nifras and massacre crowded her mind—fear and anger. The bear stood up onto his back paws, looming four feet above her head. Ever so gently, he reached out a massive paw and placed it on her shoulder. Tekoa's words echoed through her mind, *"If ever you need a light Kaia, just remember the one that burns within you never goes out."*

A rush of feeling stormed through her, driving out the icy terror that clung to her. Odriel's strength enveloped her like sturdy arms, shouldering her buried grief and steeling her against the weight of her doubts. She saw her father looking on proudly as she held fire for the first time, her face glowing with joy.

You have always had the power.

Her overcrowded thoughts fled in the face of the raw hope that flooded from Odriel to her, rushing through her veins like a river after a storm. Kaia locked eyes with the spirit guide as her chest swelled with pride and courage.

Odriel lifted his paw and eased himself back down onto the stone. **Now, think of love, and draw strength.**

Love, Kaia thought to herself, *no fear*. She thought of her family, her father, and then, to her shock, the image of Klaus came to her mind. She felt Klaus' arms around her, she saw his soft hazel eyes under his dark brows, imagined his teasing smile, and warmth filled her. The familiar heat rose within from her toes to the tips of her hair—the buzz brimming beneath her skin. She drank it in like a desert in a spring rain. She breathed deeply, savoring the sensation.

Then, with only a thought, an explosion of flames burst from the Dragon Heir's body.

A whirl of spinning fire cocooned her from head to toe, and tears sprang to Kaia's eyes as she laughed with relief—just before Gus barreled into her chest. The ragehound bathed her face with his tongue, and Kaia, still smiling, let the fire fade from her body. Had it really been so simple all along? She looked up gratefully at the monstrous bear, but her eye caught on the half-sun weakly glowing behind him. Her grin flattened into a hard line.

"What about Jago? Is he still alive?"

The bear followed her gaze to the bruised sun. **His soul has not crossed over.**

Kaia nodded solemnly, understanding the unsaid. Just because he had not crossed over, did not mean he was still alive—that's why they called them the Lost. Souls trapped by Nifras could not find their way to the other side.

"Odriel, what does Nifras want with us? Who is he?"

The bear sagged ever so slightly. His eyes seemed sad when the voice echoed in her mind again.

The demon's true name is Idriel. The thoughts halted for a brief second in her mind as the bear turned his great head to look out over the lush green forest stretching below them. **My brother.**

Kaia's eyes widened.

There are many lands, my dear Heir, and for each land, there is a spirit guide, my kin, who conducts souls from the world of the living to the world of the dead. My brother was dissatisfied with the confines of his own land. He saw himself and his people as superior—deserving of more. In his greed, he refused to let the souls depart for the afterlife, and sought out new worlds for his dead to conquer. Thus, began the great battle so many years ago. Now, he returns for revenge.

Kaia's brows knitted over her eyes, "But, how could a spirit guide be so evil?"

Odriel smiled at her as a parent might to a child. **Even I do not have all the answers. Wherever there is light, there is also shadow.** The bear turned towards the sun. **And now, my Heir, I must leave Okarria's light in your protection.**

"Wait, Odriel!" Kaia protested as the legendary being began to shift once again. His form glowed blue as he shrank and sprouted wings.

I have answered your questions, but walking this world exacts a steep toll. I must depart. Good luck, my dear Heir. Our people are depending on you.

Kaia brought her clenched fist to her heart in a silent salute as she watched an unassuming brown hawk take wing in front of her. Watching the legendary guardian spirit dissolve into the clouds, she thought of Klaus again, and a deep warmth suffused her. She let a small explosion of fire swirl around her fingers, feeling the untapped power crackle in her palm.

"Well, Gus." Kaia smiled as she stroked his shaggy fur, "Now, we turn south."

CHAPTER 22
SOUTHWARD

The setting sun bathed the mountain rocks in a vivid tangerine as Kaia picked her way down the slope, sliding on her backside over the steeper parts. Gus slipped down the loose rocks with little hops while Sunflash skipped down in the bounding, sure leaps of a mountain goat.

Kaia's breath condensed in smoky clouds as she felt for a sure foothold with her numb toes. Miraculously, she had only lost a day in the mountains, but if Klaus was pushing hard to the south, then she might not catch him. She knew the Deadlands was a week's ride to the southeast, but she would have to depend on town gossip to locate Everard and their small army. That is, if the southerners hadn't already fled north.

Step by careful step, she descended, while her mind wandered back to Klaus and his connection with her gift. The idea lightened and confused her at the same time, and fire wove between her fingers of its own accord.

Still, when Kaia thought of seeing Klaus again, her smile faltered. She hoped he didn't stay too angry with her for disappearing. After all, her intuition had served them well. Meeting Odriel had not only returned her gift, but her confidence also. She had held her vigil through the night, and yet this morning, she felt wholly restored, as if finally waking from a deep sleep.

As Kaia rounded a protruding boulder, a flash of black caught her eye from down the slope. She squinted, and the figure resolved into a cloaked rider cutting briskly across the mountainside below. The rider turned in his saddle, scanning the slope. With a start, she recognized Odriel's Tooth strapped to the saddle and the familiar movements of Klaus atop Stormshade, as if he'd been drawn by her thoughts.

Her stomach fluttered and knotted in turns. *He came for me.*

Gus barked, his tail wagging furiously beside her. *Our boy! Our boy is here!*

The Shadow Heir pulled to a sharp halt as he cast about for Gus' familiar yap.

Apprehension and excitement still warring within her, Kaia waved a hand. "Klaus!" She scrambled through the loose rocks on her chafed feet, with Sunflash leaping ahead and Gus following more slowly behind.

"Hey!" she called again, trying to stay upright as she tumbled down the mountain. "Klaus!" she yelled once more as she ran up to the elegant Stormshade. "You'll never guess—!"

She drew up short as her smiling eyes met Klaus' flinty glare. "Okay, now, don't be mad—"

"DON'T BE MAD?" Klaus roared, swinging down from Stormshade's back. "You run off in the middle of the night and tell me not to be mad? I've been tracking you through these mountains all night!"

Bristling, Kaia's grin fading. She took a step towards him. "Just let me explain—"

Klaus cut her off, waving his hand emphatically. "Without the dragon fire you could have been captured again, or even killed!"

Kaia raised her hands in exasperation. "Klaus—"

He whirled towards her, his face only inches from hers. "How is it you're constantly finding new ways to drive me crazy?"

Kaia softened as she noticed the worry etched around the Shadow Heir's eyes. Barely suppressing a smile, she lifted an empty palm between them. "It's just one of my gifts, I guess." With a *whoosh*, a perfect orb of flame spun in her palm.

Klaus' face slackened with shock as he gazed at the sphere. He looked back up at Kaia, relief lighting his features like the sun freed from the clouds. With a sudden laugh, he wrapped his arms around her, lifting her off her feet as he spun her around.

"You did it, Firefly!" he breathed, putting her down and releasing her. He looked to the sky as he ran both hands through his hair. "Thank Odriel."

"Well done, Guardian Dashul," Shadmundar purred from his usual place in the saddle bag.

Kaia beamed, her heart thrumming from Klaus' embrace. "I thought we agreed you should go south without me, Shad."

Klaus' retort was instant. "And *I* thought we agreed that no good has come of Heirs being separated."

"I was useless to you without my gift." Kaia turned her face away from him. "It was my problem to face, not yours."

Klaus grabbed her arm and squeezed it gently. "Fire or no, I could never just leave you out here on your own." His mouth curved into a wistful half-smile. "It's just you and me, after all."

Kaia returned his grin, her heart ablaze in her chest.

"I tried explaining that you needed space to find your way," Shad chimed in, obviously miffed. "But there was no talking to him."

Kaia absently scratched Gus' head as he leaned against her. "Well, I'm sure you'll both wish you had caught up earlier when I tell you what happened."

"Wait," Klaus turned to Stormshade and pulled her worn boots from a saddle bag. "I think you'll want these first."

The Dragon Heir laughed, a long ringing sound, as she shoved them on her battered feet.

The Heirs turned and walked down the rocky slope with Kaia's tale bubbling into the crisp air around them. The Shadow Heir and the cat listened raptly, drinking in every detail of her story of the caelidrake and the great spirit guide. When she finished her tale, she looked up at them expectantly. Klaus' eyes were unreadable, and Shad looked to the horizon reflectively.

"So, Nifras is a spirit guide as well," Shad murmured.

Klaus looked south. "And we still don't know what happened to Jago."

Kaia turned her eyes to the ground but said nothing.

Klaus nudged her. "We've been managing well enough without him though." He cocked an eyebrow. "But there does seem to be something different about you."

"I—"

Kaia's words died on her tongue. Beneath her feet, the world started to shake, and she grabbed Klaus' arm for balance as the ground rolled and rocks began to pound down the slope around them. The Heirs whirled towards the peak just as the cliff cracked away from the shoulder of the mountain, a slew of boulders tumbling towards them.

"RUN!" Kaia yelled over the first thunderous crashes of the darkening sky.

In seconds, the peak of the mountain came down around them. The Dalteek whinnied in panic as they hurdled down the slope, Gus close on their heels. The Heirs half-ran, half-stumbled after them.

"We won't be able to outrun it!" Klaus shouted over the clamor.

The earth beneath Kaia's feet convulsed, and she fell, slicing her back on the sharp rocks as she slid. She glanced behind her and gaped at the giant rocks bearing down on them in the near darkness. She scrambled to her feet just as Klaus grabbed her wrist and pushed her back down under a pathetically small outcropping. He dove beside her, narrowly avoiding a boulder rushing by. His breath came quick against her cheek as he pressed her up against the rock and covered their heads with his arms.

Their hearts raced against one another as the outcrop shuddered—rocks crashing up against their small shield, their momentum carrying them over and past it without crushing the two Heirs on the leeward side. She winced as the boulders grazed Klaus' hair and freed her hand to pull him closer to her under the rock shelf. Finally, a great shattering rent the air, and the crashing once again came to an end. The only sounds were the remnants of the landslide careening down the slope, like weak echoes of Nifras' thunder.

Kaia squeezed Klaus tight as she waited for the darkness to lift.

The sun will shine again. It will brighten. It will brighten. It will brighten. She thought to herself over and over.

At last, a faint glow lightened the sky, and she released a heaving sigh. Klaus lifted his head to peek over the outcrop for the last falling rocks.

He stood. "Earth below."

Kaia followed his gaze. "Oh no."

A gibbous shadow blotted out all but a golden sliver of a crescent sun. In the weak light, the sky had frozen in a perpetual dusk.

Klaus offered her a hand up. "We're running out of time."

Coming to her feet, Kaia's scanned the mountainside. "Wait, where's…" Her heart stammered as her head whipped around in a sudden panic.

Klaus put a hand on her shoulder. "Relax." He pointed down to a grove of trees where Gus and the Dalteek huddled together. "They're fine."

Breathing a sigh of relief, the Heirs jogged down to their mounts.

Hackles raised, Shad paused his pacing on Stormshade's back when he saw them. "Thank Odriel you're all right," he breathed. "The yanai barrier won't hold much longer." His whiskers trembled. "Mount up. We leave immediately."

***

For the next three days, they pushed their mounts and themselves as hard as they dared, making camp late and breaking it early with few rests in-between. Klaus, Kaia, and even Shad kept a worried eye on the sun's last shard, as if it might disappear if they looked away for even a second. As they rode south, clouds gathered about the mangled sun, and snowflakes drifted down onto the world.

After that, the cloud cover made it hard to tell the days apart from the nights. In the unnatural weather, the Heirs wrapped blankets around themselves beneath their cloaks, but the cold still bit through. On the fifth day, the steady snow grew into a blizzard, and Kaia woke from an uneasy doze in her saddle to a sheet of white swirling around them. She could barely see Gus wading through the snow right beneath Sunflash's belly.

"Klaus!" She tried to shake off the exhaustion that weighed on her eyelids. "Shad!"

"Here," a muffled voice called from close by.

The wind whipped wet flakes into Kaia's hood and collar as she squinted through the heavy snowfall. She could barely make out the silhouette of Dalteek and rider through the whiteout. She called flames to her palms to warm feeling back into her fingers and then brought her heated hands to her icy face. The numbness in her toes was harder to get rid of, but she curled them in her boots to make sure they still worked.

The voice rose above the wind again, and Kaia realized it must be Shad, cocooned in a spare shirt in his saddlebag. "We're still a day from the Deadlands, but we'll have to stop until the storm passes," he said with a sour feline growl. "I can't determine our direction of travel."

Kaia looked for shelter among the few trees that lined the road. "Stop where?"

"There's a big evergreen next to me that'll have do," Klaus said. "We can shelter in the lee of the trunk. I can't see anything else."

Kaia turned Sunflash to follow Stormshade off the left side of the road, the Dalteek lifting her hooves high to break through the snow. The base of the thick evergreen wasn't exactly dry, but the leeward side had only a thin layer of snow beneath it, and the thick branches held off the worst of the driving snow like a porous green roof.

The Shadow Heir dismounted and rubbed his hands together. "It's too wet to make a fire."

Kaia smirked halfheartedly as she climbed down from Sunflash's back. "Have a little faith, Shadow Heir." She waded over to the trunk. "Just find me something to burn."

Conjuring flame from her hands, she used the heat to dry off a small area underneath the thickest branches. Klaus broke off some of the smaller boughs and placed them at her feet. It took a minute or two, but Kaia's blaze soon dried them enough so that they caught fire and brightened their dim world.

The thick-coated Dalteek bedded down together on the edge of their little clearing, not daring to wander off into the storm. Gus shook the snow off his fur and curled up in a furry red ball as close as he dared to the crackling flames. Klaus leaned back against a tree trunk, holding his cloak close and shivering slightly.

Shad leapt from his perch atop Stormshade and padded over to Klaus. He paused for a moment; his ears pressed flat against his head in embarrassment. "It pains me to ask, but might I share your cloak?"

Without a word, Klaus opened his coat to let the cat settle into his lap before snapping it shut again over the two of them.

Kaia would have laughed but for the weariness that threatened to overtake her. She pinched the bridge of her nose, took a deep breath, and tried to ward off the siren-call of sleep.

"If you're looking for a place to rest, Shad and I could use another warm body over here." Klaus patted the bare earth beside him. "The Dragon Heir must be warmer than most, right?" he teased through chattering teeth.

Chuckling, Kaia leaned against the tree and sank down next to the Shadow

Heir. Klaus leaned his trembling form into hers, and Kaia threw her blanket over their legs. The toes of their worn boots practically touched their small campfire. Kaia's skin prickled at Klaus' closeness as she relaxed against him.

"Have I ever told you how glad I am that you can conjure fire?" he joked as he blew on his hands.

Kaia heated her palms with fire once again, letting it fade before reaching out to massage life into Klaus' icy fingers. "That must be a recent change of heart, because that's not what you used to say when we were small."

"Yes, but you were such a cocky little thing."

"I was not!" she protested, her teeth chattering despite herself.

"You were so." He adjusted his hood to keep the snow out. "Every day you wanted to fight."

"That's because you were always teasing me!"

"But I still tease you now."

"With the Lost and the necromancer running about… who has time to scrap with you anymore?"

Klaus fell silent for a moment as they watched the white curtain of snow fall and fizzle into their bustling fire. His fingers tightened around hers before she could withdraw them. "Things have changed a lot since those days. I never really thought it would come to this, and so quickly."

Kaia nodded. "A few moons ago all I wanted to do was go to the village dance with friends like a normal girl."

He grinned. "And now all you want is to save Okarria."

"I've danced, and I've made friends." Kaia closed her eyes and stifled a yawn. "So, defending the land is obviously next on the list." She turned her face into Klaus' shoulder to shield it from the stinging wind. "And what do you want?"

"I wish…" he began. "I wish I had more time. There's still so much of the world I haven't seen. I want to swim with the oceanfolk, tame a griffin, duel the fire spirits…."

Kaia peeked out at the millions of ice crystals swirling in the dark. It was hard to imagine such wondrous things when the world was frigid and black.

"But, it looks as though the world might freeze over before Nifras even gets here," he finished bitterly.

Kaia thought of Odriel and squeezed Klaus' hand, wishing she could share with him the same confidence the spirit guide had poured into her. "It's going to be ok, you know. We're going to defeat Nifras, the sun will shine whole again, and you can go do all of those things."

When Klaus turned to her, his eyes softened, but he did not smile. He opened his mouth to say something, but then closed it again and looked back at the fire. "I hope you're right, Firefly." He lowered his head to rest it against hers.

The dragon fire stirred restlessly within as the Shadow Heir leaned against her. She considered, wearily, that this might be their last chance to talk before reaching the Deadlands, but she couldn't sort her feelings into words. How could she explain how much he had meant to her in the past months?

The bond between them seemed palpable, so strong Kaia felt she could reach out and touch it—an unbreakable tie between two that shared a past, present, and future. Hopefully, it was a future that stretched past the next season. The fire blurred as Kaia's eyes slid shut. As she fell asleep, she imagined that the small blaze was the only warmth, the only light, in their frozen world.

She hoped she was wrong.

CHAPTER 23
IDRIEL

It seemed as if Kaia had scarcely closed her eyes before Nifras' great booming woke her. Under the black sky, the snow had stopped, but the earth's quaking caused the drifts to fall from the boughs of the evergreen. As the crashes resounded around them, Kaia summoned flames to her hand as she, Klaus, Shad, and the animals scrambled to escape the small avalanche in the dark.

Just as they clambered to their feet, a shattering cacophony like they had never heard before reverberated through the air, like the breaking of a thousand mirrors echoing through the night. An eerie silence fell over them like a heavy blanket.

But the sky did not brighten.

It only took a second for Kaia to realize what had happened. She looked at Klaus with wide eyes, then turned to Shad.

The cat's hair stood straight up from his body, and his black pupils dominated his normally luminous eyes. "We must fly."

They leapt onto the Dalteek and spurred them southward. Klaus urged Stormshade to a leaping gallop and Sunflash eagerly bounded after, as if she sensed the urgency of their cause. Kaia looked back to see Gus, in full sprint, already trailing behind.

He barked as he sprang through the snow after them. I'm coming. I'm coming.

She tugged Sunflash's reigns and called out to Klaus. "Klaus, I can't keep up at this speed, Gus won't make it."

Stormshade tossed her antlers impatiently as Klaus slowed the doe to a halt. Shad's eyes turned to the red shepherd, panting happily as he caught up to them.

I'm here. Why are we stopping?

"Firefly…" Klaus grappled for the words.

Kaia tilted her head as she waited.

"Kaia," Shad said, his voice rough with tenderness. "You must leave Gus behind."

The words didn't sink in. "What?"

"He won't be needed in the Deadlands," Shad went on.

"No." Kaia shook her head incredulously, looking from Klaus to Shad and back. "I can't just leave him here." Kaia illuminated the road around them, tears welling in her eyes. "Not in the freezing dark!"

Klaus ran a hand through his hair. "He'll be safer here than where we're going, Firefly."

Gus looked back and forth between them, tail wagging. I'm ready. Where to next?

Sunflash pawed the ground in agitation, urging them to hurry.

"Maybe we could take him to a village," Kaia protested, her voice catching.

Shad shook his head. "You know we haven't the time."

Kaia swiped at her eyes with a battered forearm, willing the nightmare away. They still had miles yet to run through the pitch black and ice to meet an undead army. An army she wanted nowhere near her beloved companion.

With a cry of frustration, Kaia bowed her head with clenched fists. She slid off Sunflash's back with trembling lips. She knew they didn't have time for her sentimentality, but Klaus and Shad said nothing as she knelt on the ground before the ragehound and wrapped her arms around his neck in a tight embrace.

She remembered the day he was born, almost four years ago—just a puff of wriggly red fur squeaking in the straw. No matter where their journey had taken them—haunted forests, dank cellars, bloody battlefields—he had been there, always happy, never complaining. Now, she had to leave him on his own in this sunless, unfamiliar land. With a sob, she released him and grabbed her blanket from her saddlebag, knotting it about Gus' neck like a cape. She knew it wouldn't stay on, but she could hardly bear the thought of him out here in the cold.

Klaus fidgeted restlessly atop Stormshade, haste and compassion warring within him. "I'm sure he'll be fine."

Kaia hugged Gus once more. "Stay safe, my friend," her voice wavered as tears spilled down her face. "I love you, Gussy."

Gus gave her face a lick and cocked his head, his tail still wagging blithely. Why are you sad, my girl?

Kaia wished Mackie were here to make Gus understand…wished Mackie were alive anywhere. She kissed Gus between his brown eyes. "I promise I'll find you."

With that, Kaia stood and turned to mount Sunflash. Without looking at Klaus or Shad, she spurred the Dalteek into a gallop with Stormshade following close behind. As they rode into the night, Kaia looked behind her to see Gus trailing them.

He barked uncertainly. *Wait, my girl! I'm coming! Wait for me.*

Kaia's loyal hound fell further and further behind, until at last, he was swallowed by the darkness.

***

The hooves of the Dalteek beat the ground like overzealous war drums as they raced south. They rode for hours, the Naerami beasts living up to their tireless reputation, but without the sun or stars, it was impossible to tell how much time had passed. The only light came from the lit branch that Klaus held in front of him and Kaia's own outstretched hand as she tried to illuminate their path. They passed only a few scattered villagers fleeing north in panic.

The pressing, suffocating need to rush south had dried Kaia's tears, and a nauseating dread roiled within her, consuming her thoughts. Were they too late? Would they find their allies already dead and Idriel's Lost free to suck the marrow from their world? She concentrated on Odriel to keep herself calm, pictured the glowing blue bear and imagined his calming voice in her mind. She had to believe they would win. *This is why I was born. My time is now.*

A familiar white ball of light in the distance disrupted her thoughts.

"Everard!" she cried, urging Sunflash even faster. As they crested a small hill, Kaia gasped, the breath stolen from her lungs. Ringing filled her ears, and her limbs went numb.

Idriel didn't have an army.

He had *ten* armies. A multitude. A legion that swallowed the landscape before her, illuminated by Everard's light.

A sea of black eyes in warped skeleton skulls covered the snow-coated desert. The red sand had already born these foes once before, centuries ago, and now it groaned under their mass once again. These Lost, no flesh on their gleaming white bones to speak of, clanked in their armor and rushed forward with disturbing agility—a heaving, twitching ocean of dead surging towards the beacon of yanaa.

Lurking behind their ranks, a great black dragon writhed and roared with malice. So unlike the elegant, joyful creature Kaia had witnessed on the mountainside, this dragon bristled with spikes, claws, and teeth. Great wings folded on its back, it loomed larger than two houses stacked on top of one another, with spines protruding from every scale. She could feel the emanation of sheer hate as it thrashed in orgiastic fury, whipping the host of Lost forward in an unstoppable killing wave. Idriel, brother to Odriel, had come to consume this world.

As she watched, the Okarrian army—no, their band of warriors, of allies, of friends—closed ranks further down the ridge, preparing to meet the flood of evil. Shad alighted from his saddle bag to the ground. There would be no place for the cursed cat down there. The ancient flames within Kaia roiled furiously at the sight of the tidal wave of Lost threatening to wash away Everard's small glow.

She turned to Klaus beside her, her voice sharp. "Kill Idriel. I'll take care of the rest."

Klaus' eyes locked with hers. "Kaia…" Still atop Stormshade, he leaned over to grasp her arm and pulled her to him. His lips met hers in a hard, searching kiss. Her warmth rose to meet his cold mouth as the dragon fire sparked and crackled within her. He softened as he pulled away, lingering for a moment they didn't have, letting their breath come and go together as one.

A first kiss that felt like a last.

His eyes brimmed with unspoken words as they locked on hers, his hazel irises swirling gold and gray in her fire's reflection—sparking facets she had never noticed before—overflowing with a longing kept long hidden behind dark lashes.

But they were out of time.

"Burn bright," he managed roughly, and then he was gone, galloping down the hill towards the black dragon.

Kaia stared for a moment where he had been, letting her electrifying emotions course through every inch of her body, stoking the scorching heat within her.

"Odriel's wings," she whispered.

With that, she turned Sunflash and thundered along the ridge to join Okarria's bravest. She resisted the urge to touch her mouth where the hot press of Klaus' lips lingered. As she remembered the sweet taste of him, her heart nearly burst with passion. With an effort, she shoved the jumble of desire to the back of her mind. She would see Klaus again and tell him how she felt. She had to believe it.

Kaia focused on Everard's beacon. She needed to reach the frontlines before Idriel's soldiers, or their warriors would be surrounded and overwhelmed. As she reached the rear of her army, she threw a great fireball into the air to announce her arrival. A thunderous cheer erupted as the soldiers parted to let her pass. Hands reached out to touch her boots and brush Sunflash's flanks for luck as they galloped to the front where Everard, Cressida, and Okoni awaited her.

"I hope you didn't worry too much," Kaia said breezily as she leapt from Sunflash's back.

Anger and relief struggled for control of Everard's countenance, but in the end, he only favored her with grimly pursed lips.

Cressida smiled and raised her sword in a salute. "We hunt together again."

She raised her voice loud enough for the frontlines to hear. "May the killing be swift!"

The warriors cheered her words, and Kaia turned to face their foe. The Lost were already almost in range. The ground thundered with their approach, and their keening filled the air.

She flashed a wolfish grin at the stern magus as the explosive heat surged through her body. "Any last words of advice?"

The magus sighed deeply. "I am over a thousand years old, and I am not the oldest being on this world by half." he paused as Idriel shook the sands with an ear-shattering roar. "How is it that the fate of Okarria has come to rest on the shoulders of a seventeen-year-old human child?"

"Actually, Everard." She walked out into the glistening white field. "I think I'm eighteen now." With that, she raised her hands in front of her, and in an instant, images of Layf, her mother, Gus, Tekoa, Fiola, and Klaus bloomed in her mind. She thought of Okarria—its marvelous creatures, brilliant mountains, and verdant forests. As the caged fire rampaged within, she set her hardened gaze on the army before her.

And exploded.

With a deafening BOOM, she unleashed the Dragon Rage.

A towering wall of flame billowed out in front of her with great reaching fingers. The snow evaporated before the roiling curtain of heat, steam billowing up to reveal the scarlet sand beneath. A searing shockwave blasted through the leading wave of Lost, incinerating them without a trace. The blast knocked back the second, third, and fourth rows, leaving them flaming in the sand.

For a moment, the battlefield silenced. Kaia looked back at her dazed allies with a smirk of satisfaction. When they saw her clear eyes and smiling face, they realized the rage had not consumed her and another raucous cheer, louder than the first, echoed across the bloodshot desert.

In their bolstered fervor, the army jostled to push forward while the enemy was down, but Everard and Cressida steadied them. It would not do to go rushing into the enemy's open arms. Kaia had killed hundreds and knocked down a thousand, but the other thousands already scrambled to step over their downed comrades and fill the empty spaces at the front.

Idriel bellowed again, and the Lost rushed forward even faster. Kaia would be able to keep those directly in front of her at bay, but the far left and right flanks were out of range. It wouldn't be long before they were surrounded. They had to stick together.

I just have to stall the attack and keep us alive long enough for Klaus to kill Idriel. Kill the puppeteer, and the marionettes will fall. She took a deep breath as she glanced at the massive dragon pacing behind his endless army, flashing its man-sized teeth and raking its claws through the sand. But how would Klaus be able to kill *that*?

As the dead army closed the distance with her own, Kaia released three successive explosions in an arc around her in an attempt to keep the horde from circling behind them. But where one skeleton disappeared, another three took its place. For every one that fell, five stampeded over it in their voracity. With one hand after the other, Kaia released successive streams of fire into the endless dead. The inferno coming easier to her hands than ever before—every blast totally in her control—she no longer had to fear her strength, no longer had to hold back.

But, despite the constant river of flame, the mob of dead circled, clashing with her army from the right and left. The sounds of battle cries—human, Dracour, and Maldibor rang in Kaia's ears. Cressida called for the warriors to hold formation. If they didn't stay together, they'd be swallowed.

Idriel lashed his tail and stomped the ground, urging his pawns forward with throaty growls and roars. For every explosive boom that erupted from Kaia's hands, the shadowy beast would answer with his own threatening bellow. It was difficult to believe that the monster could be kin to the small turtle Gus had found by the mountain lake.

Snow began to fall again as the battle raged. Kaia was grateful for the chill as her body overheated, her skin steaming and her heavy panting creating small clouds in the frosty air. As she dispatched the skeletal warriors in a burning bath, she noticed these Lost were different than Conrad's stock. Intelligence sparked in the bottomless eye sockets of these creatures, and they seemed to have a greater instinct for survival than the ones she had faced before.

Thankfully, her meager army rose to the task. Her comrades arranged themselves at her flanks and rear in a semicircle, clashing with the wings of Lost that managed to outflank Kaia's blaze. Idriel remained behind his army—whether fearful of Kaia's gift, suspicious of a hidden attack from Klaus, or just waiting for the right moment to strike, Kaia didn't know.

After an hour, her shoulders drooped, and sweat stung her eyes. *Hurry Klaus! I don't know how much longer we can hold out.*

She screamed a hoarse battle cry, and another swirling inferno of flame exploded from her hands to rip a hole in the shadowy mass before her. Spreading her arms wide, she launched two fireballs at the Lost trying to move around her range. She sucked air greedily as she tried to regain her breath and squinted in the dim light at the sinuous dragon. He had stopped his pacing and seemed distracted now, thrashing every which way and keeping his spiky head trained to the ground.

"Everard!" she called back behind her. "Klaus is engaging Nifras!"

The great magus strode purposefully to stand behind her. His dark eyes surveyed the scene tensely. "He is having difficulty."

"What?" Kaia's voice pitched with anxiety. How could the magus even see that far? "If Kallar could do it, Klaus can too!"

"He cannot fend off the dead and battle the demon at the same time. They will overwhelm him. You need to get closer to distract the horde."

"I *am* distracting the horde!" she snapped. *In Odriel's name, what else can I do?*

Everard's dark eyes locked on hers. "You have to get closer."

"And leave the army?"

"Kaia," Everard said sharply. "Every soul in this army knew they would die here. As will Klaus. As will you." Kaia opened her mouth to protest, but Everard continued before she could object. "What is important is that the demon dies here, as well. If he dies, there is still a chance for this land. The living will be able to deal with the remaining dead."

Kaia shook her head in disbelief, shock numbing her feelings as the magus spoke. *So, there was never hope after all?*

She heard the voice of a child escape her mouth. "E- everyone is going to die?"

Everard rested a heavy hand on her shoulder. "Okarria will survive. Your family will survive. The future will survive. You must do this for them, Guardian Dashul."

Kaia looked at the ground for a moment and took a deep breath. There was hope—but not for her, not for Klaus. This was her destiny. She looked up into Everard's solemn countenance and nodded.

"I'll see you on the other side, magus."

And with that, she ran into the sea of dead.

CHAPTER 24
IDRIEL'S ACE

Kaia rushed headlong into the ranks of the Lost...and was immediately swamped. Drawn to her power, they dashed towards her, reaching out with long fingernails and gnashing yellow teeth. She encased herself in flames and every few steps, she'd permit the nimbus to burst outward in a globe of destruction—at once clearing her path and protecting her from the encroaching horde.

It was exhausting, but the danger lent Kaia strength. With the air choked with death, Kaia became hyperaware of the life humming within her. She was fighting not only for her survival but for the survival of Okarria. As Kaia rushed across the dark field, the snow swirled, and the unending waves of dead crashed into her fiery shield again and again, like a surreal nightmare she might awake from at any moment, with Layf calling her for breakfast.

As she sent another fiery pulse through the swarming corpses, Idriel reared up before her, a typhoon of yanaa and fury. He had abandoned his dragon body and glowed green as he shape-shifted from one form to another. First a lion, then an eagle, a wolf, now a griffin. Again and again, he morphed as he exchanged blows with some unknown enemy, his hate too consuming or his pride too great to consider retreat. Idriel viciously clawed and snapped at the air, his yellow eyes darting from side to side.

If there's a match for a Shadow Heir with a blessed sword, this is it.

And if that challenge wasn't enough for Klaus, Idriel's Lost clustered around their master, trying to seek out the invisible foe. Now, Kaia understood Everard's words. With scores of enemies surrounding his target, Klaus had no room to move. Without space, they would find him soon. It was up to her to draw them away. It was the duty of the Dragon Heir. She smiled to herself. Time to burn bright.

Pushing back her creeping fatigue, she built the heat within her, turning away from Idriel. She glanced briefly at their struggling army, now thousands of bodies away from her. Whatever battle plan Everard had designed, it had evaporated like the snow. The Lost had broken through their thin lines, and now every man, beast, and Dracour faced a desperate fight for survival. Kaia's heart swelled on their behalf as she thought of those brave warriors walking into a battle with no hope of returning.

Just like the first Heirs.

But like the Heirs, these people, too, deserved to return to their families. As she watched through her swirling flame, a dozen more fell, and the fire in Kaia boiled and screamed.

I don't care what Everard says. I can protect them. They can survive.

With an earsplitting blast, Kaia erupted like an avenging volcano, flames shooting into the dark sky in a monstrous column of fire that lit the faces of all those warring in the snow-spotted desert. Then, it fell back to earth in a flood of magma that washed over the aberrations in an all-consuming tidal wave.

A thousand unholy voices wailed in one despairing scream as Kaia fell to her knees in exhaustion. She looked back towards Idriel to see that her spectacle had indeed gotten his attention. The glowing griffin shrieked as its minions abandoned their spirit guide to race towards the Dragon Heir—the real threat. Or so they thought. In Idriel's moment of distraction, a silent shadow darted behind him and thrust his blade through the demon's chest. Kaia's heart soared.

Then, something familiar caught her attention from the corner of her eye.

A cornflower luminescence billowed only paces from where the great Idriel writhed in his death throes. *Another spirit guide?* Panic clutched Kaia's throat. She craned her neck to spy the new source of yanaa, releasing another globe of flame to cut through the mobbing Lost.

She had seen this azure aura before. But where?

Then it hit her.

Jago.

No, her brain wasn't working correctly. Jago? Jago was here? As she considered it, Kaia's heart leapt. No wonder Klaus had been able to survive Idriel's onslaught. Jago was healing him! And he could heal her, too. He could restore her yanaa, she could wipe out the rest of the Lost army, and then everyone would be able to go home.

With a glowing grin and renewed hope, Kaia rushed towards him. He was clearly silhouetted within a sphere of glowing blue light, and she grinned as she blazed through the last few bodies standing between them. With nearly unbearable anticipation, she stepped into his light....

...and her heart nearly stopped beating. The smile died on her face, and all hope shriveled. This was not the dark-skinned, handsome youth of her childhood. Jago—or what used to be Jago—swayed before her with one arm missing, skin torn, bones poking through fingers and elbows, and a bloody, gaping hole instead of a stomach.

The Lost wore Jago's tattered body like an ill-fitting costume with a mask-like grin on his face. The rotting miasma of death overpowered Kaia, and she collapsed in the sand, gagging uncontrollably. She gasped as the horror dawned on her. Jago was healing Idriel, fueling his transformations, filling him with unnatural stamina. She heard a squawking from behind her and looked to see the griffin, whole and unharmed once again, rise into the air, searching for prey.

"No," she whispered. She looked back into Jago's black pit eyes. "How could you!" she screamed—not entirely sure if she screamed at Jago or the darkness that corrupted him. She staggered to her feet and sent a gush of fire at the Lost once again clambering to surround her.

Kaia knew what she had to do. As long as Jago's head was attached to his body, Idriel would be able to endlessly shift, never tiring, never dying. Klaus wouldn't have a chance. Kaia drew her sword and stepped towards her childhood friend and mentor—the third of their trio, the sweet one, the good one. Her heart screamed in despair, as if it, too, burned alive. She lifted her sword, but as she gazed at Jago, she saw sadness in the pits of his eyes—pain.

She cringed at the sight of it. *It's too late. I can't save him.* She tried to shake off the heartsickness that roiled through her. *Why did it have to be Jago?*

Then, to Kaia's horror, the Time Heir opened his misshapen mouth and spoke. "Kai," he mumbled, his dead lips struggling to form the words. "Take— care—fami—" As the words of resignation escaped him, a single, impossible tear ran down his ravaged cheek.

Kaia's mouth hung open. Somehow, Jago was still trapped in there, fighting the darkness. And that made it all the worse.

She nodded. "I will." Then, with the dead circling her once again, Kaia couldn't stall anymore. "I'm sorry, Jago," She swallowed a sob as she stepped forward. "May Odriel guide you."

A green wash of yanaa flowed over Jago, and his jaws unhinged, unleashing a wrathful screech as Idriel reclaimed his puppet and forced him towards Kaia on shambling legs.

The Dragon Heir raised her sword. "Odriel, bless my blade!" With a mighty stroke, she cleaved through Jago's neck with a single blow. His head rolled from his shoulders, and his body fell to the side—lifeless and free of Idriel's grasp—as it was meant to be.

With another anguished yell, Kaia whirled and attacked the mob of Lost around her with wild, erratic bursts of fire. Her fatigue had caught up with her now, and she could no longer control her flames as they burst forth weakly. She fought blindly as maddening, despairing thoughts clawed at her mind, weariness sapping her hope.

She stole a glance at the demon Idriel, the source of all her pain and loss, and she stopped her desperate thrashing. Her mind buzzed with alarm...*the Shadow Heir was no longer invisible.*

A bleeding and spent Klaus flickered in and out of sight before an enormous black serpent, their epic match now one-sided. Kaia gasped as the dripping fangs of the snake struck impossibly fast at the weary warrior. Klaus managed to deflect the first strike with his blade, and dove to the side to avoid the second. He wasn't even trying to use his gift anymore.

Klaus' gaze flicked to meet hers, and in his hazel eyes, exhausted as they were, gleamed life and hope. They weren't done fighting yet.

White-hot fire blazed in a searing globe around Kaia, and she charged Idriel with her sword raised high. As she ran, she let her encasing flames grow larger and larger until they swirled around her with cyclonic fury. With her free hand, she hurled a fireball at the demon, only to see it swatted away like a fly. Undeterred, Kaia rushed onward, desperate to keep Idriel's attention. The Shadow Heir could no longer hide; visible, he had no chance of surviving.

Then it came to her. "Klaus, shield your eyes!"

The Shadow Heir threw an arm over his face as a bright flash of fire erupted from Kaia's hands towards the diamond head of the snake. Once again, Idriel absorbed the blow with little effect, but Kaia had not aimed to harm the demon this time. Kaia sustained the flickering flames as long as she could before allowing them to extinguish. The world once again plunged into shadow, illuminated only by Everard's dim light half a battlefield away.

Kaia let her arms fall heavily to her sides as she glanced anxiously up at the serpent, spots dotting her vision. Idriel seemed to be affected as well. He whipped his head around, trying to refocus his own narrow eyes.

"NOW!" she yelled.

Idriel whipped his head toward her voice, trying to find her with his blinded yellow eyes. A distant awareness that she should get away from the shapeshifter tickled Kaia's sluggish mind, but her heavy legs remained rooted in place. She caught a glimpse of movement as a quick shadow darted behind the snake. Kaia looked back up at the serpent, and its cold eyes locked on her at last. It bared its man-sized fangs and reared high above her.

Kaia threw up her hands as Idriel lunged.

Then a bloodcurdling screech escaped its gaping jaws, splitting the air and shaking the ground. Klaus straddled the back of the serpent, stabbing again and again. The snake coiled and writhed under the obsidian steel. Not daring to hope, Kaia watched numbly, but there was no Jago to heal Idriel this time. The horrific keening ceased as the lifeblood gushed out of the torn adder, and its struggle stilled.

Klaus stepped away from the steaming carcass, but Kaia refused to take her eyes off the demon. Idriel, who had been responsible for the deaths of so many, would not escape this time. His hateful topaz eyes locked on hers and to Kaia's shock, a hissing voice emerged from the snake's gaping jaws.

"I may be dying," it choked. "But my children will avenge me."

In his final act, Idriel whipped its gigantic tail towards Kaia and knocked her flying into the air. She fell heavily on her side in the sand with a sickening crunch. Pain shot through her ribcage and black spotted her vision as she tried to get her bearings.

The blow from Idriel's tail had knocked her into the middle of the milling ranks of Lost. Still animated by evil and hungry for yanaa, they encircled her. Smelling blood, they closed in.

Kaia instinctively brought flames to her hands, but no more than a lantern's glow lighted her fingertips. Ignoring the pain that lanced through her ribs, she unsheathed her sword in a sweeping slash that decapitated the closest Lost. Fighting for survival, she whirled and hacked off the eager outstretched arms of two more skeletal warriors pawing at her back, but there were far too many attackers. She looked desperately for help, but she could barely even see the remaining knot of their army hidden among the dead. Fifty paces to her right, Klaus battled towards her. So far, so far away.

At least they still have a chance.

Kaia slashed frantically as the Lost, unaware or uncaring of their leader's demise, remorselessly pressed forward.

Suddenly, she felt a warmth on her skin that had nothing to do with her gift. She looked to the sky and saw the dark veil lifting. As Kaia's movements became slower and slower, the sun showed its round beaming face, shining down on all of them in effulgent glory.

At least I got to see the sun one last time. At least my world is safe.

Ignorant of this newfound peace, the howling horde continued its relentless, mindless attack. Fingers, nails, and swords clawed her now, faster than she could beat them away. Overwhelmed by the madness and dizzy with exhaustion, Kaia thought she saw Mogens' leer among the onslaught. But with another swipe of her blade, the apparition vanished in the tidal wave of dead crashing against her.

Klaus screamed her name as he hacked at the Lost, but he was no closer than before. She gave him the slightest curve of a delirious smile. *You've always been the strong one.*

Swinging clumsily at the demons and all reserves of yanaa drained, she felt a pang of regret that she wouldn't be able to see all the wonderful things Klaus had spoken of. She wouldn't even be able to look after Jago's family like she promised, but she had done her duty as the Dragon Heir, and soon she would be joining her father. She slashed at a hand tearing at her hair. But the weariness had soaked into her bones. She was just so tired....

Then, out of the corner of her eye, Kaia glimpsed a flash. On the hill to the north, a single rider raced down towards them and smashed directly into the throng of Lost. The silver shield crashed into the dead ahead of him as he cut a path through the ranks. A cheer echoed across the plain as the rider rode into their midst.

Her arms too sluggish to defend herself, the dead tore at her flesh in earnest now. As the pain threatened to overcome her, Klaus yelled her name in despair. He slashed through the Lost in a last frantic bid to reach her, but he wasn't going to make it. She gave him one final smile just as her bright world once more went black.

CHAPTER 25
PROMISES

Kaia dreamed she floated above the battlefield, as if watching from a bird's sharp eyes as her body disappeared under a mass of howling Lost.

Klaus howled as the Lost swarmed over her. "KAIA!" he roared, sword cleaving the air with relentless fury, the Lost tumbling before him.

Further away, a silver coated Dorinar galloped across the battlefield in a wide circle on a heaving horse. As he cut through the Lost, they turned their hungry eyes towards this fresh source of yanaa. Without their brutal Master, the shining sphere drew them like bees to honey, and they abandoned her still form, the desperate Shadow Heir, and their tired army. Like a flock of migrating birds, they turned as one and followed the shining beacon into the heart of the Deadlands.

Breaking through the straggling Lost, the Shadow Heir knelt on the ground and pulled her torn body into his lap. Silent tears traced through the blood and grime on his cheeks as he cradled her still form to his chest. "I'm sorry." He swallowed a sob. "I was supposed to save you this time."

Klaus looked across the sand, watching as the dead trailed into the desert and the Okarrian army dispatched the remaining strays. "It's over now, Firefly, but this isn't right." He looked at the full, burning sun above them. "I would rather fight beside you in the darkness than live without you in the sun." His voice trembled as he smoothed her bloodied hair. "Kaia, you can't go off without me." His gritty tears splashed on her forehead. "I'm lost without you."

A sizzling sound drew his eye to her arm. There, a silver armlet glowed red as it burned through her bloody sleeve. The smell of scorched flesh wafted into the air as the whimsical pattern of the metal branded her skin. With a small crack, the armlet broke in two, revealing the scarred flesh beneath.

The dream faded as a searing pain ripped through Kaia's arm. Her eyes shot open as she gasped for air and found herself looking straight into Klaus' tear-stained faced.

Dazed, nauseous, and skin crawling with a maddening itch, she turned her head aside as a bout of coughs racked her body. Still disoriented, she sucked in long breaths of air and tried to get her bearings.

She lay in Klaus' lap, but the Lost were nowhere to be seen. Across the field, Dalteek trotted towards them from the exhausted army, but her bleary eyes couldn't focus on the riders.

"Firefly" Klaus squeezed her to him. "You're alive!"

Her body still screaming with agony, she turned to him with a grimace, her voice hoarse. "Is that why I'm in so much pain?"

"But how?" Klaus scanned her bloodied body. She bled from uncounted gashes, but he couldn't see any mortal wounds. "You weren't breathing, I'm sure of it."

Kaia looked down at the scarred flesh on her arm to where Dorinar's broken armlet lay on the ground. "That magus." She closed her eyes. "Dorn said the silver had 'mild restorative properties.'"

As the words left her tongue, the Heirs broke into identical, ridiculous smiles. Klaus burst into relieved laughter, and a giggle bubbled out of Kaia before she could contain it. She smothered a groan as the mirth shook her broken body.

Klaus wiped the tears of joy and grief from his face, gathered her gently in his arms and stood up, still cradling her to his chest.

"Tears?" Kaia traced a finger across his grizzled cheek. "I thought the Shadow Heir gave nothing away."

In answer, Klaus bowed his head and brushed his mouth against hers. "I'll give anything to you, Firefly." He murmured, kissing her with smiling lips. "Only for you."

Just before blackness consumed Kaia once again, she saw a plain brown hawk circling above them.

***

The next day, the sun dawned hot and bright on the Deadlands. For the third time that year, Kaia, covered in bandages and splints, stood among the survivors as they gathered to honor the dead. Okarria had paid dearly for the victory. Of the six hundred warriors that had gathered for the battle, only eighty-eight survived: thirty-seven men, eleven Maldibor, thirty-eight Dracours, and two Heirs. Though Kaia was aggrieved to find Cressida and Okoni among the dead, she sent a prayer of thanks to Odriel for keeping Bram and Tekoa safe.

Kaia stood with the other survivors gathered in front of the fresh graves, as they named the dead once again. She felt stiff in the casts that covered her from head to toe and woozy from the medicine Fiola had forced down on her. The only thing keeping her upright was Klaus' arm wrapped firmly around her waist. Kaia absently reached out to stroke Gus' big ears, only to remember for the tenth time that day that his spot at her side was empty. It was a loss she just couldn't seem to absorb. She fought back against the tears welling in her eyes and tried to focus for a few more minutes.

She had one last task to accomplish before she could sleep. After the tribes honored their fallen, Kaia and Klaus stepped forward to the small pyre resting in the desert sand with Jago's remains hidden amidst the kindling. Solemnly, Kaia extended a hand and a fiery jet erupted to engulf the Time Heir in flames. She watched the blaze crackle to life before turning to face the warriors. Still leaning heavily on Klaus, she began to speak—old words her father had read at her bedside. From *The Heirs' Way*, Chapter 4, Passage 21:

The war is over but many will remain,
They have fallen but will not be forgot,
Though we leave them behind, we feel their pain,
With their lives, their sacrifice, peace was bought.

The Time Heir, too, travels to the unknown,
Only his legacy is left behind,
But go we must, once the spirit has flown,
May Odriel grace us with peace of mind.

The silence that followed lingered until only ashes remained.

***

As the sun blazed triumphantly overhead in the azure sky, Kaia sat next to Klaus on the back of the packed supply wagon and allowed Fiola to fuss over them. Felix, Mackie's daycoon, chattered unintelligibly at them from his perch on the old woman's shoulder while Shad stretched out on the driver's bench. As they gazed over the barren desert, a cloud of dust appeared in the distance. Kaia squinted in the bright sun, and the dust cloud resolved into the magus Dorinar, riding towards them.

Wobbling ever so slightly, Kaia stood up in the wagon bed. "So it was Dorinar," she murmured. "Who'd have guessed that?"

The magus rode up to them on the stocky gelding Kaia had seen in his barn. He glared at Kaia under his tangled mop of hair.

"I see you managed to break the priceless artifact I entrusted to you." He blew his unruly curls out of his eyes. "But I'm glad that you remembered to wear it."

This time Kaia could see through the pretend outrage to the well of concern that lay beneath. She bowed as deeply as her bandages would allow. "My greatest thanks, Dorinar. We are all in your debt."

"But you could've come more quickly," Shad growled as he padded up behind them on the wagon bed.

"It takes time to cast a shielding spell of that magnitude!" the magus huffed. "Ingredients must be gathered! Precise calculations must be conducted! Besides,"—he wagged a finger at them—" I haven't cast that spell in thousands of years. You should be grateful that I document my work."

Kaia's eyebrows knitted as she sat back down, a flash of Mogens' twisted smile still prickling her mind. "But where are the dead now, Dorinar?"

The magus looked out into the desert. "Unfortunately, I could only draw them away. It will be up to you to hunt them down." He waved a dismissive hand. "But that is your duty after all." With that, he clicked his tongue for the horse to move on.

"Once you recover," Fiola added firmly, moving to check the bandage on her leg.

"Dorinar," Klaus called after the retreating magus, "What made you change your mind?"

Dorinar paused. "Raeza would have loved to write about this." He sighed. "Even in memory, she is a force to be reckoned with."

"You should travel back with us, Dory," Fiola offered, her amber eyes twinkling. Felix chirped in agreement.

The magus made a sound of disgust, "I would rather walk than be forced to listen to your inane human chatter for days on end."

The Heirs rolled their eyes at each other. "Safe travels till our next visit then," Klaus jibed, winking at Kaia.

"I've told you I do *not* allow visitors!" Dorinar shrieked. "Next time, go barge into someone else's cottage." Still grumbling to himself about the absurdity of humans, Dorn urged his sturdy horse into a trot and rode northeast out of the desert.

Klaus drummed his fingers on the wagon. "It's odd to think that Nifras is really gone."

Kaia only nodded as she watched Everard and Bram walk towards them. The smoke billowed from the burning bodies of Idriel and his dead army behind them. The remnants of their allies had already departed, and she had been sad to see them go. The departure of the Maldibor had especially wrung her heart. Thirty-six of the brave warriors had left their home in the shadow of the mountains, and only eleven would return. Her only consolation had been Tekoa's assurances they would meet again in gladder times. She knew better than to doubt her shaggy friend.

"Indeed," Fiola agreed as she finished re-bandaging Kaia's leg and reached out to grasp Everard's hand with a smile. "We can all return home with the sun on our faces."

Everard wagged a stern finger at them. "Just until you recover." He looked from Kaia to Klaus as he mounted his sorrel Dalteek. "There is still much work to be done here."

"There always is," added Shadmundar in a bored tone as he leapt into the front of the wagon once again.

Covered in bandages himself, Bram leaned against the wagon next to Kaia and rapped his knuckles against the wood. "Kai," he didn't meet her eyes. "I—I just want to say that I was wrong." He looked up at her. Aged with sorrow and battle, he looked years older than he had at the Spring Festival. He resembled their father so closely now, Kaia almost felt she was talking with a ghost. He reached out and took her hand. "You were always meant to be the Dragon Heir."

Kaia slid down from the wagon and pulled her brother into a fierce hug. "When I need courage," she whispered. "I think of you."

Everard nodded at them. "Tam would've been proud."

Bram pulled away, looking from Kaia to Everard to Klaus. "I know I'm not an Heir, but perhaps I could help with all the..." He waved at the black smoke curling into the desert wind. "Work."

Klaus leaned over and gripped his shoulder with a grin. "Of course. We could always use another sharp blade."

Fiola smiled over her shoulder as she climbed into the driver's bench next to Shad. "So much to do and still so young." She jerked a thumb. "You best get on the cart so you can get started."

With his broad hands around her waist, Bram helped Kaia back to her place next to Klaus before he mounted his tall tan stallion. Fiola clicked her tongue to urge the wagon mules along, with Sunflash and Stormshade following as loyally as hounds.

Out of habit, Kaia searched for Gus to make sure he was coming before she caught herself once again. He wasn't there.

"I still have to look for Gus." She looked to Everard wearily. "And I need to visit Jago's family on the way back. To tell them what happened," Kaia closed her eyes with a grimace as she recalled Jago's last heartbreaking moments—another scene that would be seared in her memory forever. "Then, I have to face my mother." Her voice was barely above a whisper. "How am I going to face them?"

Klaus pulled her closer. "Not alone."

She looked up at him. "You'd do that?"

The Shadow Heir drew back so he could meet her eyes, and took her hand in his, speaking low so only she could hear. "Kaia, I know you're grieving the fallen, but all I can think about is what we've been gifted. When we parted on the hill, I didn't think we'd ever see each other again." He looked at their linked hands and gently rubbed his calloused thumb across her skin. "But when I held your still body, out there on the sand… I couldn't imagine my future without you." He grinned. "Now, here you are, my walking miracle, and I cannot help but smile."

A rogue tear crept down Kaia's cheek as a glowing smile spread across her face. Klaus reached out a hand and brushed the tear away. "So yes, if you'll have me, I'll stay right here next to you, and we can face those things together."

Beaming, she grabbed a handful of Klaus' shirt and gently tugged him into a soft kiss. She pulled away slowly, her eyes twinkling with mischief. "Well, I guess I'll have you."

Klaus rolled his eyes with a smile. "Aren't you generous today? That blow to the head must have really gotten to you."

"But you'll have to keep up with me," she said in mock seriousness. "I plan to see the world."

"Ha," he scoffed. "I could catch you even if you had a week's head start."

"If I wasn't smothered in bandages, I would leave you in the dust."

"Is that your excuse today?"

"Just wait till the spring!"

Shad shook his head with a soft chuckle as the Heirs continued their bickering, and Bram rolled his eyes. Fiola exchanged a glance with Everard. The wisp of a smile, as rare as a lily in winter, ghosted across the magus' face.

As Kaia laughed and joked with the gentle sun warm on her face, she offered one last silent prayer of thanks. The world was safe, and they were free to be young once again.

CHAPTER 26
HOME

The sun glowed orange as it dipped below the horizon on the Summerbanks Snowmelt Festival. Butterflies drifted about, chasing the blue petals of the Naerami star blooms that swirled thickly through the fragrant mountain air. Kaia stood among the bustling crowds of townsfolk and watched the newly turned seventeen-year-olds of the town undergoing the coming-of-age ritual. Fiola, being a war hero, had been given the honor this year of calling out the names. Felix peeked out from behind her slim leg on the wooden stage.

Kaia stretched and fingered the strange scar that ringed her upper arm. Her body had taken months to heal, and it felt delightful to finally be free of bandages and splints. Fiola had coaxed Kaia into a fine violet dress, and she watched with distant curiosity as smiling boys and girls, dressed in their finest clothes, stepped forward onto the small stage.

Had it only been a year ago that she had snuck into town to see this very event? The crowd erupted in cheers as Fiola presented each youth to the village as a new adult. A lilting tune played and the tempting aroma of sweets and bread mixed in the air. The distant bark of an excited dog made Kaia's heart clench, blowing the sails of her thoughts back to the autumn's end.

She thought of Jago's widow squeezing their tiny daughter tight as the Heirs told her of her husband's fate. She thought of searching their route endlessly for Gus, calling for him for days. Her yell had sounded no louder than a whisper when Klaus finally convinced her to travel homeward. Even now, when she reached for the missing dog at her side, she still pictured him wandering, lost, and waiting for her to return for him.

She thought about her mother's open arms and relieved face when she and Bram had walked in the door. Of Layf and Eleni's gasping sobs as they tackled her in a hug. And of more tears, as they had gathered around the fire to remember Tam. Through it all, Klaus had been by her side, his fingers locked with hers as she choked out their story. Seeing Layf and her family again had been a salve, and after months of wandering, the familiar blusheep farm of her childhood had been a welcome change.

But, once Klaus left to visit his own home, the house felt too large. In Bram's silence, she knew he felt it too. They were not the children they had been when they left. She found herself sorely missing Shad, Fiola, and Klaus—realizing they had become a second family to her. When the early lilacs bloomed, Layf and Eleni laughed and played with their friends while her mother threw herself back into farm work. Kaia's gaze found Bram's, and a shared understanding passed from one to the other and back. Arimoke could no longer hold them.

Finally, she thought about Klaus. They had parted with a long embrace and the promise to meet at Fiola's cottage on the first day of spring, but it had been almost a week, and the Shadow Heir had not showed. Kaia alternatively worried that something had happened to him or that perhaps he had forgotten his promise.

She pushed the worry from her mind as Fiola finished calling the names of the town youths and announced the official start of the annual Snowmelt festival to the cheering crowd. The old woman looked brilliant in her shimmering blue dress. Fiola had offered to formally introduce Kaia to the town as the Dragon Heir, blessed protector of Okarria, but she had declined. She wanted only to enjoy the festival as any normal villager might—to be a part of the spectacle she had only ever been able to gaze upon from afar.

Another thundering shout went up from the crowd as Fiola called for the first dance of the year, and the musicians struck up a cheerful tune. By tradition, no one could dance until all the honored youths found partners. In Kaia's fantasies as a girl, she had always dreamed she was picked first. How innocent she had been…. Her eyes glazed wistfully for a moment before she shook it away with a toss of her head.

When Kaia looked up again, dancers were already whirling around the town square. Her eyes searched for Fiola, and she laughed aloud when she spotted the old woman. Her face lit with a luminous smile, she swirled around the stage with none other than Everard, dressed in a fine indigo dress robe. *Skies above, that crotchety old magus never ceases to amaze.* With another laugh, Kaia watched Everard twirl and dip Fiola, while nearby Bram bowed to a pretty brunette. She even spotted Shad observing the celebration from a low rooftop.

Kaia absently rubbed at a loose hair tickling her earlobe as she watched the juggler toss torches into the air to the awe of the crowd. In a single deft movement, he leapt onto the back of the chair, balancing carefully while he spun the burning brands above him. Kaia clapped appreciatively with the rest of the spectators before scratching at the back of her arm where something brushed up against it. When she felt the brush on her neck, she suppressed a smile, and her eyes glanced right and left suspiciously. Listening for a moment, she reached out into the air and closed her fingers around a handful of invisible shirt.

"You're late," she admonished, smiling.

With a chuckle, the Shadow Heir appeared before her. Like Everard, he too was dressed in fine clothes. He wore a sharp black tunic over a white shirt, with a long black coat and black breeches. His jaw was smooth, and it looked like he had at least tried to tame his bristly hair. The sight of him took her breath away.

Seeing her surprise, Klaus smiled. "Do I look that good?"

Kaia recovered with a smirk and crossed her arms. "I'm just surprised you're clean, is all."

"Well, I did hear the Dragon Heir was coming to this festival, and they say she practically glows with beauty." He leaned in conspiratorially. "Do you think you could help me find her?"

Kaia rolled her eyes and moved to walk away, but Klaus caught her hand and drew her back. "Oh, here she is. Right next to me all along." With a smile, he pulled her into a quiet side street. He leaned against a wall next to the inn's stables and brought her close for a kiss of lost time. The warmth of his body pressed against her as his mouth met hers again and again—searching, yearning, aching—filling a void that Kaia had never know she had. Heat bubbled up within her, as lips and tongues entwined in a passion that she had never known before.

At last, she pulled back to regain her stolen breath. "What took you so long?" She rested her forehead on his muscled chest, feeling his thrumming heart beneath his shirt. "I've missed you."

The Shadow Heir kissed her neck softly. "It's a surprise."

Kaia narrowed her eyes. "What kind of surprise?"

He reached out and opened the stable door next to him. "This kind."

Kaia peeked around the doorjamb and gasped as Gus flew into her arms. The massive ragehound wriggled and whined like a puppy. My girl! My girl! My girl!

Kaia rolled with him on the cobblestones, laughing and crying into his neck as she ran her fingers through his red fur.

"Where have you been?" she asked the dog, looking into his shining eyes. "I searched everywhere for you!" She turned to Klaus in disbelief. "But how did you find him?"

Klaus shrugged with a smirk, "I went town to town." He leaned down to give Gus a scratch. "A farmer's family had found him on the road and taken him in. They were rather awed when I told them who he belonged to."

"That must've taken weeks!" Kaia gasped.

"For that reaction, it was worth it."

Kaia released Gus and threw her arms around Klaus. "I can't thank you enough. You've brought back a piece of my life."

"Luckily, I was able to find him before Dorinar could grab him and hide him in another deep dark cave."

Kaia laughed, tears still streaming down her face. She reached down and Gus pressed his familiar wet nose into her palm. We are together now. We are whole.

She glanced up at Klaus. "I was worried that you'd forgotten to come."

"Nah, I'm afraid you're stuck with me, Firefly." His crinkled hazel eyes met hers. "I can't leave you for long when you hold my heart in your hand." He lifted her hand to his mouth and kissed the inside of her wrist, then cocked his head as the music started up again. "And I believe you wanted a dance." He pulled her into the center of the abandoned street.

He lifted her hand for a twirl, and Kaia giggled, spinning close to him. "And just when I thought I couldn't love you more...."

He pressed his cheek to hers, his words tickling her ear. "I hope you always say that, Firefly, because I will never tire of hearing it."

Gus barked and pranced around them as the Heirs whirled to the music. Kaia looked into the gold flecks winking in Klaus' hazel eyes and took it all back. This was exactly where she was supposed to be. Thank Odriel for her six-minute head start.

EPILOGUE

In the gathering dusk, Idriel's Children gazed down on the Summerbanks festival from a jagged cliff jutting out of the mountainside. One was tall and blonde, dressed in an expensive suit, with his hair perfectly combed atop his head. His handsome features twisted with hate as he watched the village below.

"She killed my father, you know." Valente sneered. "Burned him alive right in front of my eyes."

His companion moved jerkily, as if his movements weren't his own. His lidless eyes were blank and unblinking, lifeless but for the dark spark that glittered unnaturally in the pits of his pupils. His lipless mouth gaped in an eternal smile, showing his gnashing teeth. "Patience," he gurgled, as if his tongue didn't quite work. "She knows nothing of your secret." He cocked his head to the side as a fly landed on one of his bulging eyes. His words were sluggish and thick. "We must gather strength, set the trap, and they will come."

"How's that?" Valente snarled, the smoke of green yanaa twisting around his fingers.

Mogen's dead eyes followed the Heirs as they danced below. "All you need is the right bait."

AUTHOR'S NOTE

Thanks so much for reading! I hope you enjoyed Odriel's Heirs. If you have time to leave a review on Amazon or your favorite book site, I would be so grateful to any words you'd be willing to leave. Even just a line or two can make a huge difference. Reviews are vital for any author, but as an indie author especially, encouragement from readers like you keeps me going and gives these stories wings.

If you're interested in reading more, you can find updates on the sequel, Idriel's Children, as well as my other works on my website at hayleyreesechow.com. You can also connect with me on Twitter or Instagram @HayleyReeseChow.

ACKNOWLEDGMENTS

It took me three months to write this book and eight years to gather the courage to self-publish. I would never have been able to take that next step without my little writing village.

First off, I have to thank my husband, Adam, for being my rock and keeping me grounded. For reading everything I put in front of him and always being honest. Whenever I get lost in my head, you're always the beacon that guides me back home. I love you more than all the words could ever say.

To my wild boys, Decker & Dashiell, for inspiring to me to take the leap and reminding me there is always room to grow.

To my dad, who has shown me just what it means to pursue your passions, who first told me to "create something" and who introduced me to griegals.

To my mom, for her ceaseless encouragement. For teaching me never to give up, and the hard things are the things most worth doing.

To my editor, Mica, for her invaluable wordsmithing and story-crafting wisdom. For keeping it real and taking this story to the next level.

To my sister, Drew, for motivating me through revision with her keen insights.

To my critique partner, Maria, for her careful eye and boundless positivity.

To my cover designer, Dominique, for bringing my characters to life.

To my audiobook narrator, Claire, for giving my characters a voice.

To my photographer, Cheryl, whose magic camera captured the best in me.

To my beta readers, Mindy, Kayla, Randy and Sheri, for taking the time to read my words—your support lifts me up.

And to all the others who have given their kind encouragement—thank you so much. Trust me when I say, your words have given me the confidence to make this book a reality.

ABOUT THE AUTHOR

Hayley Reese Chow has done of lot of things that have nothing at all to do with writing. Her hat collection includes mother, wife, engineer, USAF veteran, reservist, four-time All American fencer, 100 mile ultramarathoner, world traveler, voracious reader, and super nerd.

Hayley currently lives in Florida with two small wild boys, her long-suffering husband, and her miniature ragehound.

But in the night, when the house is still, she writes.

Made in the USA
Middletown, DE
29 February 2020